A. Louage

A course of philosophy

Embracing logic, mataphysics and ethics

A. Louage

A course of philosophy
Embracing logic, mataphysics and ethics

ISBN/EAN: 9783741189036

Manufactured in Europe, USA, Canada, Australia, Japa

Cover: Foto ©Andreas Hilbeck / pixelio.de

Manufactured and distributed by brebook publishing software
(www.brebook.com)

A. Louage

A course of philosophy

A COURSE

OF

PHILOSOPHY.

EMBRACING

LOGIC, MATAPHYSICS AND ETHICS.

A TEXT-BOOK FOR USE IN SCHOOLS.

FOURTH EDITION.

REVISED AND ENLARGED.

BY

VERY REV. A. LOUAGE, C.S.C.

PROVINCIAL OF CANADA.

Afterwards Bishop of Dacca, East Bengal, India.

DIED 1894.

P. J. KENEDY & SONS

44 BARCLAY STREET, NEW YORK

DACCA, Sept. 22nd, 1893.

To P. J. KENEDY, Publisher,
    5 Barclay Street, New York.

DEAR SIR:

I herewith send to you the preface to the
FOURTH EDITION. You will remark from it that
it is quite out of the question for me to now have the
alterations or additions ready, since my eyes are entirely too weak. *You can, however, freely proceed in
the publishing of the fourth edition.*

Most sincerely yours,

PREFACE TO THE FOURTH EDITION.

When the Second Edition of this Manual of Moral Philosophy was issued, the author was Provincial of the Congregation of Holy Cross, for the province of Canada. Three years ago he has been appointed as Bishop of Dacca, East Bengal, India. During the interval from the time of the issue of the second edition, the author had been preparing the outlines for a number of additions and alterations to be made in a third edition, impelled as he felt himself to do so, not only by a conscientious desire to present to the student and to the public as correct and exact a Manual of Moral Philosophy as could be desired, but also through the encouragement given on account of the very generous favor and welcome the Manual has found in many parts of the United States, where it has been accepted as a text-book for the class-room.

The author is reluctantly forced to state, that he was not aware of a third edition having been prepared wherein his intended alterations should have been made,—and this through the failure of John B. Piet & Co., who had published the 1st and 2nd editions,—so that the planned and digested changes had therefore to remain untouched.

The author laments very much the fact that since one-half year his eyesight has become so severely affected, that for the time being he finds himself unable to arrange or order neither his alterations as to certain points, particularly on Ontology and Logic, nor to revise the necessary additions which had seemed to him most advisable. He hopes, however, that his Manual in its fourth edition shall be welcomed with the same warmth and cordiality as it has been in the past, and by expressing to the public his sincere thanks for the appreciation of his work, he at the same time promises with no uncertain words that he will, as soon as his eyesight shall permit, arrange the notes and papers bearing upon this Course of Moral Philosophy, so that they shall be ready any time for a subsequent edition of the Manual.*

---

* Bishop Louage died in 1894, about six months after writing above Preface.—Publisher.

PREFACE TO THE SECOND EDITION.

WHEN the first edition of this Philosophy appeared, we made known to the public that we originally did not have an intention of publishing, in the form of a manual, the notes which we had gathered and dictated to our pupils. We had been intrusted with a class, in which besides philosophy, we were to teach other matters in one scholastic session of five months. At the end of our course, our notes were reviewed and prepared for the press by another person and sent to a publisher almost without our knowledge. The urgent need of a manual and the alterations made by the reviewer, whose chief aim was to be elegant, partly explain the precipitancy employed in producing the work, and also account for certain inaccurate expressions it contained. The responsibility of the principal errors, especially those in Ontology, we ourselves assume; and we here take the opportunity of thanking the author of an analytical and just criticism which appeared in the "CATHOLIC WORLD," one year after the publication of our Philosophy, for his suggestions. We have profited by that criticism and have made many corrections and additions, principally in Logic and Metaphysics.

We have now presented to the public a book we believe worthy of its title; a manual that will prove acceptable in the schools.

1*

PREFACE TO THE FIRST EDITION.

IT is the unanimous opinion of those best qualified to judge, that a knowledge of the first principles of Philosophy is necessary to complete any course of classical or scientific studies. Experience as well as reason teaches that those who complete their education with a course of sound Philosophy, thus acquire an accurate method for the continuation of their studies, for the instruction of others, or for the pursuit of any calling to which they may devote their talents.

The man who learns what truth is, learns also to love it; and will not be easily led astray by the systems of error which are everywhere paraded before him, labelled with the false appellation of Philosophy: he despises the contradictions of pseudo-philosophers, he abhors the repulsive doctrines of the wicked, and avoids with care the corruption of morals which always accompanies them. Everywhere and always he perceives the presence of the Divinity, and is accordingly filled with awe and reverence: he sees also, with consolation, the excellence of his own soul and its future destiny, and not only preserves it from the contamination of vice, but also adorns it with every virtue; thus conscientiously discharging all the duties of his station in life, he must ascend higher and higher in the scale of being.

When we thus point out the abundant and inestimable fruits of Philosophy, it is evident that we do not speak of that so-called Philosophy which ignores the light of Divine revelation, but of that true Christian Philosophy which is guided as far as possible by reason, but which freely admits the light of faith where that of reason fails: for, as we shall see, reason alone is not capable of completely solving some of the most serious problems which concern the salvation of man.

The young man who, while at college, has either

wholly neglected to study the rules of judging and knowing, or who has not engraven them deeply on his mind, wanders without a guide through dark and devious ways, and is "carried about by every wind of doctrine." He reads indiscriminately every book, good or bad, that chance throws in his way, and peruses them with little attention or reflection. Hence he fills his mind with imperfect notions of things, without any order; everywhere he sees contradictory systems, and in the midst of this general darkness he remains uncertain of the truth, and even becomes doubtful of the very existence of certitude. Soon the truth of religion appears to him as not sufficiently proved; and, owing to the prejudices to which he has yielded, he begins to deny that there is any excellence in virtue or any turpitude in vice. Passions rise in his heart, which, not being restrained, but rather flattered and excited by many causes, soon lead to deplorable results; for they shake his reason, which is already weak and deprived of its natural support, they destroy the vigor of his physical system, they deprave his nature, and finally carry the unfortunate youth to utter destruction.

That this is not an overdrawn picture is plain to any one who chooses to look around him with an unprejudiced eye; and it shows conclusively the importance of a knowledge of the primary principles of Philosophy. On this knowledge, in truth, depends the progress which we shall make in science, the solidity of our mind, our love of truth and detestation of falsehood, our sagacity in choosing what is best, the integrity of our morals, the peace of families, the well-being of society, in a word, our happiness both in public and in private life.

The teacher, therefore, who is incompetent, negligent or dishonest, is the cause of an irreparable loss to those under his care; while he who is learned, diligent and consistent in his instruction, sows in the minds of those committed to his charge the seeds of truth and virtue which will bring forth an abundant harvest of the richest fruits of a good education. To attain so desirable an end, the pupil should be guided, not by obscure and uncertain precepts, but by those which are established upon the clearest principles of reason : even as a child as yet unacquainted with the way is guided, not by the hand of an ignorant or a dangerous man, but by that of his father.

We do not approve of the method of teaching Philosophy by lecture ; for long lectures, however well developed, are not always understood by the student and are very easily forgotten : we are rather in favor of placing in the hands of the pupil a small but comprehensive text-book, which he can readily commit to memory, and easily retain. Such a text-book should be concise without being obscure, so that the attention of the student may be sufficiently attracted and exercised ; more than all, a book written for this object should be exact.

An elementary book of this kind is not often found ; indeed it may be doubted whether one possessing all the qualities mentioned above exists in any modern tongue. Some excellent compendiums written in the Latin language have been published since 1825 ; but they cannot serve our purpose, which requires a manual of Philosophy adapted particularly to the wants of those who are not acquainted with the classics. To unlock the treasures of Philosophy for them, we concluded that it would be well to prepare a text-book having as far as possible the requisites mentioned above.

During the preparation of our manual we have diligently consulted the best works on the subject; and we now submit the result of our labors in the form of an elementary text-book on Philosophy, which we trust will meet the requirements of those for whom it is intended : and may God grant that, owing to the good intentions of the author, this book may be the means of advancing the best interests of the youths for whom it was written.   S. N. D. B.

CONTENTS.

SECOND DISSERTATION.—ON JUDGMENT.

THIRD DISSERTATION.—ON REASONING.

FOURTH DISSERTATION.—ON METHOD.

FIFTH DISSERTATION.—ON CERTITUDE.

PART II.—METAPHYSICS.

FIRST DISSERTATION.—ON ONTOLOGY.

SECOND DISSERTATION.—ON THEODICY.

THIRD DISSERTATION.—ON PSYCHOLOGY.

PART I.—EXPERIMENTAL PSYCHOLOGY.

2

NOTES.

A

COURSE OF PHILOSOPHY.

INTRODUCTORY.

BEFORE entering the sanctuary of Philosophy, a few words are necessary by way of introduction. We shall arrange these preliminary remarks under four heads. Under the *first* we shall give the DEFINITIONS of several WORDS of common occurrence: under the *second* we shall examine the DEFINITIONS OF PHILOSOPHY: under the *third* we shall give the DIVISIONS OF PHILOSOPHY: and under the *fourth* we shall say something of ARGUMENT.

I.

DEFINITIONS OF WORDS.

NOTE.—These definitions are more fully developed in Ontology. See page 103.

A BEING or THING is that which *exists* or *may exist:* it is therefore twofold, real or possible.

EXISTENCE is the *real union* of the parts or attributes which constitute a being.

POSSIBILITY is the *non-repugnance* of the essential attributes which constitute a being in such a way that its existence does not involve any contradiction.

The ATTRIBUTES are the *qualities* of a being: they are *essential* or *constitutive* when the thing cannot exist without them, and *accidental* when the thing can exist without them.

The essence of a being is that which constitutes a being. It is the "ratio essendi," or simply "ratio," of a being: thus reasonable animality is the "ratio" of man. The essence of a thing is also called its *nature;* although the word *nature* is more extensive than *essence,* since the nature of a being sometimes includes its accidental as well as its essential attributes. *Nature* is also used to signify the whole collection of corporeal beings.

A GENUS is a collection of beings having one or more attributes common to each. A genus must be sufficiently general to be divided into subordinate classes, called *species.*

A SPECIES, therefore, is a collection of beings belonging to one and the same genus, but having particular and constitutive properties by which they are distinguished from any other collection of beings of the same genus.

In Philosophy, *Genus* and *Species* are two universals, and are defined: the first, "a ratio which can be found in many things, and be predicated of each of them when an incomplete answer is given to the question, 'What is it?'" The second is a "ratio which can be found in many things, and be predicated of each of them when a complete answer is given to the question, 'What is it?'"

For example, *being* * is divided into two species, *cor-*

---

* "*Being*," as we say in Ontology, does not constitute a genus; it is above all genus, and, accordingly, is called "transcendental." If "*being*" were a genus, nothing could save us from pantheism.

poreal and *incorporeal* beings. These two species are each divided into other species, and consequently they are genera with reference to the subsequent divisions. Corporeal bodies form two species—things *with life* and things *without life*. Things with life, considered with reference to a further division, form a genus which is divided into two species, *animals* and *vegetables*.

The genus may be either *remote* or *proximate*. It is remote when there is at least one division intervening between the species and the genus referred to. For instance, when I say, *Man* is a rational *being*, the genus, *being*, is remote; but it is proximate when I say, *Man* is a rational *animal*.

Each species must have an *essential attribute*, which makes it distinct from every other species of the same genus: this attribute is called the DIFFERENCE. When this difference consists of an attribute which separates every being of the species from every being of another species, it is called the SPECIFIC DIFFERENCE. We have an example of this difference in the following definition: Man is a rational animal, where the word *rational* indicates the specific difference, distinguishing man from any other species of the genus animal.

INDIVIDUALS are those beings to which, considered separately, the *same genus* and the *same difference* pertain.

In *Ontology* we shall give the definitions of *Substance, Modification, Subject*, and *Object;* also of *Order* and *Relation*.

SCIENCE * is a series of notions deduced from principles firmly established, disposed in a methodical order, and referring to one and the same object.

---

*See at the end of the Fourth Dissertation in Logic.

Science is either *subjective* or *objective;* subjective when we consider it as existing in our own minds, and objective when we consider the objects, the knowledge of which we want to acquire—their properties and relations: it is again either *speculative* or *practical.*

Practical science is the source of *art.*

ART, which is defined: a right method of making anything, is commonly the application of some special science to external things, according to determined rules. We will here observe that the same species of knowledge may be at the same time a science and an art. Arithmetic and Geometry, considered in themselves, are sciences; but applied to external things they are arts. Logic, considered in itself, is a science; but applied to the investigation of truth and its manifestation, according to determined rules, as in the method of Aristotle, it is the Art of Reasoning, or the Art of Thinking.

KNOWLEDGE, in general, is the representation taking place in the mind, of something, in some manner; it differs very little from *idea,* as we shall see. It is *intuitive* when the object appears so clearly to our intellect that we perceive it without reasoning, and *discursive* when we need some demonstration to perceive the object.

Knowledge has for its objects either natural or supernatural things.

FAITH, in general, is the assent of the mind to some truth, on the testimony of another person. When this assent is founded upon the authority of God, it is Divine Faith; it is Human Faith when established upon the testimony of men.

II.

DEFINITIONS OF PHILOSOPHY.

It often becomes necessary to give *definitions*, in order to avoid obscurity or uncertainty. A DEFINITION is an explanation of a *word* or of a *thing*. The definition of a word is said to be *etymological* when its origin is given, and *significative* when its meaning is explained.

The definition of a thing is that which shows the nature of the thing. It may be merely descriptive, and then the definition is called *imperfect*; or it may be *accurate* and *perfect*, and this only deserves the name of definition. Description is suitable to oratory, but definition belongs especially to Philosophy: it gives precisely what is necessary in order that the thing may be understood and distinguished from every other thing, by enumerating its essential qualities.

Three conditions are requisite to a perfect definition: 1st, It must be *clear*, that is, free from any obscure or ambiguous expression; 2d, It must be *brief*, that is, free from all unnecessary words; and 3d, It must give the *proximate genus* and the *specific difference*. When these three conditions are found, the definition applies to the thing defined, and to nothing else, so that the thing and its definition are reciprocals.

PHILOSOPHY has been defined as " the science of things knowable by the light of reason," or "the science of reason."

But these definitions, while they distinguish Philosophy from theology, do not separate it from the physical and mathematical sciences; and in our day these sciences have been so far extended that they have ceased to belong to Philosophy, as it is now taught in the schools. The following definition of Philosophy is found in several text-books: "The science of supersensible things knowable by the light of reason." This definition has the three requisite marks: it is *clear*, *short*, and contains the *proximate genus*, "science," and the *specific difference*, "supersensible," which word distinguishes Philosophy from the physical sciences, and "knowable by the light of reason," which words distinguish Philosophy from theology.

Philosophy is the study of wisdom. To be wise, in a moral sense, is to act always rationally. Wisdom, then, is, in that sense, the conformity to duty.

The wisdom of the philosopher is not the rectitude of a well-regulated will, but the rectitude of the intellect, which knows truth with certainty. The word wisdom is here synonymous to science; and the wise is he who, fathoming the reason of things, comes to form upon them well-defined notions.

The name of science is confined to an ensemble of notions which, on all points of space and duration, commend themselves to the intellect as an absolute and invariable rule of truth.

Among all the sciences, there are some that are more general than others; the notions which they have for object can be more or less complex, more or less simple.

All explicative reason of things rests upon ulterior reasons even to the last, beyond which the mind cannot penetrate. These reasons enter in the explanation of all, without being capable to be explained by other reasons. The science which proposes them to itself for object is then the science *par excellence*. To it is the name of wisdom confined; it is philosophy which we may define to be "The science of the first principles, or the ultimate reasons of things, inasmuch as we can acquire it by our natural means of knowledge."

III.

DIVISIONS OF PHILOSOPHY.

DIVISION, in general, is the distribution of a whole into its parts. A WHOLE is that which is formed of parts really or logically distinct. The whole is said to be *metaphysical, physical,* or *logical,* according as its parts belong to one or other of these orders.

The division, to be accurate, must have these three conditions: 1st, It must be *adequate,* that is, it must include as many members as there are in the whole which is to be divided; 2d, It must be *distinct,* that is, one part must not be included in another; 3d, The parts must be *proximate,* otherwise there would be confusion; the following division, for instance, would be wrong: Living beings are divided into three classes, men, beasts, and plants. A proximate division would be: Living beings are divided into two classes, animals and vegetables, and so continue, always giving first the proximate, or nearest division, and the subdivisions in like order.

Philosophy, as we have learned, is the science of supersensible things. In order to proceed methodically in the acquisition of this science, we must first give the rules for the investigation of truth, and then investigate the things which form the object of this science, beginning with the most important, namely, God and the soul. The nature of God and the soul being known, we may examine the relations existing between God and the soul, between the soul and the body, and finally the relations of men to each other considered as social beings. We have then three parts, which form the DIVISIONS OF PHILOSOPHY, namely, *Logic, Metaphysics,* and *Ethics.*

IV.

THE USEFULNESS OF PHILOSOPHY.

It is incontestable that the knowledge of the first truths, such as reason by itself can acquire it, is of a very great usefulness. We must, however, protest against those immoderate pretensions which would make of Philosophy a science entirely independent and sufficient by itself to bring man to his end.

Philosophy treats of the human soul and of God, hence it should examine the ties which unite them. Some minds thought that, without having recourse to revelation, they might confide themselves only to philosophy in order to attain their destiny ; but they forgot that by the formal will of God man has a supernatural obligatory end, which his reason cannot conceive and at which he cannot arrive with nature only as his guide. Without speaking of the supernatural order, the experience of ages and the study of our soul prove that reason, too weak in the present state, even in the natural order, is not a guide sufficiently safe to abandon ourselves to it without reserve.

Philosophy is not an enemy to religion. The church has at all times applied herself to it with a care altogether special to her. The foundations of our dogmas are grounded on reason, and the more reason is cultivated the more revelation finds itself fixed solidly on it.

The special object of revelation is the supernatural, properly so called—the divine. But the divine surpasses our understanding, and we do not directly conceive it. To seize it like a shadow, to express it, we must have recourse to analogy, we must bring ourselves back to the created world. Moreover, when religion speaks to us of revelation, she supposes already the existence of a revealing God, as well as the existence of an intelligent soul to whom this revelation is made, and faith borrows of nature all those truths which it needs as preambles. By the science of the first principles we forge arms which will serve to reply to the objections against religion.

Philosophy, then, renders services to religion and to revealed science; but this is not the only science which owes obligations to it, for it is useful to all the sciences indistinctly. All the sciences tend to philosophy where they find their centre, that is to say, where they find the first principles on which those sciences are grounded. It is through philosophy, again, that they develop themselves, or, in other words, attain their object, which cannot be done without knowing the laws which rule the operations of the mind. Method is indispensable to all scientific pursuits, in order to realize a serious progress; and it is logic, a branch of philosophy, which is the science of method. Hence the sciences must seek in philosophy, along with the lights of metaphysical truths, the rules of reasoning.

Moreover, philosophy is useful in a practical point of view. Conduct is closely allied to knowledge; it is very important that we should have just ideas on morals. Philosophy, enlightened by revelation, gives a solid basis to morals in showing their wisdom, and hence their practice becomes easier.

Therefore we cannot insist too much on the importance of the higher studies well directed, and particularly on the importance of philosophy, provided only that it be Christian.

V.

ARGUMENT.

The different points to be treated under this head will be given in *Logic*. We will here say only a few words in regard to equivocal propositions, which we may sometimes have to deal with.

1st. We must distinguish and point out clearly the equivocal expressions.

2d. If these expressions are not clear of themselves, we must define and explain them.

3d. We must concede the proposition in the sense in which it is true, and deny it in the sense in which it is false; and in both cases give our reasons for doing so, if necessary.

PART I.

LOGIC.

DEFINITION—DIVISION.

FOR the acquisition of science the human mind must first be provided with rules, and so be enabled to avoid error and establish truth on the solid foundation of reason.

The word philosophy, as we have seen, is as universal as the word science itself, and logic is the key of this science. Logic is consequently the first part of Philosophy—the part which treats of the first operations of the human mind to discover truth, and afterwards gives rules by which this truth may be demonstrated. We may therefore define Logic to be, "The science which directs the operations of our mind in the investigation and demonstration of truth."

When this science is put in practice it becomes "The Art of Reasoning," which words may be accepted as a definition of logic, considered as an art.

In the foregoing definitions we find the three requisite conditions of a good definition: 1st, clearness; 2d, conciseness, and 3d, reciprocity, that is, the proximate genus and the specific difference are given.

There are two kinds of logic: *natural* or *innate*, and *artificial* or *acquired*.

The summary knowledge of the laws of the mind and the use made thereof, without previous reflection, con-

27

stitute *natural logic;* when, by attention, we better
define those laws in their nature, and extend further
their application, we are said to possess *artificial logic.*
Aristotle is the father of *artificial logic;* his "οργανον"
ruled supreme in the schools until the beginning of the
seventeenth century.

Bacon was the first who opposed the *syllogism;* in his
"Novum Organum" he substituted a new method;
and, in truth, he made some useful innovations, for by
summoning the mind to the field of sensible observation he hastened the progressive march of the physical
sciences.

Logic possesses an incontestable utility; and if, for a
time, it did not enjoy much popularity, it was owing to
the exaggerations of Raymond Lulle, who multiplied
unnecessarily the rules which govern its use.

Nobody objects to *natural logic;* as for artificial, it
is always useful and sometimes indispensable.

The natural order observed by the mind in the investigation of truth may be described as follows: We
first represent objects to ourselves, we next judge of
them, we then compare our judgments and draw conclusions, and, finally, we arrange these conclusions in a
certain order. Hence we have in the science of logic
four different parts or divisions; the first treating of
our Ideas of objects, the second of our Judgments
concerning those ideas, the third of our Reasoning
concerning the judgments, and the fourth of the
Method in which we dispose of the conclusions of our
reasoning.

As soon as we have considered these four divisions
of the science we shall apply it to the investigation of
the existence of truth, or Certitude; and, logically
speaking, this question comes first. Is there anything

certain, is there any certitude? and if so, how can we prove its existence? Although this question, in reality, forms the introduction to the study of Philosophy, since without an affirmative answer to it we cannot make one step in the science, yet some authors treat it as a part of logic; and we adopt this plan as more convenient, and shall, therefore, treat of certitude as the fifth part of logic.

FIRST DISSERTATION.

ON IDEAS.

An idea may be considered as existing either in the mind or in its terms; consequently this first dissertation may be divided into two chapters.

CHAPTER FIRST.

OF IDEAS CONSIDERED AS EXISTING IN THE MIND.

"An idea is the mere representation in the mind of some object." We cannot, therefore, have an idea of *nothing;* for *nothing* has no property or attribute by which it might be represented in the mind. The idea is the simplest element of our knowledge. We have no other means to understand in what it consists than by having recourse to analogy. Thus it is that we may consider it as a sort of spiritual image (*ιιδος*), which retraces in our mind a reality considered in its proper manner of being.

Bossuet, in his "Logic," defines the idea to be "that which represents to the understanding the truth of the object understood. Placed before sensible objects, the imagination represents them to itself according to their

3 *

appearance. In another order, the understanding represents objects to itself according to their truth. We may also define the idea, "The sign in the mind of an understood object."

The idea is a sign either natural or formal. The idea expresses itself sensibly in a word. We may say, in like manner, that it is the word of the mind. Consequently, the word, properly said, is also a sign—the sign of the idea, and, indirectly, the sign of the object.*

All common notion, in fact, is relative to the essence of objects, or to something which is superadded thereto. The *ensemble* of the characters which constitute the essence total is called species. There are as many species as there are distinct natures among the beings.

The species may be divided into two parts: collection of characters common to many species constitutes the genus; and that essential quality which restricts the genus to one determinate species constitutes the specific difference.

That which is added to the essence may be a quality which, without being the essence, is necessarily deduced from it; and, as a consequence, is always added to it; it is the *quality proper*.

The quality added to the essence may have no necessary link with it, and be suitable to the object only in a fortuitous manner: it is *the accident*, "Man, a rational animal, endowed with the faculty of speaking, be he ignorant or learned." In this example the five universals are contained.

---

* There are five kinds of universal ideas; that is to say, five kinds of ideas capable of being united to many subjects, and afterwards of bringing them together in one and same group. We call them, in the school, the five universals.

The definition of an idea being given, we have now to examine, 1st, the division of ideas; 2d, their properties; and 3d, the operations of our mind in regard to them.

§ I. THE DIVISION OF IDEAS.

In regard to their *origin*, some authors divide ideas into three classes: First, *innate* ideas, or those born with us; second, *adventitious* ideas, or those coming to us from various causes in the course of time; and third, *factitious* ideas, or those formed by ourselves.

In regard to their *object*, we have, first, the idea of *substance*, when we consider the substance of a thing as abstracted from its modifications; second, the idea of *modification*, when we consider the modifications of a thing as abstracted from its substance (these two ideas are called *abstract* ideas); and third, the idea of *modified substance*, which is called a *concrete* idea.

Concrete ideas may be produced by sensation or by the imagination. They are produced by sensation when they represent objects which strike our senses, and which, therefore, really exist: they are produced by the imagination when they represent objects which may exist, but which do not strike our senses.

All these ideas are called ideas of sensible things when their objects are sensible things; and they are called ideas of intellectual things when the objects which they represent cannot affect the senses: the ideas of moral things belong to this second class.

An idea is *simple* when the object represented cannot be divided, as, "an affirmation;" *complex* when the object is qualified, as, "a good man;" *compound* when the object may be divided into several parts, as, "a horse," "a tree;" *collective* when the object is a unity formed of several objects belonging to the same species,

as, "an army;" *universal* when the object represents
all the beings of the same species, as, "man in general;"
particular when the object represents only a part of the
beings belonging to the same species, as, "several men;"
singular when the object refers to one individual of a
collection, as, "Peter," "John;" and *adequate* when
the object appears with all its attributes: God only has
adequate ideas; we have but inadequate ones.

Besides the preceding divisions, it is customary to
indicate still another one, according to the very nature
of the ideas. They are divided into *contingent* ideas
and *necessary* ideas.

A thing is said to be contingent when, though existing, it might not be.

A thing is said to be necessary when it could not but
be.

Hence, it follows that our ideas, with regard to their
existence in us, could never be said to be necessary.
Being modifications of our mind, they could not be
necessary in a subject which is itself contingent. Let
even the soul be given, there are yet no absolutely necessary ideas; for the soul, contrarily to the opinion of
Descartes, cannot be defined by the actual thought, but
by the power of thinking. It, then, can be conceived
without any actually developed idea.

There is, however, a certain number of very general
ideas which the mind apprehends from the very first
awakening of reason, and are supposed to be in the comprehension of all the others. It is, then, necessary that
they should exist at first. In this sense we will call
necessary, of a relative necessity, the ideas of being, of
cause, of time, of space, etc., etc.

§ II. PROPERTIES OF IDEAS.

Ideas are, first, either *true* or *false*. They are true when they conform with their objects, false when they do not. But since this conformity is always with the objects as they show themselves, and not as they may be in reality, we may, with this explanation, admit the opinion of those who pretend that there are no false ideas. Ideas are, in the second place, either *clear* or *obscure*, and these words need no explanation. Thirdly, they are either *distinct* or *confused*. An idea is distinct when it represents distinctly its object in all its particulars, as the idea of "a certain *house*" or of "a certain *person ;*" and it is confused when the object cannot be distinctly determined. If I say, "Many *persons* are standing at a distance from me, and I cannot see whether they are armed or not," I have a confused idea.

The *comprehension* of an idea signifies the sum of the attributes which constitute the nature of the object. The comprehension of the idea of man includes everything necessary to constitute a man, as man, thus distinguishing him from everything else, as a tree or a stone.

The *extension* of an idea is the range of its universality, and consequently applies itself to all the individuals which the same idea embraces. The extension of the idea of man includes all those beings that have the human nature, that is, all men.

§ III. OPERATIONS OF THE MIND IN REGARD TO IDEAS.

The principal operations of the mind in reference to ideas are attention, abstraction, and comparison.

Attention is that operation of the mind by which we lay our ideas, as it were, before the eyes of the mind, in order to examine them with care and master them.

C

Attention and reflection constitute the foundation of science and the source of learning.

Abstraction is that operation of the mind by which we consider one or more qualities of an object, the other qualities being laid aside. Abstraction is not only possible, and even easy of attainment, but it is also necessary.

Having examined several qualities, and found that they belong to a certain object, if we unite these qualities in order to form this object again, we perform an operation which is called *synthesis*: on the contrary, if an object is given us to study, and we divide it into its parts, examining successively each part, we perform an operation which is called *analysis*. We may, therefore, see that analysis is a decomposition, while synthesis is a recomposition.

When, in order to form a species, we reduce particulars to their genera, leaving aside whatever is individual, and retaining that which is common, we perform an operation which is called *generalization*.

When we consider two or more ideas, in order to find their consistency or their inconsistency, we perform an operation which is called *comparison*. This operation is, of course, the most important; without it, we could not improve in any branch of science or art.

CHAPTER SECOND.

OF IDEAS CONSIDERED IN THEIR TERMS.

There are three ways by which we may express what we represent to our mind, namely, gestures, speech, and writing; and these three are designated by the general appellation of *signs*.

For the development of this chapter see the remarks on the "Origin of Language," in experimental Psychology.

SECOND DISSERTATION.

ON JUDGMENT.

When the mind, after having compared two ideas, declares their consistency or their inconsistency, it makes a *judgment*. Consequently "Judgment is that operation of the mind affirming the mutual inclusion or exclusion of two objective terms as apprehended, and consequently declaring that a certain quality exists or does not exist in a certain object." That there may be a judgment formed, it is not sufficient to bring nearer together, to compare, two ideas. All comparison does not constitute a judgment properly so called. Comparison consists, in fact, in considering two objects placed side by side, either in the point of view of quantity or in that of quality. Thus a mountain and a hill may be compared in regard to elevation. In these sorts of comparisons we bring nearer together two subjects determined by their attributes. It is, then, rather a comparison of judgment than a comparison preparatory to a judgment. In the latter the two terms are necessarily a subject and an attribute.

It is asked sometimes if all judgment supposes an anterior comparison. It suffices for the solution of this question to make a distinction. Does all judgment suppose a slow and well considered comparison, in such a manner that the two terms are always considered separately, previous to their being formally united or separated? No; for in all immediate judgments, not only those of the experimental order, but also those of the rational order, the affirmation or the negation of the relation between the two terms is made, as it were, spontaneously. "This body is dark." "I am." But however sudden be the effects of these perceptions, it is evident that in these judgments, as indeed in all judgment, there must always be two terms, either united or separated, and it is indispensable that we should have understood them previously. We may readily understand that our errors proceed from mistaken judgments only, for we cannot err in perceiving or in feeling.

Here again we may consider judgment as existing either in the mind or out of it, and consequently this dissertation is also divided into two chapters.

CHAPTER FIRST.

Of Judgment Considered as Existing in the Mind.

Judgment is a positive act of the mind, and not a mere sensation, as Condillac said, or a perception, according to the opinion of Malebranche. It is an act, since we judge and pronounce, and we can do neither without acting; it is, besides, a simple act, since it consists of an affirmation or a negation, and, consequently, cannot be divided.

The judgment is a simple act of the intellect, just as much as conception is, since it is, in last resort, like the latter, but a mere perception. Undoubtedly, to express a judgment, it is necessary to mention several ideas; nevertheless it has, in itself, for object only the common link which exists among them, and it consequently remains indivisible.

In an act of the judgment, some philosophers contend that we should sometime consider separately the perception and the affirmation. Descartes and others attribute perception to the intellect and affirmation to the will. But who does not see that a clear perception supposes the assent of the mind, and that thus the judgment is found complete, independently of all ulterior act, especially of an act belonging to another faculty. Inasmuch as the understanding maintains the existence of a relation clearly perceived, even when the will rejects it, it is certain that the will is complete in the sole assent of the mind. The will belongs to intellectual, and not at all to moral, activity. This fact, however, does not prevent moral activity from influencing intellectual activity, as it happens in those judgments where passion leads the understanding astray.

A judgment is either *necessary* or *free*. A necessary judgment is one formed when the mind is so strongly impelled to judge that it cannot refrain from judging. "I exist," is a necessary judgment. A free judgment is one which the mind is not forced to pronounce.

There is another way of considering the necessary judgments. The necessary judgments are those in which the relation of the ideas could not be denied without contradiction; and such a thing happens when the attribute is found in the essence of the subject. Example: "Man is rational." These judgments are thus opposed to the contingent judgments, that is, to those in which the relation exists, without, however, being necessary when the attribute is a pure accident. Example: "There are learned men."

Judgments are *possible* when the attribute can be joined to the subject, even when it would not be so joined in reality. The necessary and the contingent judgments are always possible judgments: "Ab actu ad posse valet consecutio." On the other hand, the possible judgments are not for that either contingent or necessary judgments: "A posse ad actum non valet consecutio."

Finally, a judgment is *impossible* when two ideas are repugnant to each other and cannot be joined. This

4

Impossibility is absolute, if the contradiction be in the very essence of things. It is relative, when the repugnance exists only by circumstance.

A judgment is, again, either *true* or *false*, depending on the fact as to whether the things are or are not as the mind declares them to be.

Thirdly, a judgment is *certain* when it is established on an infallible foundation, as, "Our Lord died," "Bodies exist."

Fourthly, a judgment is *evident* when it rests upon a clear and distinct perception of the consistency or the inconsistency of two ideas, as, "Two and two equal four."

Lastly, a *probable* judgment is one established on trustworthy, but not infallible, reasons, as, "It is probable that a sick man will recover when several good physicians are of opinion that such will be the case."

CHAPTER SECOND.

OF JUDGMENT CONSIDERED AS EXISTING OUT OF THE MIND.

When we express our judgment we form what is called a *proposition*. To constitute a proposition three terms are necessary, a *subject*, a *verb*, and an *attribute*, one or even two of which may be understood.

In every proposition the attribute always expresses a notion more extensive than the subject. Aristotle gives ten classifications of attributes, which he calls *de categoriis;* Kant gives but four.

A proposition is *universal* when the subject is taken in all its extension, as, "Every substance is divisible," "No spirit is mortal."

A proposition is *particular* when the subject is not taken in its full extension, as, "Some men are learned."

Even such expressions as "All young men are fickle" are but particular propositions.

A proposition is *singular* when the subject is but one individual, as, "Cæsar was a great general."

A proposition is *affirmative* when the attribute is declared to be consistent with the subject, *negative* when declared inconsistent.

The following axioms in reference to affirmative and negative propositions are given in this connection; we shall need them further on:

1st Axiom. The attribute of an affirmative proposition is taken in its entire comprehension, but not in its entire extension; consequently, the attribute of an affirmative proposition is a particular term. For example, if I say, "All angels are spirits," the attribute "spirits" is taken in its entire comprehension, but not in its entire extension, for other beings than angels may be spirits.

2d Axiom. The attribute of a negative proposition is not taken in its entire comprehension, but is taken in its entire extension; consequently, the attribute of a negative proposition is a universal term. For example, if I say, "A man is not a stone," the attribute "stone" is not taken in its entire comprehension, since both "man" and "stone" have the comprehension of material substance; but it is taken in its whole extension, for no stone whatever is a man.

A proposition is *grammatical* when we consider only the terms as abstracted from the sense, and *logical* when we consider the proposition as having a determined sense.

The sense of a logical proposition may be *proper* or *foreign*: it is proper, or natural, when we give to the words their ordinary meaning, and it is foreign when we give to the terms a signification which is not their own.

The sense may also be either *divided* or *composite ;* or, to use the Latin expressions, the proposition may be taken either in *sensu diviso* or in *sensu composito.* For instance, if I say, " The blind may see," the proposition is true in *sensu diviso*, but false in *sensu composito.* In the first sense the proposition means, " The blind, if restored to sight, may see ; " in the second it means, " The blind, though remaining blind, may see." In the course of this work we shall have more to say of this distinction.

A proposition is *true* when it declares its subject to be as it is in reality, as, " God is powerful," and *false* when it declares its subject to be as it is not in reality, as, " God is cruel."

Sometimes a proposition has two senses, and then it is called *equivocal.* To obtain the true sense of a proposition it is often necessary to state the proposition in a different manner, to change the order in which the terms have been first presented ; sometimes also when two propositions are given and compared it becomes necessary to judge of the contrary or the contradictory of one of them ; it is, therefore, necessary for us to learn something of the conversion and the opposition of propositions.

§ I. Conversion of Propositions.

The *conversion* of a proposition is the changing of it into another proposition of the same meaning.

This conversion is *simple* when the whole attribute is substituted for the subject, and the subject for the attribute ; and it is *accidental* when a part only of the attribute takes the place of the subject.

The following rules must be observed in the conversion of propositions.

RULE I. The quality and the quantity of the proposition must be retained in the conversion.

RULE II. A universal negative proposition and a particular affirmative proposition may both be converted by simple conversion: for, in the first, both terms are universal (2d Axiom), and in the second, both are particula.' (1st Axiom); consequently, the quality and the quantity are kept in the conversion. Examples of simple conversion:

No man is a stone; no stone is a man.

Some men are good persons; some good persons are men.

RULE III. A universal affirmative proposition cannot be converted by simple conversion, for its attribute is a particular term (1st Axiom), except in necessary and reciprocal statements, that is, when they are identical in regard to the sense, as is the case in definitions. For example, " All priests are men " is not equivalent to " All men are priests," but to " Some men are priests." But " All circles are round " is equivalent to its reciprocal, " All round figures are circles."

RULE IV. A particular negative proposition cannot be converted either simply or accidentally; for such a conversion would violate the first rule, by changing the quality or the quantity of one of the terms.

§ II. OPPOSITION OF PROPOSITIONS.

When I say, " Peter is a learned man," and " Peter is not a learned man," I have two propositions which are *opposite*.

Opposition is, therefore, the negation in one proposition, and the affirmation in another, of the same attri-

4 *

bute, concerning the same subject and with the same reference. Consequently, in these two propositions, "Peter is good" and "Paul is not good," there is no opposition; nor is there any opposition in the following, "Peter is learned in philosophy" and "Peter is not learned in theology." To conclude, two propositions are in opposition when one of them denies what the other affirms. It follows that two negative propositions cannot be in opposition.

Two propositions are said to be *contrary* when in one of them more is said than is necessary to refute the other. Example: "All men are just. No man is just."

Two propositions are called *contradictory* when in one is said precisely what is necessary to refute the other; as, "All men are just. A certain man is not just."

Evidently two contradictory propositions cannot both be either true or false; for, if so, the same thing would be and not be at the same time; that is, the same attribute would be consistent and not consistent with the subject, which is absurd.

As a corollary, since two contradictory propositions cannot be true and false at the same time, it follows that when one is true the other is false, and vice versa.

Two contrary propositions cannot both be true at the same time, but both may be false; for, as two contradictory propositions cannot both be true at the same time, since in one of them is said precisely what is sufficient for the refutation of the other; so, *a fortiori*, two contrary propositions cannot both be true at the same time, since in one of those propositions more is said than is needed for the refutation of the other: also, since in one of the two contrary propositions more is said than is necessary to refute the other, there may be a middle term which is the true one; and consequently the two contrary propositions may both be false.

Examples: "All men are just. No man is just,"— both false. The middle term, "some men," is the true subject; and "some men are just" is the true proposition.

THIRD DISSERTATION.

ON REASONING.

When after comparing several judgments we draw a conclusion from them we are said to reason. *Reasoning* is, therefore, an act of the mind deducing a judgment from other judgments; and when expressed in words it forms an *Argument*. Argument then is to reasoning what the proposition is to judgment, namely, its formal expression in words.

When a judgment is certain, *a priori*, we can affirm or deny, at once, the conveniency between the two ideas which are brought near each other.

All the art of reasoning consists in bringing successively nearer to the subject and the attribute a third idea, which serves as a means to unite or to separate them.

This is the application of the general principle of identity: " *Quæ sunt eadem uni tertio, sunt eadem inter se;* " and of this principle of contrariety: " *Quorum unum est idem uni tertio, aliud vero non idem, non sunt eadem inter se.*"

The process of reasoning always supposes three judgments: 1st, A judgment to bring nearer the middle to the attribute; 2d, Another judgment to bring nearer the middle to the subject; 3d, Another judgment still to unite or to separate the subject and the attribute.

In these three judgments there is one which is universal, and which serves as a principle. The conclusion enters in this principle, as in a particular case. The second judgment serves to demonstrate it.

Reasoning may be *a priori*, when we set down at first the principle or the cause which accounts for the consequence or the effect; it is said to be *a posteriori* when, from the effect necessarily linked to a cause, we go up to the cause.

Reasoning is wholly *abstract*, when from rational premises a consequence of the same nature is drawn. It is purely *empirical*, when the principle is of a contingent order, and can be applied only to contingent objects.

Finally, reasoning is of a *mixed* nature, when we make the application of a principle necessary to physical realities.

Reasoning affects only *formal* truth; hence, if we assume a false principle, we shall, by good reasoning, deduce a false conclusion.

There are many sorts of argument, of which the syllogism is the most common.

We shall divide this dissertation into five chapters. In the first we shall treat of the syllogism and its rules; in the second, of the different kinds of syllogisms; in the third, of the forms of argument other than the syllogism; in the fourth, of sophisms; and in the fifth, of the sources of sophisms.

CHAPTER FIRST.

Of the Syllogism and its Rules.

The syllogism is an argument consisting of three propositions, so arranged that from the first two, called the premises, the third necessarily follows as a conclusion.

In every syllogism there are three terms: the *major*, or greater, the *minor*, or less, and the *middle*.

The major term is the attribute of the conclusion, of which the minor is the subject: as we have already learned, the attribute is always a greater term than the subject. The middle term, which is the term of comparison, is not found in the conclusion.

The first proposition of the syllogism is called the *major* proposition, because it contains the major term; the second is called the *minor*, because it contains the minor term; and the third, which, as we have just seen, contains both the major and the minor term, is called the *conclusion*.

The major and the minor are together called the *premises*, or the *antecedent*; and the conclusion is also called the *consequent*.

Example.

Middle Term.	Major Term.	
Major. ALL BAD MEN ARE MISERABLE;		Premises, or
Minor Term.	Middle Term.	Antecedents.
Minor. ALL TYRANTS ARE BAD MEN;		

Conclusion. All tyrants are miserable. Consequent.

The minor premise may precede the major.

Rules of the Syllogism:

1st. The syllogism must have but three terms.

2d. No term must be greater in the conclusion than it is in the premises.

3d. The middle term must be at least once a general term.

4th. No conclusion can be deduced from two premises which are either negative or particular.

5th. Two affirmative propositions cannot produce a negative conclusion.

6th. The conclusion follows the weaker premise. That is, when one of the premises is a negative proposition the conclusion will be negative, and when one of the premises is a particular proposition the conclusion will be particular.

Examples of faulty syllogisms:

Against Rule 1st.

Every *man* is a *spirit;*

Every *substance* is *divisible.*—Four terms, no conclusion.

Against Rule 2d.

Every animal is a living being;

Every animal is a substance;

Every substance is a living being.

Every substance, in the conclusion is a general term, and it is a particular one in the minor.

Against Rule 3d.

Every man is *an animal;*

Every brute is *an animal;*

Every man is a brute.

The middle term is taken twice in a particular sense and with a different reference, which constitutes two different terms; consequently, there are four terms in the premises.

Against Rule 4th.

No man is a stone;

Man is not marble.—No conclusion.

Against Rule 6th.

The Italians are soft;

The Italians are men;

Hence (some) men are soft.

This syllogism is good, but the following would be wrong:

No man is a stone.

Marble is stone.

Marble is man.

Syllogisms may be divided into four classes, according to the position of the middle term.

In the first class—The middle term is the subject of the major and the attribute of the minor.

In the second class—The middle term is the attribute of both premises.

In the third class—The middle term is the subject of both premises.

In the fourth class—The middle term is the attribute of the major and the subject of the minor.

In the first two classes we may have four cases, or forms of syllogism; in the third class we may have six forms; and in the fourth, five forms. Each of these cases, or forms, is designated by a word containing three vowels. The first two vowels indicate the quantity of the premises, and the third indicates the quantity of the consequent.

There are, as we have seen, four kinds of propositions, which are indicated as follows:

1st. Universal affirmative—by the vowel *a*.

2d. Particular affirmative—by the vowel *i*.

3d. Universal negative—by the vowel *e*.

4th. Particular negative—by the vowel *o*.

We will illustrate the use of these vowels by two examples:

First. All VIRTUOUS MEN are happy;
All good men are VIRTUOUS;
All good men are happy.

One form of the first class.

Second.

No vicious conduct is PRAISEWORTHY; ^{Middle.}

All truly heroic conduct is PRAISEWORTHY; ^{Middle.}
No truly heroic conduct is vicious.

One form of the second class.

In the first example, both of the premises and the conclusion are universal affirmative propositions, and, by the notation given above, must each be indicated by the vowel *a*. Hence the word used to designate this example must contain the vowel *a* three times. *Barbara* is the word used for this purpose.

In the second example, the major premise is universal negative, and therefore indicated by *e ;* the minor is universal affirmative, and hence indicated by *a ;* while the conclusion, universal negative, is designed by *e :* the word *celarent*, therefore, designates the form represented by this example.

It will now be enough, without further explanation, to give the words used to designate each form in the four classes of syllogisms:

1st CLASS.	2d CLASS.	3d CLASS.	4th CLASS.
Barbara,	Celarent,	Darapti,	Bramantip,
Cesare,	Camestres,	Disamis,	Camenes,
Darii,	Festino,	Datisi,	Dimaris,
Ferio.	Fakoro.	Felapton,	Fesapo,
		Dokamo,	Fresison.
		Feriso.	

CHAPTER SECOND.

OF THE DIFFERENT SORTS OF SYLLOGISMS.

The syllogism may be simple, complex, or compound. The *simple* syllogism is that of which we have treated in the preceding chapter. A *complex* syllogism is one

whose conclusion contains complex terms; it may always
be reduced to a simple syllogism.

Example:

Complex. {
Divine law obliges us to honor the pastors
 of the Church;
Benedict is a pastor of the Church;
Hence, divine law obliges us to honor him.
}

This syllogism is equivalent to the following:

Simple. {
Our pastors ought to be honored;
Benedict is our pastor;
Hence, he ought to be honored.
}

The syllogism is *compound* when the major is a conditional, disjunctive, or negative conjunctive proposition.

I. The major is *conditional* when it consists of two
parts, the one called the antecedent and the other the
consequent, united by *if*. In this case, when we concede the antecedent in the minor we must affirm the
consequent in the conclusion, and when we deny the
consequent in the minor we must also deny the antecedent in the conclusion—*verum prius, ergo et pos-
terius; falsum consequens, ergo et antecedens*—that is,
the first being true, the second is true; and the second
being false, the first is also false.

Example:
If Peter is wise he will stay away from gambling
houses;

1st. But Peter is wise; hence, he will stay away, etc.

2d. But Peter will not stay away, etc.; hence, Peter
is not, etc.

II. The major is *disjunctive* when it consists of two
or more parts incompatible with one another, and united
by *either—or*. In this case, when one part is affirmed
in the minor the other is denied in the conclusion. The

parts forming the major must be contradictory propositions.

Example :

We must either restrain our passions or yield to them ;

But we must restrain them (since reason and religion teach us to do so) ;

Hence, we must not yield to them.

Since the two propositions forming the major ought to be contradictories, there should be no middle term between them.

Example :

We must either obey governments commanding evil to be done, or we must revolt against them ;

But we must not obey governments commanding evil, etc. ;

Hence, we must revolt against them.

Here the major term, which should consist of two contradictories, is made up of two contraries, both of which, as we have seen, may be false ; hence, the error in this example. The truth is contained in a middle proposition, " We must suffer persecution."

III. The major is *negative conjunctive* when it consists of two contrary propositions. In this case, when we affirm in the minor we must deny in the conclusion, for both propositions cannot be true ; but if we deny in the minor we cannot absolutely affirm in the conclusion, for two contrary propositions may both be false. The rule is, therefore, as follows : One part ought to be affirmed in the minor and the other denied in the conclusion.

Example :

No one can serve God and mammon ;

The avaricious man serves mammon ;

Hence, he does not serve God.

CHAPTER THIRD.

OF THE FORMS OF ARGUMENT OTHER THAN THE SYLLOGISM.

1st. The *Enthymeme.*—This is an abbreviated syllogism, in which one of the premises is omitted.

Example:

God is good;

Hence, he should be loved.

The major, " We should love those who are good," is omitted.

2d. The *Epichireme.*—This is a syllogism whose major and minor are accompanied with proofs. The substance of Cicero's beautiful " Oration for Milo " is given in the following Epichireme:

It is lawful to kill those who lie in wait to kill us (this is proved by the natural law and by the laws of nations—many examples);

But Clodius lay in wait to kill Milo (this is proved by the number of armed men who accompanied Clodius, his absence from Rome at the time of the attack, etc.);

Hence, it was lawful for Milo to kill Clodius.

An Epichireme may be reduced to a simple syllogism.

3d. The *Sorites.*—This is an accumulation of propositions, so connected that the attribute of each is made the subject of that which follows, and the subject of the first becomes the attribute of the last.

The propositions must be well "chained," so that there may be no middle term between the attribute of one proposition and the subject of the following; and no equivocal proposition should be employed.

Example:

Avaricious men desire many things;

Those who desire many things are in need of many things;

Those who are in need of many things are dissatisfied with their condition;

Those who are dissatisfied with their condition are not happy;

Hence, avaricious men are not happy.

4th. The *Dilemma.*—This is an argument in which we conclude of the whole major, which is generally a disjunctive proposition, what we have concluded of each part. It is called a horned argument, because it strikes on both sides.

Example:

When the wicked die, either they are utterly destroyed or their souls are immortal;

If they are utterly destroyed there is no hope of eternal happiness for them;

If their souls are immortal there is also no hope of eternal happiness for them, since God is just;

Hence, there is no hope of happiness for the wicked after death.

To have the dilemma good no middle term must be possible in the major, and the conclusion must be true after each part.

5th. *Induction* or *Enumeration.*—This is an argument in which the major is an enumeration of particulars, from which a universal conclusion is deduced. That the argument may be absolutely conclusive, the enumeration must be complete.

6th. The *Example.*—This is a common form of argument, in which a single conclusion is drawn from a single proposition. This may be done in three ways: by similitude, or comparison (*a pari*), by opposition, or contrast (*e contrario*), and by superiority (*a fortiori*).

Examples:

1st, *a pari.* God forgave David when he repented; *a pari*, He will forgive me.

2d, *e contrario.* Intemperance is hurtful to health; *e contrario*, Temperance is favorable to health.

3d, *a fortiori.* John's conversation for even one hour is tedious; *a fortiori*, It would be tedious for a whole day.

CHAPTER FOURTH.

Of Sophisms.

The word *sophism* comes from the Greek *sophizo,* which signifies *to teach wisdom;* and the Greek noun *sophismos* means *wise invention.* From this etymology it is easy to understand that the word sophism had not in the beginning the meaning which it has at present. Men of subtle intellects, falsely called philosophers, have abused their powers of reasoning so far as to construct a theory for reasoning falsely, a theory by which fallacies are logically established as if they were truths. This is what is now called sophistry. A *sophism*, then, is a false reasoning, with the intention of deceiving. When the sophism results from ignorance in the reasoner, it is called a *paralogism.*

Aristotle divides sophisms into three classes: 1st, formal sophisms; 2d, material sophisms, or sophisms *extra dictionem;* and 3d, verbal sophisms, *in dictione,* that is, sophisms existing in the words used.

Formal sophisms are syllogisms badly constructed. Of these we have already spoken.

Material sophisms are the following:

(a) *Ignorantia elenchi,* which may be translated, "ignorance of the subject." This occurs when we prove what is not in question, or what is not denied

5 *

by our opponents; also when we suppose them to be actuated by principles which they disavow, or when we draw from their words or actions inferences which they would not admit. This sophism is of common occurrence; it comes from precipitation, prejudice, and feelings of pride or hatred towards our opponents, but still more from equivocation in terms not well defined. In order to avoid this last source of error, we must know both the precise sense and the exact extent of the expressions used by our opponents.

(b) *Petitio principii,* or "begging the question." This species of false reasoning takes place when we suppose as proved that which is to be proved. There is no substantial difference between this sophism and that called the vicious circle (*circulus vitiosus*), or arguing in a circle, which consists in proving two propositions by one another, neither of them being otherwise proved.

Examples:

The earth is immovable, because the sun moves around it.

Evidence is infallible, because God is infinitely true; and God is infinitely true, because it is evident, etc.

(c) *Non causa pro causa,* or, "Not the cause for the cause." This sophism occurs whenever we give as the cause of some effect that which is not its cause. This happens frequently, especially in the case of *"Post hoc, ergo propter hoc,"*—after this, therefore on account of this.

(d) Imperfect enumeration. No explanation needs to be given of this kind of false argument.

(e) Fallacy of objection. This sophism results when we consider as a cause, or as an essential, that which is only an accident.

The following are examples of the fallacy of objection:

(1) Philosophy rendered many men impious; then philosophy is a bad thing.

(2) False miracles have been believed; then no faith ought to be given to miracles, etc.

Verbal sophisms, or sophisms *in dictione*, are the following:

(a) Fallacy of division and composition. Passing from a distributive to a collective sense in the use of words.

Example:

Two and one are even and odd;

But two and one are three;

Therefore three is even and odd.

One and two are even and odd when divided (*in sensu diviso*), but not when united (*in sensu composito*). This distinction is the only one to be given in such cases. We may see that in the above sophism there are four terms: two and one are taken *in sensu diviso*, or distributively, in the major: and *in sensu composito*, or collectively, in the minor. Hence the syllogism involves an error against the 1st rule.

2d. Passing from a collective to a distributive sense; or attributing to several parts of a collection what is true only of the collection itself.

Example:

The Apostles were twelve;

Peter and James were Apostles;

Therefore Peter and James were twelve.

Here again we have four terms in the premises. The Apostles are taken together (*in sensu composito*) in the major; and separately (*in sensu diviso*) in the minor,—and no conclusion can be drawn.

(b) **Fallacy of accident.** This consists in asserting something of a subject in a general sense, in one of the premises; while in the other premise we connect with that subject some accidental peculiarity.

Example:

You now have the same feet that you always had;

But you once had small feet;

Therefore you now have small feet.

Putting this sophism in the form of a regular syllogism, we shall perceive that there are four terms in the premises.

Your present feet are those of your childhood;

The feet of your childhood were small feet;

Therefore your present feet are small feet.

In the major, the "feet of childhood" means the *essence* of those feet, while in the minor it means their *form* or *shape.* Hence, the middle term being taken in two different senses, we have four terms in the premises and can draw no conclusion.

Besides these two kinds of verbal sophisms, we have (c) that of Equivocation, (d) that of Amphibology, and (e) that of Figure.

Example of a sophism of figure:

No creature laughs but man;

But a meadow laughs;

Hence a meadow is a man.

We may observe that "meadow" is first taken in a figurative sense and then in a literal.

Doctor Ubaghs, speaking of these last three sophisms (c, d, and e), says that they do not deserve to be mentioned, since they could embarrass no one but a child or a person of very dull mind.

CHAPTER FIFTH.

Of the Sources of Sophisms.

The sources of sophisms are:

1st. Precipitation. We are liable to commit a sophism whenever we pronounce a judgment on anything which we have not well considered, or which is not sufficiently well known.

2d. Prejudice. In this case we form a judgment in accordance with our wishes and without previous examination.

3d. Our passions. There are impressions violently agitating our mind and forcing it in different directions.*

4th. Our senses. The senses have been given to us by God that we may judge of external bodies, not as they are in themselves, but as they appear to us.

5th. Our imagination. The imagination is that faculty of the mind which pictures to itself material objects that do not affect the senses.

Although the human mind is very imperfect, still it would never be deceived if we always acted prudently in the investigation of truth, abstaining from judging until the truth shows itself manifestly to the mind. We should then be ignorant of many things, and know others imperfectly; but we should not err.

---

* See, for the development of these terms, Passions, Senses, Imagination, at the Psychology.

FOURTH DISSERTATION.

ON METHOD.

We have now explained the notions of Ideas, the nature of Judgment and of Reasoning, and we have given rules for judging and reasoning correctly. It remains for us to examine in what order we should arrange these mental operations for the investigation and manifestation of truth. This arrangement and order is called Method, or "The way we must go in order to reach the end we have in view."

Definition.—*Method* is the ensemble of the rules disposed in that order which is most suitable for detecting the truth which we do not know, and showing it as soon as we know it.

Evidently the necessity of method shows the weakness of our mind; but without it progress cannot be made, nor can pleasure be found, in the reading of books or the teaching of masters.

Method being the application of the science of logic, is consequently an art; and this art is acquired rather by practice and experience than by precept, and it depends more on the rectitude and attention of our mind than on rules.

Division.—Before we proceed to indicate the different ramifications of method, according to the sciences to which it applies, it is important to show its most general characters.

Sometimes, the point of departure is a universal notion, and we seek to make clear through it some particular cases which are connected with it. And at other times, the starting-point is a particular truth which we wish to abstract and generalize. In the first case, we proceed from the simple to the compound; in the second case, we go up from the compound to the simple and the universal. The first method is called synthetic; the second, analytic.

The analytic method ought, amid variable conditions, to determine the fixed element which corresponds to the very nature of an observed object. Hence the name of analytic given to this branch of the method. Analysis (ἀνά λύω) consists in separating the elements of a whole, in order to study them better. Synthesis, on the contrary, starting from a simple formula, in its universality, imparts to particular cases the true principles in its generality. Now, these particular truths imply a new element joined to the comprehension of the principle. It is necessary, then, to unite several elements in order to form a whole. Hence the word synthesis (σύν τίθημι) used to characterize this method.

In the proceedings of dialectics, there are some which hold closer to analysis, whilst others lean more on synthesis. Abstraction, generalization, are analytic proceedings; deduction is synthetical. There is no science, in its entirety, which does not, at the same time, make use of both analysis and synthesis; for, in every one of them, we need sometimes to rise up to principles, and at other times to make application of them. The analytic method often takes the name of method of invention; the synthetic method is called method of doctrine.

Whatever be the method made use of, there are general rules from which the mind ought never to depart.

1st. Before all, we should form a just idea of the question proposed, and to have recourse, if needs be, to an exact definition of the terms which serve to express it.

2d. We should divide the question in all its points of view, so as not to embrace too much at one time.

3d. We should put apart, in order to consider them more particularly, the points of view which have a closer relation to the essence of the question.

4th. We should study each of the parts in reverting them to the ensemble, in order to know them as they are, and as they should be known.

5th. We should go from the more to the less known; from the more simple to the more compound; for the most general notions are the most easily understood.

6th. We should never support arguments except by notions which are evident *a priori*, or which are sufficiently demonstrated.

7th. We should apply to each question the method which is suitable to it.

First Division, the Method of Invention.

The difference between observation and induction may be stated thus: When our attention is directed towards a phenomenon or a fact, in order only to know it, we make an observation; but when that attention is directed to the same fact or phenomenon, in order to discover some law, or to deduce some conclusion from principles, we make, in the first case, an induction; and in the second, a deduction.

The method of deduction is synthetic, and the method of induction analytic.

To the first method belong the exact sciences of the mathematical order. The method of induction, or of observation, ought to be followed in the physical and natural sciences.

As to the science of spirits, we have the Theodicy, which is treated by deduction, and Psychology, where we ought to proceed by induction.

The science of the being, or general metaphysics, is a rational or deductive science.

Observation is, consequently, a serious attention of the mind, in order to know some fact, which fact may be either exterior or interior.

In order to observe well, four operations are necessary: First, attention; and this attention must be intense, persevering, and free from prejudice; second, distinct perception of the fact, that is, we must determine well the circumstances of its existence, and its essential elements; third, analysis, which should be complete, the examination being minute and exhaustive; and fourth, synthesis, which should also be complete, the recapitulation being made in proper order. These rules ought to be followed not only in observing, but also in making experiments.

Induction, which always supposes previous observation, is an operation of the mind affirming of things not observed that which we have observed in similar things.

Induction takes place not only in physical sciences, but also in all intellectual labor. The ancients had a knowledge of induction; Plato and Aristotle, as well as Bacon and Descartes, make mention of it. The last two were able to describe it with more insistence in the relations to the natural sciences. They, however, did not do it more exactly; at least, they invented nothing. There is a difference between induction and classification.

Classification consists in arranging the subjects which are related to a genus, a species, or a group of facts.

Four conditions are necessary in order that the induction may be good: "First, *abstraction;* second, *comparison;* third, *generalization* (this, as we have seen, signifies the discovery of a quality common to several similar objects; and this common quality serves as a distinguishing mark for the class in which all the similar objects are contained. *Classification* is the formation of these classes, and we may see that generalization

6

affords the materials for classification); and fourth, *induction*, properly so called, which is the extension of the common quality discovered by generalization to other objects of a similar kind."

NOTE.—This method leads us to a certain knowledge of the truth. There are other modes of investigation which lead us, not to a sure, but to a more or less probable knowledge of the truth; these are: analogy, hypothesis, and the calculation of probabilities.

Analogy is an operation of the mind attributing to one object some quality observed in another. In other words, analogy is the resemblance of two objects of a different order. Hence it is not a resemblance of identity. Analogy being a constant law in nature, judgment through analogy brings us to certitude.

Analogy helps the mind greatly in putting it on the way to precious hypotheses.

Example: A certain medicine has proved to be good for a certain sick person; analogy would lead us to believe that it would be good for another person sick in like manner.

Analogy must be grounded on obvious resemblance, and the resemblance must have necessary connection with the conclusion which we draw. Hence the science called cranioscopy, and others of that kind, are false.

Hypothesis is the supposition of a cause, in order to explain several effects of which the cause is concealed. An hypothesis is also called a *postulate*.

Example: The hypothesis of the existence of a neutral electric fluid in all bodies, in order to explain electric phenomena.

There are several laws to be consulted in the use of a hypothesis.

1st. The hypothesis ought not to be absurd, and evidently not false.

2d. The hypothesis must be brought forward only when there are no certain principles.

3d. The hypothesis must be apt to explain that for which it is given; it ought to follow, and not to precede observation.

4th. Every hypothesis should be verified as much as is possible by experimentation.

Hypotheses are very useful, but subject to many serious inconveniences. In order to proceed wisely when we form an hypothesis, we must first examine well the case which we wish to explain by hypothesis, and notice all its circumstances; for the degree of probability of an hypothesis depends on the number of circumstances which it explains: and, in the second place, we should choose out of those circumstances that which is most important, and try to explain it by the hypothesis; but although our hypothesis may explain this most important circumstance, yet if it be in contradiction to any other circumstance it must be rejected.

The *calculation of probabilities*, so far as it has reference to philosophy, will be spoken of in several other places, especially in Ethics.

SECOND DIVISION—THE METHOD OF DEMONSTRATION, OR DIALECTICS.

To demonstrate is to prove; and a *demonstration* is an argument in which the truth of a proposition is deduced from one or more propositions which are known to be true. The proposition from which the conclusion is drawn is called the principle of the demonstration; and as this principle may be either sure or probable, the deduction will be accordingly either certain or only probable.

The parts of a demonstration are as follows:

1st. The question, or proposition to be demonstrated. When the question is concerning a truth to be demonstrated, it is called a *theorem*, a *thesis*, or simply a *proposition;* and when it is concerning a truth to be discovered, it is called a *problem.* The question must be defined, divided into its parts, precise, and well arranged.

Example: The question is: is the human soul immortal? Immortality must be defined; and the question must be divided into its two parts concerning internal immortality and external immortality.

The first part of the question may be passed over, as evident; and then the real question comes, which is, whether the soul, after the death of the body, will pass to another life, a life without end. We next arrange this question into its two parts, (a) whether the soul, on leaving the body, will pass to another life, and (b) whether that life is eternal.

2d. The principle of the demonstration. This principle, or these principles, must be certain and connected with the question. They may be axioms, or facts of experience, or simply postulates. These first two parts, the question and the principle, are called the *matter* of the demonstration.

3d. The form of the demonstration, or the connection of the conclusion with the principle. This connection must first be accurate, that is, nothing should be used in the argument which does not belong to the question; and second, it must be clear.

The demonstration may be:

1st. *Analytical*, ascending, going from the question to some general principle; or *synthetical*, descending, starting from some general principle and coming to the question.

2d. *Direct* or *indirect.*

3d. *A priori*, the effects being proved by the cause; or *a posteriori*, the cause being proved by the effects.

4th. *Absolute*, resulting from a true principle; or *relative*, grounded on a principle admitted as true by our opponent, whether really true or not. This last demonstration does not prove that the conclusion is absolutely true, but only that it cannot be denied by those who admit the principle on which it is based: it is therefore called the *argumentum ad hominem.*

THIRD DIVISION—SCIENCE.

Science, or the certain knowledge acquired by reasoning, can be defined: The certain knowledge of a necessary truth understood by means of its own proper cause.

This necessity is absolute in analytical judgments, *a priori;* it is relative in analytical judgments, *a posteriori.*

Science supposes that things are known by their cause, for our mind is satisfied only on condition that it takes cognizance of what it observes.

In the physical order these causes are efficient, material, formal, and final.

In the metaphysical order, nature is the unique cause.

There is no science without principle; still these principles are not science, but its source. Notions deducted from these principles form the body of science, that is, the science itself.

Sciences are divided into *exact sciences*, or those which have for their source a judgment *a priori;* and *sciences deduced from observation*, having for their source a synthetical judgment.

Science is again divided into *speculative* and *practical* science; the former has for its end the contemplation of investigated truth; the latter is that which we endeavor to know in order that we may act.

Science is acquired by study and by teaching, for teaching aids the labor of the reason. The collection of particular sciences forms an encyclopedia.

St. Thomas divided science into five classes, according to the different degrees of abstraction. (Note I.)

Bacon has a subjective division. He divides science into three branches, corresponding to the three faculties of the soul: reason, imagination, and memory. This division is, however, faulty, because it is arbitrary; no science depends exclusively on any one of these faculties. Each one of the faculties of the soul has its field of action in all the sciences.

APPENDIX.

Of Universal Conceptions or of the Universals— Of Principles and Axioms.

1. *Of Universals, Nominalism, and Realism.* Intellectual knowledge is necessarily marked by the character of the absolute or universal; but created beings, the only ones we know, are individuals; and knowledge is true only when it is conformable to its object. How could we reconcile a universal knowledge with individual objects? Is the universal but a word? Some philosophers have affirmed it is. They are the nominalists, who are divided into two classes, the Nominalists, properly so-called, and the Conceptualists.

Others again have denied it, that is to say, that the universal is a real being. They are the Realists, who are also divided into two classes: the Exaggerated Realists and the True Realists. The Exaggerated Realists are again sub-divided into two branches; the one says that the Real Universal is out of nature, the other says that it is in nature.

The Sensualists of all ages are to be classified with the Nominalists. Conceptualism was maintained by Abailard and William of Occam in the fourteenth century. This system is found in the teachings of the Stoics.

Plato is the great champion of Exaggerated Realism. The Ontologists are Realists of the same type. Realism, which puts the Universal in the world, had for its principal advocate William of Champeaux. True or mitigated Realism was maintained by the greatest doctors of the school, and specially by St. Thomas.

(a) *Nominalism.*

Pure nominalism may be rejected. *The word,* for pure nominalism, is the common sign of the things which it represents. But this cannot be admitted, for the word in itself signifies nothing, and it is brought to the dignity of a sign only by the idea which it represents. As regards Conceptualism, instead of the word it is the idea which becomes the common sign of the beings which the idea represents. But the idea is idea only in the measure in which it connects itself with its object; when there exists no foundation for universality in things there is no more of it in ideas. Rightly, then, Leibnitz said that Nominalism destroys science and opens the way to scepticism.

(b) *Realism.*

Plato and the Ontologists place the Universal beyond the physical world. Plato's system would have that our science be no more the science of real beings, but its object would be absolute types of which existence is independent.

Ontologism showing us God in all things (God being their prototype, and this prototype of beings being real) leads us to Pantheism.

The Realism of Champeaux contains an apparent contradiction. Essence would be common, and, at the same time, individualized. 1st. The individual separated from its essence could no more be a determined being. 2d. Nature would be "sui juris," and the subjects which are its participants could never reclaim its property. This Realism again leads to Pantheism.

There remains, then, but True Realism, the theory of which is given us by St. Thomas.

There is nothing real in the world excepting singular existences. Real beings have their nature individualized; hence, there is no line of demarcation between pure essence and its individualization; they are inseparable things.

This individuality is not a necessary element of the nature of beings, it is but a condition of their actuation; neither is multiplicity essential, or else it would be altered by individualization. Therefore, nature is outside of number. Isolated in itself, nature is a determined principle by quality and not by quantity. Hence, there is no repugnance that it be considered, making abstraction of all individual conditions, Pure nature; the direct universal is, on account of the abstraction, the object of the conception of the mind. This pure concept of the mind can be adapted to all individuals of the species to which it will serve as commonplace.

This Realism, this pure concept, is not Nominalism, for, although giving to the mind its part in the constitution of the universal, it rests itself on the objects; it is even the objects which we know under the cover of a determined form, by an abstraction of the mind.

II. Of Principles or Axioms.

Principles are judgments which are at the foundation of sciences (principium), and which serve for the demonstration of truths, without having need themselves to be logically demonstrated; they are universal and of first evidence, they occupy a place entirely apart from all other judgments, they have a dignity altogether superior. Whence also the name of axiom (ἄξιος, worthy), employed as synonym of principle. General truths can belong to two distinct orders; they may be of a rational evidence, and again of an experimental induction. They may be necessary or contingent. Hence, two kinds of principles, *analytical* or *a priori* and *synthetical* or *a posteriori*.

In *a priori* judgments, coming from analytical principles, a necessary tie between the subject and the attribute is implied; while in *a posteriori* judgments we affirm of the subject an attribute which its concept does not contain.

Synthetic axioms are authoritative when connected with an analytical principle.

There is a difference between the axioms and supreme principles of each particular science, which are the propositions which determine its object and explain its mental attributes.

Analytical principles, according to their definition, are such that the conception of the subject and the attribute is evident by enunciation only.

Synthetical principles are made known to us by induction coming from observation.

Analytical principles suppose a common axiom, the principle of contradiction. Synthetical principles are supported by the principle of causality.

FIFTH DISSERTATION.

ON CERTITUDE.

CHAPTER FIRST.

PRELIMINARY NOTIONS—DEFINITIONS.

Certitude is the firm adhesion of the mind to the truth made known to it. Certitude does not admit of the actual possibility of a contrary judgment. Let one be certain of the existence of the world, he, by this very fact, rejects in his thought the judgment which would contest his existence.

Truth is, "that which is." Truth is either necessary or contingent. *Necessary truth* is that which cannot but be, and which cannot but be as it is. Such is the truth of the existence of God.

A *contingent truth* is one which, although it may exist, yet might not have existed, or might have existed in a different manner.

Truth cannot be known by the intellect unless it is cognoscible. That by which truth is cognoscible, or rendered capable of being perceived by the intellect, is called *evidence.* Evidence has an objective sense, as the term has been used by all good philosophers; although some have pretended that evidence being a perception has only a subjective sense.

Certitude is *subjective* when considered as existing in the mind; and it is *objective* when considered as existing in the object, in which case it is the same as truth itself, inasmuch as it is surely known or inasmuch as it is the object of our certitude.

Evidently subjective certitude cannot exist without

the objective; but objective certitude may exist without the subjective.

Evidence is also subjective as well as objective. Objective evidence is that which is perceived by the mind; it is objective evidence that is defined above. Objective evidence is the *visibility of truth*, and subjective evidence is the *vision of truth*.

Certitude is *implicit;* that is, direct, common, or spontaneous, when the mind adheres to the truth from what is only an implicit knowledge of the motion or cause which determines that adhesion. Certitude is *explicit*, philosophical or scientific, when the mind adheres to the truth from an explicit knowledge of the motion or cause which determines that adhesion. Both implicit and explicit certitude are true.

Certitude is *rational* or *experimental.* It is *rational* when it depends directly on reason, *experimental* when it comes to us from conscience or the senses. Rational certitude is again divided into rational certitude (properly so called), or immediate, and logical certitude, or mediate.

Certitude is *immediate* when the evidence of the truth is intuitive, and *mediate* when the evidence is discursive, or the result of a course of reasoning.

Evidence is itself immediate or intuitive when a truth manifests itself to the mind without the aid of another truth, as in the axiom. The whole is greater than any of its parts; and it is mediate or discursive when truth is made manifest by the aid of reasoning.

Note.—Mediate evidence is formed from that which is immediate, and requires more labor from our minds for its perception.

It is not possible by noting the manner in which the perception takes place in our mind to fix the line between intuitive and discursive evidence; we must, for this purpose, accept the definitions, and take them as rules for making the distinction between the two kinds of evidence.

A *primary truth* is one which is intuitively evident; and a *secondary truth* is one which is discursively evident.

Metaphysical certitude is that which is based upon the essence of things, and which can on no hypothesis be different from what it is.

Physical certitude is that which is based upon the laws of nature, and which cannot be other than it is except by a miracle.

Moral certitude is that which is based upon the laws of our moral constitution, and which cannot be otherwise without affecting the condition of humanity.

Moral certitude, more subject to be contradicted, does not establish an adhesion so firm as the others. It is thus that we have come to represent by the same name something radically different—a great probability.

Probability differs essentially from certitude. It is a character of opinions; and opinions are personal judgments, the truth of which is not incontestable. The mind, in presence of an opinion, remains in suspense—it doubts.

We would accordingly define probability the character of an opinion, which, without excluding the contrary opinion, commends itself the more to the intellect.

In regard to the subject, certitude is one and the same for all, though it admits of several degrees in the clearness of our perception of the truth, and in the intensity of our adhesion to it.

CHAPTER SECOND.

Of the Criterion of Certitude.

A criterion is a sign by which something may be distinguished from everything else; consequently, the *criterion of certitude* is the sign by which certitude is perfectly distinguished from error. Evidently such a sign must exist; but in order to proceed methodically, let us first examine what is the criterion of truth.

I. Proposition. *Objective evidence is the criterion of truth.* To prove this proposition we proceed as follows:

That which is so evidently the characteristic of truth that it cannot be attributed to falsehood, is the criterion of truth.

Such a characteristic is objective evidence,—that is, the property by which truth is cognoscible to our minds, and consequently by which truth is distinguished from what is not truth; for if evidence could be attributed to falsehood as well as to truth it would not be that by which what is true is distinguished from what is not true.

Hence, evidence, taken objectively, is the criterion of truth.

In order to meet objections that may be brought against this proposition, let us observe that there is a difference between judging and perceiving. We judge sometimes that such a thing is so and so, and perceive afterwards that we have made a mistake. In the first case we *judge* erroneously of something, which afterwards, on account of evidence, we *perceive* exactly as it is.

II. The criterion of certitude differs from the criterion of truth. The criterion of truth is the character proper to truth, and consequently something essentially objective; but the criterion of certitude is the character proper to our knowledge, and consequently something both objective and subjective. It is, after all, the criterion of truth applied to our mind, the criterion of truth being the cause of our certitude.

7

In order to determine in what the criterion of certitude consists, let us first see what are the conditions or marks which ought to be found in such a criterion.

This criterion ought to be : 1st, necessarily connected with truth ; 2d, known by itself; and 3d, universal, that is, it ought to be the last reason of certitude.

Proposition. *A clear perception is the only criterion of certitude.* Argument:

That is a criterion of certitude which has the requisite qualities for establishing such a criterion ;

But a clear perception has such qualities ;

Hence, a clear perception is the criterion of certitude.

Proof of the minor. 1st. Such a clear perception has a necessary connection with truth ; what we clearly perceive is evident, and it cannot be evident, as we have said, unless it be true. 2d. It is something known by itself, since it is a perception ; for nothing is more known to us than what we see. 3d. It is the last reason of certitude ; for the last reason which we can give for our certitude is this : " I see," " I perceive clearly."

We have said that this clear perception is the only motive of certitude ; for the other motives of certitude, of which we shall speak hereafter, are all grounded on this criterion. The last reason which we bring forward is always, " I see clearly."

CHAPTER THIRD.

Of the Existence of Certitude.

Some philosophers have altogether denied the existence of certitude, while others have established erroneous systems concerning its attributes. The following are the schools which we shall refute by the exposition of the true philosophical doctrine concerning the existence and the motives of certitude:

1st. Universal or subjective scepticism, also called Pyrrhonism. This denies, or at least doubts, the existence of subjective certitude; and since one who doubts his own existence may doubt anything, this subjective scepticism is called universal scepticism.

This was the system of the sophist Pyrrho and his disciples, and also of the "new sceptics," a sect that renewed the errors of Pyrrho at the beginning of the Christian era. Among modern philosophers, Montaigne (1533-1592), Bayle (1647-1706), author of "Dictionnaire Philosophique," which prepared the way to Voltaire and the Encyclopedists, and Hume (1711-1776), who wrote a "History of England" and some philosophic works, have indirectly adhered to the same system.

2d. Objective scepticism, or Kantism. This is the doctrine of those who accept subjective, but reject objective certitude. It is the system of the modern German school, represented by Kant, Hermes, and Fichte. Some French philosophers, of the school of Jouffroy, have accepted the doctrine of Kant with modifications.

3d. Idealism and Empiricism. The idealists are those philosophers who, extolling too much the certitude of pure reason, destroy in part the certitude of experience. Berkeley and Malebranche are the chief representatives of this system. Descartes adhered more or less to the system of Malebranche, and he was also of opinion that the perception of the senses, of itself, could not produce certitude.

The empiricists reject the certitude of pure reason, and teach that sensation is the only cause of certitude;

they are also called materialists and sensists. Of this class were Condillac and Helvetius, and in our time Augustus Comte, Littre, etc.

4th. Historical scepticism. This is the system of all those who attack historical certitude. It is of two kinds—general, when it rejects all historical certitude, and particular, when it refuses to admit some particular historical fact. We find this system, in regard to its principles, in Bayle, and in the writings of Craig, a Scotch mathematician, and also of Laplace and Lacroix.

A branch of this system has been called the theory of Mythism, which is mythism applied to history and religion. Philosophers, or rather infidel writers, try to explain in a mythical way the best authenticated facts of history. This system appears in the dangerous writings of Vico, Michelet, Dupuis, Volney, Strauss, Hegel, and, lately, Renan.

The arguments of scepticism, besides being inconsistent with themselves, soon disappear when they are reduced to their real worth.

1. The human reason, say the Sceptics, being fallible, can always err; and, consequently, we never possess that firm assurance which constitutes certitude.

Man is fallible in this sense, that he is not by nature, and in a necessary manner, exempt from all error. But it is equally false that on every question, and in every circumstance, he is subject to error. He may be mistaken for want of exterior evidence and lack of attention; but there are cases where the object appears to him sufficiently manifest as to engender, by a mediate or immediate evidence, a complete certitude. Then, although fallible, he is not deceived, and is certain that he is not mistaken. There is no need of having recourse to scepticism.

2. Doubt must continue until demonstration is obtained. Demonstration, which supposes a certain principle, bears, in its turn, on another demonstration, and so on indefinitely; but, as there must be a point of departure for this series, the initial principle will remain doubtful, and, therefore, all the consequences that flow from it.

The fallacy of this argumentation is easy to understand. It takes for granted that there is no primary evidence.

3. Sceptics also say: We are so apt to be deceived that, without discussing further the question of certitude, it would be wiser to doubt always. That would be like the reasoning of a man who, fearing to be poisoned, would consider it wiser, in practice, not to eat at all. Our frequent errors, our possible illusions, dictate the necessity for us to be prudent in our affirmations, to avoid precipitate judgments; however, we remain in full possession of the right to trust to certitude in the face of evidence.

All these reasonings, and others of the same kind, can, then, in no way, according to our principles, make scepticism acceptable. Scepticism cannot maintain itself, except in deserting the common ground of reason; in other words, it is a kind of insanity in the philosophic order. We must, then, leave the sceptics alone, and not lose our time in arguing with such silly persons.

5th. Rationalism. This is the doctrine of those who do not admit any revealed truth, and try to explain in a natural manner the miracles and mysteries of revealed religion. We shall see hereafter that revelation is possible, that it is an infallible motive of judging, that the doctrine revealed by God may be perceived by human reason, etc.

7 *

The system of rationalism is widespread. It has been taught in France by Cousin, Jouffroy, and Damiron.

6th. Fideism. This is the doctrine of several philosophers who think that genuine certitude cannot be obtained except by faith, either human or divine. As we may see, it is directly opposed to rationalism.

Philosophers have been found who denied the possibility of personal certitude, and, by a natural consequence, the existence of a *criterion*.

Huet, the learned bishop of Avranches, and in our days the abbé Beautain, in a moment of frailty, admitted as possible no certitude but that based on the word of God.

It is certain that God alone enjoys *absolute infallibility;* but man can possess certitude, and even *relative infallibility*, without enjoying absolute infallibility. God sees all things in an unobstructed view. The shadows that obscure our light of reason do not permit us to see or know all things. There are always truths which appear sufficiently evident to exact our enlightened consent. This, then, is the limit of our certitude. Such, for example, are the first principles and their immediate consequences; such are all the truths which have been called "the preambles of Faith." If we had nothing but revelation to justify our judgments, how would it be possible to demonstrate the existence of God, and to establish our own? How would we prove Divine truth and criticise the testimony of its interpreters? What assurance can revelation give us as long as those truths which are its foundation are able to be contested? To refuse reason all personal certitude, is to put to hazard all possible certitudes, not excepting revelation itself. It is true that, in fact, human reason too often remains beyond that natural capacity which it has preserved. Whence the moral necessity of a revealed doctrine to

remedy an infirmity which different causes, notably the
passions, may have aggravated. But a proof that it is
not impossible to arrive at certitude, is that there has
hardly been any philosopher of antiquity who either has
not brought to light some truth or refuted some error;
so much so that reason more than once rectified the
errors of reason.

La Mennais and his school brought forth another criterion. Mistrusting individual reason, he admitted it
to be possibly certain only when its judgments would
be confirmed by the judgments of all mankind—by universal consent. This it is that La Mennais called common
sense, which he pretended to be the last reason of our
certitude. In human nature there are many truths which
all ages have admitted. They belong chiefly to the moral
order. They have as characters: universality without
limit, constant duration, absolute invariability. Far
from rejecting which, reason adheres to them more
firmly. Their presence in all minds can be explained
by none of those causes which engender error, such as
corruption of morals or superstition. Consequently it
must be admitted that they are the appeal of a just and
good nature.

"Omni in re," says Cicero, "consentio omnium gentium lex naturae putanda est." Add to this that these
truths, intimately connected with our destiny, were not
left to the mercy of our fallen reason. Providence, as
always wisely disposing affairs, preserved them inviolate
in that great doctrinal current which dates back to the
origin of the world, and which we call tradition. Primitive tradition, successively confirmed and perfectioned
by the Mosaic and Christian, is a rule of faith destined
to supply our deficiences. Traditions kept otherwise in
the memory of people, or in books considered as sacred,

are deficient in many respects. They nevertheless agree among themselves, and with true tradition on certain dogmas, *v. g.* the existence of God, the immortality of the soul, the future life, the moral order, the sanction of laws.

Hence, whether we trust to the cry of nature or the authority of tradition, it would be absurd to contradict those truths of common sense; and in this regard we have the right to summon individual errors to the judgment of that tribunal. La Mennais, making of the authority of common sense a necessary criterion of all truths, as well rational as speculative and practical, extends it to a greater degree.

If common reason would act as a powerful organism, or each reason would intervene as a single element, concurring to the *ensemble*, we might be tempted to attribute to it a power of knowledge which we should refuse to individuals. But common reason is but the total expression of the separate work of each individual intelligence. Its power, then, could not exceed that of individual reasons; and it possesses no other certitude than that which belongs to themselves.

This unanimous consent, far from being the criterion of individual reason, is a striking confirmation of the certitude of each individual mind. Undoubtedly there cannot be common errors; therefore we shall not err in following the sentiment of the whole mankind, as we have already said.

But previous to being personally certain through common sense, it was necessary that we should first be personally certain in order to give rise to common sense.

Besides, how could we, if we cannot be certain by ourselves, come to know that what we think, what others say, is a truth of common sense? How shall we come to justify, as undeniable, that criterion of certitude? On this point of view again, personal certitude is supposed on the strength of the certitude of the common sense; and the latter never could exist if it had not the former for solid foundation.

This system was reconstructed lately under a modified form; and some authors have given to it the name of traditionalism, or the system of those who think that tradition, that is, the revelation made to man, and handed down by the testimony of men, is necessary to us, in order that we should have a certain knowledge of the truths of the natural order. This is the system which the provincial council of Rheims, held in 1853, condemned, and this condemnation was approved by Pope Pius IX., who at the same time condemned the following propositions:

(*a.*) They err who teach that human reason is, by its nature, inimical to divine revelation or opposed to it.

(*b.*) They err who teach that the force of human reason, in the present condition of our fallen nature, has been almost destroyed or rendered powerless.

(*c.*) They err who teach that no interior power has been left man by which he may acquire truth, or that all truths and notions come to us from exterior source— by speech and revelation.

(*d.*) They err who affirm that man cannot, with his reasoning powers, perceive and demonstrate certain truths of the metaphysical and moral order.

(*e.*) They err who teach that man cannot naturally admit any metaphysical or moral truth unless he has first believed by an act of supernatural faith through divine revelation.

(*f.*) They err who do not admit a distinction between the natural divine law and the positive divine law.

F

7th. *Sentimentalism.* We shall furthermore make mention of the German school of Jacobi (1743–1819). This philosopher lays down, as a basis to the certitude of our judgments, a certain interior attraction which renders us sympathetic with truth and hostile to error.

This exaggerated sentimentalism lays certitude on a blind force; for sentimentalism, previous to formal knowledge, is but an unreflected attraction. Besides, we would ask: what fixity could have our judgments left at the discretion of our humor? Nothing is less stable than are our impressions; and our judgments would be just as changeable as they if they depended on them.

Having named and described the systems according to which certitude is either disfigured or its existence totally denied, it now remains that we should affirm and demonstrate it. For this purpose the following propositions are stated and demonstrated:

First Proposition.—Certitude Exists.

It is certain that certitude exists if there are any truths which the mind accepts without any fear of erring; for then it perceives these truths clearly, and this clear perception is the criterion of certitude. But there are such truths; for when we say "Two and two are equal to four," the mind accepts the fact without any fear of erring. Hence certitude exists.

Second Proposition.

The existence of certitude is a fact which cannot be rigidly demonstrated, but which nevertheless becomes clearly manifest on mere statement or representation to the mind.

Certitude is a fact which cannot be demonstrated, if it be necessary for its demonstration that we should take as a principle that which is to be demonstrated. But such is the case in regard to the existence of certitude; for to demonstrate it we should first have to take as granted certain premises, which assumption would of itself suppose the existence of certitude; but this would be the *petitio principii*, or begging the question. It is enough, then, to show or state the existence of certitude; for this is so clear of itself that no one can seriously doubt it when thus presented to the mind.

Third Proposition.

No one can doubt the existence of certitude without falling into a contradiction.

He who supposes in the premises what he wishes to deny in the conclusion, contradicts himself. But such is the case with one denying the existence of certitude; for his conclusion would be the affirmation of his belief in the non-existence of certitude, and as an affirmation is the expression of a certitude it follows that he contradicts himself.

Sceptics bring many objections against this thesis. They say that we may find arguments both for and against every proposition, and that therefore we must doubt; and, again, that the human mind is fallible and knows nothing fully, and that for this reason, also, we should doubt. It is true that we must sometimes doubt, but not always; and hence certitude does exist. When they add that perhaps life is a dream, we need not stop to answer them.

This thesis refutes both subjective and objective scepticism.

CHAPTER FOURTH.

Of the Motives of Certitude.

A *motive*, in general, is that which disposes the mind to adhere firmly to some truth. We have seen that evidence clearly perceived is the general motive of certitude; but this evidence affects the mind diversely in regard to its adhesion to the truth, according to the different orders of truth. Hence there are different motives, which we shall examine successively:

First Motive.—The Certitude of Pure Reason.

Pure reason, or simply reason, is the faculty by which our mind perceives what is absolutely necessary. We have already seen what is meant by a necessary truth, and have shown that the evidence which pertains to necessary truth is the evidence of contradiction, that is, an evidence which does not allow us to suppose that the truth is other than it is without contradicting ourselves, or saying implicitly that the same thing may be and not be at the same time.

Reason has for its principle all necessary truths, that is, all truths which are intuitively evident. These truths are the sources from which all other truths are derived, and it is on this account that they are called the principles of pure reason. These principles have been also called axioms; and, although some writers have made a distinction between axioms and principles, we shall consider the two words as synonymous.

We may define an *axiom*, or *principle of pure reason*, to be a necessary and self-evident truth, from which other truths proceed.

These principles are: 1st. The principle of identity,

or essence; namely, "What is, is." This is the same
as the principle of contradiction; namely, "The same
thing cannot be and not be at the same time," a principle
implicitly contained in every necessary truth. 2d. The
principle of equality and inequality; namely, "Two
things which are each equal to a third are equal to each
other;" and "Two things, of which one is equal to a
third, while the other is not equal to this third, are
unequal to each other." 3d. The principle of substance;
namely, "The mode supposes the substance." 4th. The
principle of causality; namely, "That which has a beginning has a cause."

These axioms being given, we prove the following

Proposition.—*Pure reason gives certitude of necessary truths.*

(a) This proposition is clear, according to the very
definition of reason. Reason is perceiving; but if the
mind could never adhere to truth, reason would at the
same time be perceiving and not perceiving. It would
be perceiving according to the hypothesis, and it would
not be perceiving, because we should always doubt;
that is, the same thing would, at the same time, both
be and not be, which involves a contradiction. Hence,
when reason perceives clearly it gives true certitude.

(b) This proposition cannot be seriously opposed, if
it be false argument to suppose as true what we attack
as false. But such is the case with any argument con-
trived against the legitimacy of reason, since he who
would argue against reason would suppose that reasoning is a lawful mode for the attainment of certitude.

SECOND MOTIVE.—CONSCIOUSNESS.

Consciousness is the interior feeling by which our
mind is aware of its present condition or state.

8

Proposition.—*Consciousness produces a true certitude in regard to our interior feelings and affections.*

Consciousness gives a true certitude, if there is a necessary connection between it and the truth of the judgments formed by it. But such is the case, since the object and the subject are the same individual; consequently, consciousness cannot be deceived. Hence consciousness gives true certitude; and the judgments formed by it concerning the appearances of things which have affected it are essentially true, since they express the present state of the soul.

Here, again, we cannot demonstrate the truth, but simply show it; for any truth which we could bring forward as a principle of demonstration would rest on reason and on consciousness, which latter is aware of the evidence produced in our mind. These two motives, reason and consciousness, are, as we see, chained together.

Our own existence is, in regard to ourselves, the first truth known of itself, or self-evident.

Third Motive.—The Evidence of the Senses.

The evidence of the senses is that to which necessarily yields that invincible propensity which induces us to refer our sensations to the bodies which, according to our convictions, have been the causes of them; and by which, therefore, we judge of the existence of the bodies themselves.

Our senses lead us into many errors and illusions, and consequently some philosophers have refused to acknowledge that our senses may give us true certitude. Hence, the origin of objective scepticism, of idealism, and of traditionalism. Against those philosophers we establish the following

Proposition.—*By the evidence of the senses we can judge infallibly of the existence of bodies in general.*

That is infallibly true which we are irresistibly forced by nature to believe as true. But we are irresistibly forced by nature to believe in the truth of the existence of bodies in general, which we perceive by our senses. Hence, by the evidence of the senses we can judge infallibly of the existence of bodies in general.

We prove the minor as follows: A propensity which is universal, constant, and irresistible may be considered to be the effect of truth, or the voice of nature, and consequently to exclude every doubt. But that propensity by which we are led to judge of the existence of bodies in general is universal, constant, and irresistible. It is universal, since we find it in all men; constant, for all men have it during their whole life; and irresistible, since we cannot overcome it whatever efforts we make. It is then the voice of nature, the expression of truth.

Indirect demonstration.—If there were no bodies, there would be no difference between the phantoms of our imagination and real bodies; but we know that this difference does exist, and hence bodies must exist.

The evidence of the senses, according to the more probable opinion, gives immediate certitude; and, consequently, in regard to the strength of the conviction produced in our mind, the certitude given by the evidence of the senses is equal to that given by reason or by consciousness, from which it differs only in regard to the object, which is metaphysical in one case and physical in the other.

The propensity by which we are led to believe in the

existence of bodies in general, will also enable us to judge in favor of the existence of bodies and external events in particular; for the same argument may be brought forward in this second part of the thesis as in the first. But in this case four conditions are required in order that the evidence of the senses may be an infallible motive of certitude:

1st. The organs of sense must be sound and in their normal condition.

2d. The bodies themselves must be within the limits of the perception of our senses.

3d. Nothing must intervene between the organs of sense and the bodies, so as to interfere with the ordinary laws of their action.

4th. Each of the senses must be exerted upon an object upon which it cannot properly act.

These conditions being observed, the evidence of the senses gives a true certitude in judging of the relative properties of bodies in particular, but not of their essence; that is, we may judge of them as they appear to us, but not as they are in themselves.

Fourth Motive.—The Consent of Mankind in Things of the Moral Order.

By the *consent of mankind*, we do not mean unanimity, or metaphysical universality, but that general consent which is called moral, being the consent of the greater and sounder part of mankind.

This consent is the result of common sense, and *common sense* is nothing else than that source of general knowledge of first notions or principles which is found in all men, extending to all conclusions that are evident but informal, and especially to moral dictates.

In order that such a consent may be a criterion of

certitude, it must be constant, uniform, reasonable, and not indifferent in regard to its object.

Proposition.— *The consent of mankind, with the conditions prescribed above, is an infallible motive of judging, in regard to several moral truths.*

1st. Either such a consent ought to be admitted as a criterion of certitude, or some private opinion should be preferred to it; but such a preference would be absurd, and therefore the general consent must be admitted.

2d. A man who would defend an opinion contrary to common sense ought to defend it with irresistible arguments; but he could not find such arguments (a) in his reason, for his reason must be in harmony with universal reason; nor (b) in the consent of mankind, for he rejects this motive of certitude : he would, then, be obliged to admit this consent or be in contradiction with himself.

3d. Direct argument.—It would be absurd to admit that the majority of men, and most sound part of humanity, would deceive, or could be deceived; but if one should deny the proposition under consideration this absurdity would result. Consequently the general consent must be accepted as an expression of the truth.

4th. This consent has been accepted in all ages and at all times as an infallible motive of judging. To show this, it will be sufficient to quote the following from Cicero : "What is established upon the laws of nature must be true, if anything is true; but a general consent of mankind, which is constant, uniform, and refers to something of great importance, as the existence of a Supreme Being, the necessity of worshipping the Deity, etc., is the voice of nature."

To solve any objections to this proposition, we have only to refer to the four conditions already indicated.

8 *

FIFTH MOTIVE.—THE TESTIMONY OF MEN.

As we have already said, we can judge by our senses only of those facts which we have witnessed: for other facts we must rely on the testimony of men.

Descartes seems inclined to invalidate that authority in his treatise *De Methodo*, in which he makes known his resolution to rely no longer on the judgment of others—at least in the order of rational truths—and to have confidence only in his own reflections. By thus acting, the mind would be encompassed within very narrow limits, and all the knowledge accumulated in the storehouse of ages would be imprudently rejected; and that grand law which makes the help of society necessary for our further development in every respect would be entirely disregarded; personal certitude would then be shattered, for a witness, otherwise reliable, offers us the guaranty of his reason, which is, in truth, similar to our own: and if we consider the knowledge of others doubtful, our adherence to our own knowledge will then cease to be certain.

It would be absurd to place in opposition to the imposing authority of the ancient doctors an intellect perhaps only slightly refined. For a stronger reason, it would be entirely wrong to reject the restrictive authority of revelation, which not only has reference to the transcendent mysteries that Descartes sets apart, but also teaches moral truths which man, absolutely speaking, might be able to know; yet in the investigation of these truths, on account of his weakness he is often led into gross errors.

By its nature, such testimony is not necessarily infallible; and we have to examine under what conditions it may be considered an infallible motive of certitude.

We shall first give some general notions concerning the *facts*, the *witnesses*, and the *conditions* which the testimony must have in order to be an infallible motive of certitude.

(*a.*) The facts may be: first, contemporaneous or past; second, public or private; third, of great or of little importance; fourth, favorable to the views of the people or opposed to them; fifth, clear or obscure; and sixth, natural or supernatural.

(*b.*) The witnesses may be: first, eye-witnesses or historical witnesses, and second, contemporaneous with the events or posterior to them.

(*c.*) The testimony, in order to be an infallible motive of certitude, must have the following conditions: First, the fact must be possible; second, it must be important; third, there must be several witnesses who were not deceived, who would not deceive, and who could not deceive, even if they wished; and fourth, these witnesses must speak clearly and be clearly understood.

Bayle and his followers have attacked the legitimacy of the testimony of men as an infallible motive of certitude, and have gone so far as to deny the possibility of establishing with certainty the truth of any historical fact. This system has been called Historical Pyrrhonism; and it must be rejected for the following reasons: First, it is as much repugnant to the nature and moral disposition of men as is Universal Scepticism; second, it is opposed to reason, which naturally admits that several witnesses cannot be deceived in regard to the substance of an important fact, and that they would not and could not deceive: this second part is grounded (*a*) on the love of truth, which is natural to man, and (*b*) on the principle of veracity, or the inclination which all men have to speak this truth: the impossibility of deceiving may come from the fact itself; and this takes place when many relate a fact which is hurtful or useless to them, or one concerning which their previous interests are divided; or the impossibility may come from the nature of the testimony, as when many persons relate the event in the same way, even in the smallest details; or, again, it may come from the character of the witnesses, and is very clear when they are all honest.

Pyrrhonism must, in the third place, be rejected because its acceptance would result in the subversion of religion, of society, and of private rights. The truth of religion is established by facts, while society rests upon a system of customs, laws, and forms of government, which, in regard to their origin, are based on tradition, or the testimony of men; and private rights, so far as their origin is concerned, depend upon titles and documents handed down from generation to generation by the testimony of men. Bayle's doctrine must therefore be rejected. From what has been said, it is indirectly proved that the testimony of men is sufficient authority for the existence of facts of which we have not been eye-witnesses, including historical facts.

We have now to proceed to the direct proof of the proposition that the testimony of men is an infallible motive of certitude in regard to facts. As the facts may be either natural or supernatural, it is evident that the question at issue is a double one; we shall, therefore, examine it in two sections.

§ I. Authority of the testimony of men concerning natural facts.

1st. Proposition.—*The testimony of men is an infallible motive of judging of contemporaneous facts.*

We may judge that a fact is true when the witnesses have not been deceived, and when they would not and could not deceive. But such is the case with facts which are contemporaneous and of great importance. This minor has been fully developed in the preceding remarks; therefore the testimony of men is an infallible motive, etc.

NOTE.—When we speak of facts we mean the substance of them, for we may be deceived in regard to secondary circumstances.

It is not necessary that the number of the witnesses should be great, provided, 1st, that they are honest; 2d, that their account is uniform; 3d, that they persevere in giving the same testimony at all times; and 4th, that it is evident they are not influenced by motives of interest or pleasure, or that their interests are divided, or that the fact is opposed to their interests, or that the fact is of such notoriety that any fraud might be detected by other contemporary witnesses.

We may accept the evidence of even one eye-witness when he is entirely trustworthy, and when the fact which he relates is in necessary connection with other known facts, and especially when the witness is of great wisdom and virtue, and still more if he attests by miracles the truth of his testimony.

The objections to this first proposition, given under different forms, are expressed in the following major: "If the testimony of one man gives only probability, the testimony of several men will give only several probabilities, but no certainty." We deny the major; the amount of probabilities is not to the point: the question is not concerning the value of testimonies taken separately, but concerning the value of testimonies taken together. Consequently the objection is a sophism, which we have called *ignorantia elenchi*, or a mistaking of the question at issue.

2d. Proposition.—*The testimony of men is sometimes an infallible motive of judging of past events.*

Argument: The testimony of men is an infallible motive of judging of past facts, provided there be several means by which truth comes to us. But such is the case, the means being: tradition, history, and monuments.

The force of the argument from tradition comes, first, from the moral impossibility that many men have been deceived, or that they have deceived; this has been sufficiently developed already: and, second, from the argument of prescription, according to which the actual existence of a tradition or a universal custom, the reason for which cannot be given unless the fact on which it is based be accepted, makes it necessary to accept the fact; for such a tradition could not originate in error or falsehood, it not being possible in regard to facts of a serious nature and having a serious consequence, that an error should have either suddenly appeared or slowly grown through centuries without some protestation against the falsehood. We are, therefore, justified in assenting to the truth of a fact which is attested by tradition: the argument is considered good even in respect to moral obligations.

History must be authentic, true, and entire. The authenticity of a book may be established by oral and written tradition, and also by an examination of the book itself. A book is authentic when its style is the same as the style of other books known to be by the same author, and when the contents of the book are in harmony with the known views, doctrines, and opinions of the author. An historical work is true when the facts related, whether contemporaneous or past, are of great importance, are public in their nature, and are not contradicted by any historian of the same period. A history is known to be entire, when a comparison with the original manuscripts, or the first printed editions, shows no omission or alteration of statements in regard to important circumstances. When such a comparison cannot be made, we may judge by the unity of style and plan, and the satisfactory connection of events, that the work is entire.

In regard to monuments, it is necessary that they should have a necessary connection with the events commemorated, whether erected at the same time or afterwards.

It is objected that a certitude cannot be perfect which is diminishing gradually by the lapse of time and the loss of titles, which rests upon the testimony of witnesses less trustworthy than eye-witnesses, which becomes less clear as the date of the facts becomes more remote, and which, finally, has often been the source of deception. We answer, that a certitude once established is always a certitude; and though it may not afterwards affect our sensibilities so deeply, nevertheless its intrinsic nature is not thereby changed, and we always have sufficient means to detect a falsification when this takes place.

§ II. Authority of the testimony of men concerning supernatural facts.

A *supernatural fact* differs from a natural fact only with reference to the cause and the manner of its production. In regard to the effect, or the fact itself, it is a natural one. With this explanation, we proceed to demonstrate the following

Proposition.— *The testimony of men is an infallible motive of judging of supernatural facts.*

The truth of supernatural facts may be established by

the testimony of men, provided this testimony has the same force for proving such facts that it has for proving natural facts. But such is the case; for, as we said in the introduction to this proposition, and this assertion is denied by no one, a supernatural fact, in regard to its effect an exterior motive, is only a natural fact, and consequently can be established by similar proof, so that we might here repeat the argument already given in regard to natural facts. The testimony of men is true, when many witnesses relate the same fact, whether this be a miracle or a mere natural fact, provided it be evident that these witnesses have not been deceived and have not deceived. Hence, the testimony of men is an infallible motive, etc.

The objections to this proposition rest upon the following assertion: A miracle is impossible. In this assertion there is an implied contradiction; for to pretend that all the witnesses to the miracles of our Lord were deceived or did deceive, is to assert a miracle in the moral order greater than the facts which are denied.

From what has been said, we may understand what is meant by *authority*. It is the motive by which we judge of those things which we do not know ourselves. Authority is human when it is the source of human faith or belief, and divine when our adhesion to it constitutes divine or supernatural faith.

Sixth Motive.—Memory.

Memory is that faculty by which we recall to mind feelings that are past.

There are the *sensitive memory*, which preserves and renews the sensations, and which is connected to the external perception, and the *intellectual* memory, or that memory which is relative to ideas and their relations.

Both are related to each other; and on account of that union the brain, which is the organ of the sensitive memory, becomes the organ of memory in general. Hence all violent affection of the brain has its rebound in the memory. The proper character of memory is faithfulness. Memory supposes that knowledge remains and reproduces itself such as it was. Take away that quality and there would no longer be memory.

Memory is *spontaneous* and *voluntary* according as former informations come back, as it were, of themselves, or present themselves at the call of the will.

The acts of memory take the name of *remembrances*. When remembrances remain confused and ill-defined they are called *reminiscences*.

Memory is a precious faculty. It is to it that our intellectual life owes the favor, at every moment, of surviving to itself. Hence the importance of cultivating and developing it from an early age by attention, by sensible representations, and especially by putting order in the mind and learning with method.

Proposition.—Memory is an infallible motive of judging of a past state of the mind of which we have a clear recollection.

This proposition cannot be proved; it can only be explained.

I. There is certitude where there is a clear perception of a truth; but by memory, when our recollection is distinct, we have such a perception. Hence we have certitude.

II. Judgments based upon a universal, constant, and irresistible propensity are infallible. This is admitted by every one; and were it not true we might doubt of everything, even of God himself. But by memory we form judgments which are based upon an irresistible,

9 G

constant, and universal propensity, these judgments are therefore infallible. Hence memory is an infallible motive, etc.

Memory, like consciousness, produces an immediate certitude, and consequently cannot be demonstrated, since the demonstration should rest on memory itself. It is, in fact, by memory that we call to mind the very first principles, the bases, of every demonstration.

Seventh Motive.—Induction or Analogy.

We reason by *induction* when we pass from phenomena observed and known to phenomena which are neither known nor observed. The following definition of induction may therefore be given: Induction is the operation by which, from several particular phenomena, the mind concludes the existence of a general law of nature.

The principle of induction rests upon the laws of nature. These laws may be summed up in these three axioms: 1st. There exists a constant and general order in the things which have been created, that is, in nature; 2d. Every natural cause follows a certain order in the production of its effects; 3d. The same natural cause, placed in the same circumstances, produces the same effect.

We may now proceed to establish the following proposition concerning the principle of induction.

Proposition.—*A persuasion of the constancy and generality of the laws of nature is an infallible motive of certitude.*

What is born with us must be in harmony with the truth, and consequently an infallible motive of certitude; for if a persuasion natural to our mind could be false, the very constitution of the mind itself would be false, which would be the destruction of all certitude. But a persuasion of the constancy and generality of the laws of nature is innate; for it is universal, irresistible, and anterior to reason itself, as we see in the case of children, who instinctively avoid what is hurtful; such a persuasion is therefore an infallible motive of certitude.

We have seen, from the exposition of the principles of induction, that there are in nature general laws; but is it possible to have a true certitude in regard to the existence of the laws of nature in particular? In order to solve this question we proceed to establish this

Proposition.—*Induction sometimes gives true certitude concerning the laws of nature in particular.*

We have true certitude when we clearly perceive some truth, and when we may affirm it without any fear of erring. But by induction we know surely, and consequently perceive clearly, the existence of some laws of nature in particular; for instance, that fire will burn wood, melt lead, etc.; and we affirm the existence of these laws without any fear of erring. Certitude, then, sometimes gives us true certitude, etc.

Notes.—Induction gives certitude concerning the existence of a law of nature in particular, when there is some identity of circumstances in the phenomena which are observed, and this identity may be discovered by an attentive observation.

The certitude of facts known by induction is sometimes merely conditional and sometimes absolute.

The laws of nature are contingent, and God can suspend them when this suspension is not in opposition to his attributes, but not when such suspension would be in contradiction to any of these attributes. For instance, He could not cause a multitude of persons to agree among themselves to tell an untruth which would be injurious to their own interests. From this explanation we may know when the certitude given by induction is conditional and when it is absolute.

The laws of nature are twofold, physical and psychological; the former governing corporal bodies and the latter regulating spiritual substances. Moral laws are included in the psychological laws. By induction we may learn the existence of psychological as well as of physical laws.

APPENDIX.

PROBABILITY.

Although, in itself, certitude is complete and indivisible, yet it sometimes happens that a proposition, true in itself, appears to us to approach the truth more or less nearly, according as we have more or less reason for believing it to be true. Those reasons which leave our minds in a state of uncertainty are called probabilities. When the probabilities in favor of a proposition are equal to those against it, we have what is called *doubt;* and when those in favor are more numerous than those against we have *verisimilitude. Probability,* then, is the motive which inclines us, in a greater or less degree, to believe as true that which is not completely demonstrated. As it is often very difficult to determine the degree of probability in favor of or against a given proposition, we must be cautious and not judge beyond what we perceive.

We admit historical facts which are only probable, whenever we have to doubt on account of the difficulty of criticising the sources of the history. In our daily actions, also, we often have to conduct ourselves according to information which is only probable. The further elucidation of this question belongs to theology.

In many questions relating to future events the issue depends upon a certain number of unknown possibilities; the probability of one of these possibilities may, therefore, be determined mathematically, and upon the result obtained certain calculations may be based. In this manner contracts of insurance are drawn up, certain games of chance are predicted, etc. But evidently logic has nothing further to do with this subject. Here, then, closes the First Part of this work. (Note II.)

9 *

PART II.

METAPHYSICS.

PRELIMINARY NOTIONS.

METAPHYSICS literally means *above nature*, and "nature" here signifies the physical and corporeal things. The following definition of metaphysics is generally accepted: The science of supersensible and merely speculative things, as known to us by reason. By the words "merely speculative" metaphysics is distinguished from the other parts of philosophy.

Metaphysics is divided into two parts, general and special. General metaphysics has been called *ontology*, or the science of being; and special metaphysics comprises *pneumatology*, or the science of spiritual substances, *cosmology*, and *anthropology*.

Pneumatology is divided into two parts, the first treating of God and his attributes, and the second of the human soul, its faculties and qualities. The first is called *theodicy*, or the science of God, and the second *psychology*, or a dissertation on the soul.

This order in the division of pneumatology is manifestly the proper one, for the knowledge of God and of his attributes is necessary in order to treat of various questions concerning the human soul. The destination of the soul for another life, for instance, cannot be proved until we have demonstrated the existence of

102

God and his providence with his infinite wisdom and justice, ready after this life to render to every one according to his deserts.

NOTE.—Nothing is more general than the idea of being and its properties, considered abstractly from any particular determination. Moreover, nothing is more philosophical than the science of a being or ontology.

The being appears to us in the finite beings, but these bear the mark of their dependence, and reveal a being not created and infinite.

Finite beings are divided into corporeal and spiritual. To determine the nature of those two classes of beings in their remotest principles is also the object of philosophy. These two new branches of the whole philosophical science are cosmology, which treats of bodies, and psychology, which treats of spirits.

In order to conform ourselves to the plan adopted by many authors of the present day, we will treat of cosmology in an appendix at the end of our dissertation on ontology.

FIRST DISSERTATION.

ON ONTOLOGY.

The word ontology comes from two Greek words, λόγος and ὤν, which together signify "discourse on being." Ontology may therefore be defined to be that part of philosophy which treats of being in general and of the general species and relations of being. In this dissertation we consider being as such, and therefore as existing either in the order of things or at least in the order of ideas; and as we may have a positive idea of being thus abstractedly considered, the title of this dissertation, "Ontology," or being in general, is correct.

We shall divide the subject of ontology into five chapters, treating in the first of the notion, essence, and possibility of a being in general, in the second of its causes and its effects, in the third of its species, in the fourth of its properties, and in the fifth of space and duration.

CHAPTER FIRST.

Of the Notion, Essence, and Possibility of a Being in General.

A *being* is that which exists or may exist. The notion of being is the first of all notions. We cannot think of anything unless there be some being; hence the notion of being is logically prior to our thought, the notion of being is necessarily involved in thought.

We have given the definition of being such as we find it in almost every text-book. In reality being cannot be defined, because of all ideas that of a being is the most simple and most common. This definition would, moreover, be useless, because nothing is more intelligible.

When we say that a thing is, we thereby understand that it is actually in existence. Being, therefore, signifies, in the first place, actual existence. This existence can be considered as either real or possible. Being is an attribute proper to everything that can be known. For everything, the word *being* seems as a commencement of its affirmation.

The Being, par excellence, is God. We ought not to conclude from this, as ontologists do, that we conceive nothing but in God and in the idea of God, for things have their being proper to them; they have a way of being intrinsically which permits to conceive them directly. Being is divided into *absolute being*, or that which is of itself and without any relation to something else, and *relative being*, or one that has relation to something else.

Being is also divided into *real being*, which belongs to things, and *ideal being*, or that which things have in the mind which knows them.

For not having observed the distinction between the real and the ideal, several philosophers fell into dangerous errors.

The being is further divided into the *actual being* and the *possible being*.

The *act* is understood, at first, as the action which a being exerts on another in order to produce in him some change.

This action supposes the power to act in the cause and the *power to suffer* the action. There is on the one hand the *active power* and the *passive power*.

This twofold power is evident: to deny it is to affirm the impossibility of all change.

Such is the most common meaning of the word act. This signification, however, goes further. If a being, without any extraneous action, possesses a development proper to itself, we say, then, that he is *in act* of himself.

The act which actualizes the passive power of the being upon whom it exerts itself seems to pass in him to substitute it to the simple power. Thus a cold body which is made hot seems to apprehend the act of the hot body which acts upon it : it passes from the *power* to the *act*.

We say that *habits* are *acts* with regard to the *power of acting ;* because they suppose that power to be, in a certain measure, actualized.

The form is the *act of the matter ;* and the existence the *act of the essence.*

This term *act,* which is difficult to define, as are all elementary concepts, indicates the complement in view of which a thing was but *in posse.*

The *possible* as opposed to the *actual* may be defined : " That which awaits realization."

The *essence* of a being is that without which a being can neither be nor be conceived to be. For instance, we cannot conceive the idea of a man without the notions or attributes of intelligence and animality.

Essence is the quiddity, the intrinsic form, or simply the form. In ordinary language, *formal* and *essential* are synonymous terms. Essence, the starting point of all properties, faculties, and operations, takes on this account the name of matter. Existence is the last actuation of the being, the realization of its essence.

Essence in the mind, contrary to the doctrine of Locke, is true only in so far as it is conformable with the reality : neither is *essence* an only property, as Descartes teaches.

The agreement among the essential attributes of a being forms the possibility of its existence. Consequently if certain attributes involve a contradiction they cannot constitute a being—that being is not possible. There is such a contradiction in a round square, consequently a round square is an impossibility.

The possibility, as we understand it here, abstracting it from the idea of existence, is what the philosophers call metaphysical or intrinsic possibility.

This accord among the essential attributes, which constitutes the possibility, is immutable, and consequently necessary. It is immutable, for if it could be changed there would be, at the same time, accord and discord among the essential attributes of a being; that is, the same thing would at the same time both *be* and *not be*, which involves a contradiction and which is therefore absurd. That accord is then necessary since it is immutable: hence that accord, which is the essence or possibility of a being in general, does not depend on the free will of God; but since it is immutable and necessary, like God, it has its seat or foundation in God Himself, in the divine intellect, in the very essence of God. Descartes therefore was mistaken when he said the contrary.

Possibility of itself is not a sufficient reason for existence; that is, from the fact that a being is possible we cannot conclude that it exists. Existence is more than mere possibility; and if mere possibility were a sufficient reason for existence, the effect would be greater than the cause—what is *plus* would be contained in what is *minus;* but this would involve a contradiction.

It follows, that since mere possibility is not a sufficient reason for existence, some existence must have existed before any possibility: hence, from this notion we deduce the idea of an eternal, necessary, and infinite being.

The essential attributes of a being, or its essence, either metaphysical or physical, constitutes the nature of that being. The word nature, however, has a greater extension than the word essence; it comprehends not only the attributes which are essential, but also what flows from them. Hence, those attributes are essential

without which a being can neither be nor be conceived
to be; and those attributes are natural which are formed
in a being by the force of its essence.   For instance, the
roots, the trunk, and the branches are the essential parts
of a tree; but its bulk, height, etc., are its natural
parts.

Two axioms are drawn from the considerations made
in this chapter, with regard to essence :

1st. What is, is; or, negatively, the same thing cannot *be* and *not be* at the same time.   This is generally
called the principle of contradiction.

2d.   Whatever is involved in a being must be affirmed of its essence; and whatever is excluded from a
being must be denied of its essence.

CHAPTER SECOND.

OF THE CAUSES AND THE EFFECTS OF BEINGS.

Let us first establish the difference which exists between principle and cause.   *Principle* is that which
contains the reason for the existence of something.
Our mind, for instance, is the principle of our thoughts;
that is, our thoughts could not come from a substance
different in its nature from our mind: in other words,
the substance from which thought flows is spiritual and
active.

When the principle contains the whole reason for the
possibility or the existence of a being it is called *adequate;* if the principle does not contain the whole reason
it is called *inadequate*.   The adequate principle is also
called the *sufficient reason*.

The notion of cause is a first notion.   The cause supposes an action.   The action is the relation of power to
act. It is found in the substantial constitution of a being.

Ordinarily the action is in relation with a complete subject, that is to say, with a substance which is "*sui juris.*" The cause is always the starting point of an action. A subject is a cause only when it produces, by its action, a new existence, an effect. The effect, since it depends on the cause, necessarily comes after it.

Cause is, then, that which produces something, or which concurs in the production of something. Hence, there are two kinds of causes. The first is called the *efficient cause;* and this only, properly speaking, is a real cause, for only this produces an effect. The other concurs in the production of the effect, and is only improperly called a cause.

This last, or incomplete, cause may be *material, formal, instrumental, final,* or *exemplary,* according as we consider the material, the form, the instrument, the end, or the model which has been used by the agent.

The efficient cause is either necessary or free. The cause is *necessary* when it necessarily produces its effects, and it is *free* when it may either produce them or not produce them. The human mind, in regard to its free determinations, is a free cause.

The efficient cause may also be either a first cause or a secondary cause. It is a *first cause* when it does not depend upon another cause in order to act, and a *secondary cause* when it does depend on another cause in order to act.

The efficient cause is also either physical or moral; *physical,* when it produces an effect which belongs to the physical order; and *moral,* when the effect is a moral one. The man who orders another to commit a murder is the moral cause of the death which he has ordered. The physical cause is also called the *direct* cause, and the moral cause the *indirect* cause.

10

The efficient cause is, moreover, either *general* or *particular*, which words are readily understood; and also either actual or virtual; *actual*, if we consider the effect produced, and *virtual*, if we consider the power of producing it as residing in the cause.

The efficient cause is, finally, a cause *per se*, when it produces the effect which it aims at; and a cause *per accidens*, when the effect produced is not the one intended, but an accidental one.

The notion of cause, like that of substance, has been wrongly explained by Locke, in so far as he put aside the relation of dependence, and in its stead substituted a relation of succession.

Hume removed the idea of cause in order to justify his scepticism. He pretended that the idea of cause had no real foundation; that it comes to us neither by the senses nor by conscience. This doctrine is evidently in opposition to what is manifested to us by conscience and the relation of the senses, though experimental knowledge of itself does not give us an abstract idea of cause.

Occasionalism, of which Malebranche is the principal champion, cannot be admitted. Malebranche and his followers admit only an efficient cause, the first cause, God. Everything which we call cause, beyond the consideration of this first cause, is only improperly such. Created beings produce nothing; they only give God reason to act. They are occasional causes.

We see that this is denying the activity of spirits. Spirits are active and can be a cause.

To deny the activity of spirits is to speak contrary to the evidence of the facts of conscience.

Bodies also may be cause; it is a common persuasion, and this is authoritative; there is nothing repugnant in this doctrine. God can make his creatures participants of his activity, and in doing thus He shows the immensity of his goodness.

The inactiveness of bodies is not a difficulty, since it is not a negation of the faculty of acting, but of moving itself. Occasionalism leads to Pantheism.

NO'TE.—There is a difference between the cause and the condition. Although a cause is often unable to produce its effect independently of the condition, *v. g.*, Some object kept in suspension shall not fall unless the rope which holds it be cut off, and however natural gravity attracts it toward the ground; the solution of the obstacle is a condition, *sine qua non*, for the natural cause to have its effect.

An intelligent cause does not act without aiming at some end: the *end*, then, is that which involves the reason why an action is undertaken; it has been called the *final cause*.

The end may be either *primary* or *secondary*, *proximate* or *remote, intermediate* or *final*. The end is *intermediate* when it is connected with two others, one preceding and the other following; and it is *final* when the agent, after having obtained it, is at rest, that is, has accomplished his purpose.

The *means* (media) are everything instrumental in the production of an effect. These means must be in proportion to the cause that uses them, and to the end which is aimed at. Some of them are necessary, and others only useful.

Order, in general, is the regular arrangement of causes, means, and ends. When we consider that arrangement in reference to the essence of things, we have the *metaphysical order;* when we consider it in reference to the existence of bodies, we have the *physi-*

cal order; and when we consider the same arrangement in reference to the free actions of God, of the angels, or of the souls of men, we have the *moral order.*

The moral order is called *religious* when it refers to the worship of God, *social* when it regulates the intercourse of men with one another, and *political* when its object embraces the correlative duties of the State and its citizens.

The metaphysical order is the foundation of the other two. In the whole universality of things there exists a perfect subordination of causes, means, and effects, so that all possible and existing beings are perfectly chained together.

This threefold order being the object of science, it follows that science is metaphysical, physical, and moral: and as everything which is known, or which may be known, by reason only, forms the object of philosophy, and everything which is made manifest to us by divine revelation constitutes the object of theology, it appears further that the order of science is double, natural, and supernatural.

From what has been explained in this chapter we may deduce the following axioms:

I. He who wills the end wills the means.

II. The means must be in proportion to the end.

III. There is no effect without a cause.

IV. The cause is prior to the effect.

V. The perfections of the effect cannot be greater than those of the cause.

If a perfection in the effect could exceed the perfection in the cause, that perfection would be without a cause, which is absurd.

The cause may contain its effect in a threefold manner:

1st. Formally,—as a heap of gold contains formally, or according to their nature and forms, several particles of the same metal.

2d. Virtually,—as the architect has in his mind the plan of the building which he is to erect.

3d. Eminently,—as when the cause contains all the perfections of the effect, in a most eminent manner and one quite unknown to us. God has in Himself, in a most eminent manner, all the perfections of his creatures.

The following corollaries result from the axioms given above:

I. No being can be its own cause; for, if so, it would, at the same time, be prior and posterior to itself.

II. Two beings cannot be mutually their own cause.

CHAPTER THIRD.

Of the Different Species of Being.

1st. A being exists either in itself or in another being: in the first case we have what is called *substance;* in the second, *modification.*

2d. A being is either finite or infinite.

3d. A being is either material or spiritual.

Hence the division of this chapter into three articles.

Article First.—Substance and Modification.

A *substance* is a being existing in itself: this does not mean that such a being is independent of a cause, but only that it is independent of another substance as an object in which it should lie in order to exist; thus, a stone is a substance, for it does not need another being to which it must be attached in order to exist.

A *modification* is that which needs another being to

10 * H

which it may adhere in order to exist, as color. Modification is also called accident; it is such or such determined accidental form appearing to us and determining the substance. Hence the modification is not something of a positive being added to the substance; but it is the accidental form itself, determining in such or such manner the substance. The following axiom is clear of itself: "Modification supposes substance." It follows from the foregoing definitions that modification cannot exist without substance, nor substance without modification; and that the modification, materially speaking, or considered in a material point of view, is perceived before the substance.

Substance is created or not created, and complete or not complete.

A *complete* substance is a substance *sui juris* (of its own right), that is, one which is not united to another substance in order to be perfect, and which, consequently, is the principle of its own operations, if it has any. Peter is a complete substance. A complete substance is also called a *suppositum*.

A substance is *incomplete* when it is united to another substance in order to be perfect, as the body by itself, the soul by itself.

There is a difference between a substance and a *suppositum*. A *suppositum* is always a substance, but a substance is not always a *suppositum*.

When the *suppositum* is endowed with reason it becomes a *person*.

When a person is composed of several substances, united in order to constitute it, we have the hypostasis, or hypostatic union.

From what has been said, we deduce the following axioms:

I. Actions are personal; that is, actions ought not to be attributed to each or any substance composing a person, but to the union of all, or the person itself.

II. Actions share the dignity of the person acting. Hence the actions of our Lord were of an infinite value.

III. Names belong to the persons or *suppositums*.

ARTICLE SECOND.—INFINITE AND FINITE SUBSTANCES.

Substance is infinite or finite.

Infinite substance is that having no limitation. It is the same as simple being, or absolute being (*ens simpliciter*).

Finite substance is that which is limited.

All the schoolmen divide the infinite into the infinite *actu*, or the actual infinite, that which is the highest and most perfect that can be imagined, namely, God alone; and the infinite *potentia*, or the potential or virtual infinite, which can be infinitely increased or diminished. But certainly this division cannot be accepted, since the infinite, and a substance which can be increased, are two terms involving a contradiction. That which is infinite is so of its own nature, and can therefore be neither increased nor diminished. The infinite absolutely excludes limitation; hence it is immutable. The so-called virtual infinite should be called the *indefinite*.

We shall see, further on, that the infinite being is the same as the *necessary being*, and the finite being the same as the *contingent being*.

That we have in our mind a concept of the infinite is certain, for we can define it, and it is in our mind distinct from any other notion. This concept, according to Descartes, Malebranche, Leibnitz, and Bossuet, in opposition to Locke and the other sensists, is a positive idea, but not an adequate, though a true and clear one.

Evidently it has, according to him, been placed in our mind by God himself, since the finite could not give the idea of the infinite : no one can give what he has not himself. We shall say, in the examination of the Cartesian proofs of the existence of God, and on treating the question of Ontologism, what we ought to think of this theory.

The idea of a finite being, considered materially, that is, of having a real existence, is also a positive idea; but considered formally, that is, as deprived of some reality which it might possess but does not, is a negative idea.

ARTICLE THIRD.—MATERIAL AND SPIRITUAL SUBSTANCES.

Substance is, again, either material or spiritual.

A *material being* is one which is essentially extensive and inert, and a *spiritual being* is one which is essentially active and thinking. There is, consequently, a fundamental difference between these two beings.

Matter is essentially divisible, since it is extensive; but whether matter is infinitely divisible, and what are the elements of matter, have been questions of dispute.

The opinions of Descartes and his followers is that matter is infinitely divisible; for, they say, since extension belongs to the essence of matter, as long as you have matter you have extension, and consequently divisibility. In their view, a simple element, becoming extensive by aggregation, involves a contradiction.

On the other hand, Leibnitz and his disciples are of opinion that the *monads*, which is the name given by them to the elements of matter, are simple beings; an infinite divisibility, in their view, involving a contradiction. Any composite being, they teach, is formed of composing elements; but with the system of Descartes we should have a composite substance without composing elements.

In both these systems we find at least apparent contradictions. According to the system of Descartes, the infinite is contained in the finite; while, according to the system of Leibnitz, a substance, or a simple *monad*, which is essentially unextensive, becomes extensive by aggregation.*

Spiritual substance is treble; namely, God, the angels, and the human soul.

Material substance is multiple, as may be seen in the study of Natural Philosophy.

CHAPTER FOURTH.

Of the Properties of Being.

The *properties* of a being are those parts which determine the being by modifying it; they are so called because they are its own *proper* parts (propria).

I. Some properties are common to all beings, considered in themselves; these are: unity, truth, and goodness. Every being must be one, true and good.

First, *unity*. No positive definition can be given of the unity commonly called numerical, but by the philosophers metaphysical.

The following negative definition of unity is given by the scholastics: One is that which is divided, that is, distinct, from every other being, but undivided in itself.

The metaphysical unity is found in every being; for every being must be undivided. If a being could be divided into several parts, each part would be a separate being, and there would be several beings instead of one.

---

* This question is extensively treated in Cosmology, under the head, "The Essential Constitution of the Body."

On the other hand, it is clear that every being must be distinct from every other.

This numerical or metaphysical unity may be:

1st. *Substantial Unity,* or simplicity, which belongs to substances that cannot be divided, because they exclude composition of parts. Such is the unity of the soul or of any of the spirits.

2d. *Physical Unity,* which is composed of parts united by some physical bond. Such is the unity of the human body.

3d. *Moral Unity,* which is composed of parts united by a moral tie, as the unity of a family.

Hence the following divisions of unity may be made: viz., *unity of simplicity* and *unity of composition.*

Unity of simplicity might be defined the indivisibility of the being by the absence of separable parts.

Unity of composition may be said to be the non-division of a whole formed of the assemblage of its parts. The simple being cannot, then, disappear by decomposition, whilst compound beings can cease to be by dissolution.

Unity can be further divided into *unity of gender, unity of species,* and *unity of number,* according as it indicates the non-division of the gender, the species, or the individual. Animality is a gender; humanity is a species; Peter is an individual. Individual unity is, properly speaking, the primitive element of number, which is a collection of unities.

Number supposes the multiple in the quantity; but it supposes also the resemblance, in some respect, in the quality.

When number is affixed to a determinate object, it is *concrete;* but number may be *abstract,* i. e., separated from any object.

Identity is related to unity.

Second, *truth*. A being is true when its constituent principles agree with one another. The truth of a being is its conformity with its own archetype, that is, with the idea of that being as it exists in the divine intellect. This truth, which is the metaphysical truth, is found in all beings, even those which are merely possible.

Truth is also either moral or logical, according as it refers to beings which belong to the moral or to the logical order.

The contrary of truth is falsehood, error. Error has its seat in the judgment, and consequently in the intellect. There is no objective error. Man, who cannot denaturalize his essence and counteract the plan of his Creator, has always the power to put obstacles in the way of the Divine will, by the fact that he is free. From this results a privation—a defect which is a disorder, and which constitutes, as we may say, an objective error.

Beyond this there is no error in things in spite of certain forms of expression which would tend to make us believe it.

Third, *goodness*. Goodness is the aptitude of a being to attain its own ends. It is clear that this property is found in all beings, since God is infinitely wise.

This definition is of metaphysical or absolute goodness. Moral goodness is a property of reasonable and free beings.

Goodness is also defined " the being in as much as is desirable."

The nature of the good can be indicated only by that which is liable to excite desire.

The good has for its foundation perfection, and it becomes goodness only when it excites the appetite and calls forth love.

Every being having some perfection is good; hence God is Supreme Goodness, and created beings participate of it in diverse ways.

General order comes from universal goodness. The good tends to make perfect, and in making perfect augments the Being; and enjoyment, the fruit of possession, increases in the same proportion. The good is divided into *true* and *apparent*, and again into *spiritual* and *sensible* good.

Sensible good is itself subdivided into *intellectual* and *moral* good.

The good is *true* when it is such as to produce a real improvement; it is *apparent* when it corresponds but apparently with that who desire it.

Sensible good procures some advantage to our body, whilst *spiritual* good improves our soul.

It is *intellectual* or *moral* when it has reference to the mind or to the will.

There is finally another division of the good, which is of great importance in a moral point of view. It is the *honest*, the *useful*, and the *agreeable*.

A *useful* object is that which is not as much a good in itself as it is a means of reaching it.

The *honest* is nearer the idea of the good, it is that which makes us better.

The *agreeable* is the means of enjoyment.

The contrary of the good is the evil.

Goodness does not pertain to bad actions; for a bad action, or a sin, is something merely negative, but it is not mere nothing. A bad action is an action lacking in righteousness; but the lack or absence of righteousness is nothing positive, nor is it any being, but the negative of being and of perfection.

The evil is divided into *physical* and *moral* evil,

whether it be the privation of a physical or moral perfection.

There are also the *absolute* evil (or evil in itself), and *the relative* evil, or evil on account of some accidental circumstance, as, for instance, the equitable sentence of a judge is good in itself, but evil for the man who, being guilty, becomes its victim.

BEAUTY.—We are accustomed to unite beauty with unity, truth, and goodness, on account of its close connection with goodness. Beauty, according to Plato, is the "splendor of truth." The beautiful is intimately connected with the true; but the idea of beauty adds something to that of truth.

Besides knowledge, beauty awakes a kind of satisfaction and pleasure. If the true is the "light," the beautiful is the refulgence of light, "l'eclat." Hence the beautiful can also be defined "That which is pleasing to the eyes, or rather that which pleases the understanding."

Beauty can be *sensible* when it relates to the senses, and *spiritual* when it is found in spiritual beings and in the exercise of their faculties.

There are, moreover, a *real* beautiful and an *ideal* one; the former is that which appears in a physical, spiritual, or sensible reality.

The latter is that which is conceived in the mind.

The sublime is the beautiful in a degree beyond our intelligence.

II. Some properties are merely relative; that is, they pertain to beings when compared with other beings. All beings are in continual relations with one another. We may define *relation*, in general, to be a property pertaining to a being when compared with another being. In a relation, considered in general,

11

there are three elements, a subject, a term, and a foundation. If, for instance, I compare the whiteness of paper
with that of snow, the paper is the subject, the snow is
the term to which I refer the subject, and whiteness is
the foundation or the reason for referring the first element to the second. The term and the subject are the
correlatives.

These elements are essential, or natural; or they are
arbitrary, or accidental. They are *essential* when they
flow from the very essence of things, as the relations
between a cause and its effects. They are *arbitrary*
when they are grounded on the mere opinions of men.
Such are all the symbolical objects, in relation to the
moral beings which they signify, as the relation between the olive branch and peace; and also all the moral
relations, as that existing between a king and his subjects.

Among the relations are classed identity and distinction.

Identity may be taken in several senses, but here it
is the perseverance of a being in the same entity. This
identity may be physical or moral. Living beings
have a moral identity, not a metaphysical or absolute one.

The identity of the human soul is not an accidental
one; that is, it is not an identity consisting in the main-
tainance of the similitude of modifications, but is a substantial identity.

Individuals endowed with reason retain their personal identity so long as they maintain their subsistence and rationality.

Distinction is the negative of identity. There is a
difference between distinction and diversity. What is
diverse is distinct; but that which is distinct is not
always diverse. Heaven and earth are distinct and di-

verse; Peter and Paul are distinct, but not diverse. Distinction excludes identity, and diversity excludes similitude.

Two beings entirely alike may exist, for their existence involves no contradiction.

Distinction can be *a real* distinction or a *distinction of reason*. It is *real* when it exists in the things themselves. It is called a distinction *of reason* when we examine in one thing several points of view.

Real distinction is again *substantial* and *moral*.

Substantial distinction is that which is related to substances numerically separated; or, again, when in an only substance it is related to its constitutive elements.

Distinction is *moral* whenever it exists between the moods and the substance, or between the different moods.

The distinction called *of reason* may be *virtual* or purely *mental*.

It is *virtual* whenever it has a foundation, at least in reality; thus we can consider in the soul, which is one, its vegetative, sensitive, and intellectual power.

Distinction is purely *mental* whenever the one and some reality corresponds to divert moods of apprehension. Socrates appears to us as the promoter of the philosophical movement which bears his name, as the master of Plato, etc., and these are pure conceptions of the mind, without there being in the being of Socrates, even implicitly, any corresponding distinction.

CHAPTER FIFTH.

OF SPACE AND TIME.

Space, in general, is extension, in which bodies exist, or in which they may exist or be conceived as possible.

Hence the division of space into *real space*, in which bodies actually exist, and *abstract space*, in which they are conceived as possible. Abstract space is the object of geometry.

The conception of abstract space is formed in our minds by abstraction in the same manner as we form all our conceptions of possible beings. For instance, when we see many bodies having among themselves relations of situation and position, our minds may abstract, or remove, every other property pertaining to these bodies, even their actual existence, and consider that sole property by which they may occupy various positions with regard to one another, then we have the idea of an abstract extension, or of abstract space.

Space, conceived abstractly, is eternal, necessary, and immutable, in the same manner as we conceive as eternal, necessary, and immutable all possible beings. Space is virtually (potentia) infinite, using the word "infinite" as we have before explained. It is also immense and infinitely divisible.

A *place* is a determined part or point of space.

Time is the successive duration; it is the permanence of a being's existence. Time is also defined to be the duration in which contingent beings succeed each other, or may continue those successions. Time also, we may observe, is, like space, real and abstract.

Time is divided, first, into past, present, and future; and, second, into real and abstract time, all of which words are sufficiently clear.

Eternity, properly so called, is duration without a beginning or an end;* and eternity, improperly so

---

* Here is the definition of Boëce: " Interminabilis vitæ tota simul et perfecta possessio." The total and perfect possession together of a life which is without end,

called, is duration without an end, but with a beginning : this last is the same as immortality, and by the scholastics is called eternity *a parte post*. As succession requires a first point, eternity, properly so called, has no succession, for it has no beginning. Consequently, the idea of time, as lasting from all eternity, involves a contradiction ; hence the eternal being does not exist in time, because this being does not admit of succession. We may say, however, that the eternal being, in its immutable duration, coexists with the successive mutations of contingent beings.

There have been many opinions expressed by the learned concerning the nature of space and time, the two main ones being those of Clarke and Leibnitz.

Clarke, whose opinion was accepted by Newton, taught that what he called absolute or abstract space and time are nothing else than the immensity and the eternity of God. This opinion is not acceptable, for the following reasons:

1st. We do not conceive abstract space and abstract time as things actually infinite, but only virtually so, that is, as things always admitting of increase ; while, at the same time, we conceive the eternity and the immensity of God as two attributes actually infinite, and we cannot conceive them differently. Consequently, the notions of space and time, as we conceive them, are contradictory to the notion of the infinite.

2d. We do not conceive abstract space and abstract time as things really and individually existing, but as two abstractions of the mind ; while eternity and immensity exist really and individually in God, although they cannot be separated from the divine substance.

11 *

3d. It is evident that the opinion of Clarke much favors pantheism; for since, as we have seen, space and time are not actually infinite, but only virtually so, which is the same as indefinite or finite with no determined limits, it follows that, if space and time may be considered as attributes of the divine substance, nothing can prevent us from considering the other finite beings, also, as attributes of God.

Leibnitz teaches that space and time are not beings distinct from the other contingent beings, but that they are mere relations of those beings, space being the relation of situation among bodies, and time the relation of succession among contingent beings. Consequently, if there were no contingent beings there would be neither space nor time; and when contingent beings began to exist, then, also, began the existence of space and time.

This explanation seems true, and gives full satisfaction to the mind. But Leibnitz mingles with this part of his doctrine some notions concerning the extension of matter, taken from his system of monads, which do not seem so satisfactory. Omitting these notions, we may accept the explanation given above.

Epicurus, Democritus, and several among the moderns, make space to be a substantial being which is infinite and contains all bodies. Descartes does not admit of abstract space, but teaches that space is a material and substantial being.

Kant, who denies the objectivity of bodies, applies his system to this question. His idealism has been indirectly refuted in Logic, where we established the truth that the evidence of the senses is an infallible motive of certitude.

APPENDIX.

COSMOLOGY.

Cosmology is the science of the visible world; viewed in the first principles, it is, in a manner, the preamble of the physical and natural sciences. Here we will examine but two questions, viz.: 1st. Which are the constitutive principles of the corporeal substance? 2d. In what does the life of living bodies consist?

I.

THE ESSENTIAL CONSTITUTION OF THE BODY.

We may reduce to three the systems relative to this question: Atomism, Dynamism, and the Theory of Matter and Form.

Atomism, in times gone by professed by Leucippus and Epicurus, then rejected during several centuries, was again brought to light by Descartes and Newton. According to this system, bodies are but an assemblage of *molecules,* and their mass is the essence of these bodies.

Modern Dynamism was defended by Leibnitz. It was modified by a Polish Jesuit, Boscovich; according to this system, the elements of bodies are simple forces or *monads.* Leibnitz gave them perception and appetite, and supposed them to be infinite in number. Extension resulted from their juxtaposition. Boscovich suppressed perception, appetite, and their infinite number; instead of juxtaposition, he substituted a double force of reciprocal attraction and repulsion.

The theory of Matter and Form sketched by Plato, and developed by Aristotle, has been adopted and completed by St. Augustine and all the great doctors of the Middle Ages.

Matter is that of which the body is made; but this matter does not become body except when taking intrinsically the substantial form of the body. There are consequently a first matter and a substantial form. Matter is the passive element, the root of extension. Form is the active element, the principle of unity and actualization. Corporeal substance is formed of these two elements.

The body once constituted, lends itself to accidental changements which do not modify its intimate nature—these are *alterations;* moreover, it yields to substantial modifications, which allow matter to subsist under another intrinsic form: this is *generation,* or the new information of nature.

This first matter without any form is not *nothingness;* it is something without form which passes from an informal state to one which has a form.

This informal matter can be turned into determined forms, because it is in power (in potentia) of any corporeal force; this first matter has only a subjective power; objective power and the act of production belong to a foreign cause.

This theory implies no contradiction, and it only is capable of explaining the essential properties of bodies. All bodies have extension. Atomism does not explain extension, since it indicates only the principle of divisibility, without saying anything of the principle of unity.

1st. EXTENSION.—Extension supposes that in the being there are multiple parts, the ones placed outside the others. There is no extension without divisibility. Dynamism renders extension impossible. The monad could never furnish a divisible extension of itself; it is *one* and can only unify. It could not effect it by juxtaposition, which is an absurdity, inasmuch as it occupies no place; and the action at a distance, according to Boscovich, would suppose, without explaining it, an extended space where the monads would be.

The system of Matter and Form admits, in substances, a principle which gives the reason of multiplication of corporeal elements, and thus explains extension.

2d. FIGURE.—The plurality of bodies supposes a limit for each body, and consequently an external configuration, which distinguishes the one from the other. If this configuration would arise only from the inactive mass, nothing would determine it to one mood rather than another; for the passive matter would undergo all the diverse forms coming from external action, without having in itself the principle of any in particular. Experience, on the contrary, proves that there is in bodies an intrinsic force, which constantly tends to present the same figure in the same object; hence, there is a principle of determination in matter; that is to say, a substantial form.

3d. ACTIVITY.—Bodies appear inactive, but this inactivity is not a complete passiveness. Bodies are active, and it is by this activity that they make themselves known. Resistance would, by itself alone, be a proof of it. Whence, again, the necessity of admitting in this regard the substantial form.

4th. MOBILITY.—Every body has a motive force, which is not common to any one we might suppose in each atom; otherwise these atoms would not be the elements of bodies, but distinct bodies.

Motive force, therefore, must have met with a principle *one* in the bosom of multiple matter. This principle turned into activity, carries along within its motion the whole mass. Is not this again, under another point of view, the substantial form?

I

5th. SUBSTANTIAL DETERMINATION.—It is a truth recognized by common sense that bodies are divided into a great number of species, according to a determination, which affects their substance. But with atomism and dynamism these substantial determinations cannot be explained, and we are brought back to the Theory of Matter and Form, which accounts, by its twofold principle, for the determination of objects and of their substantial transformations.

Hence, the system alone of Aristotle and of the School explains the corporeal substance in whatever way we consider it, and we are not at all surprised that Leibnitz came back to it after having rejected Dynamism, which he declares to have been but *"un jeu de son esprit,"* and Atomism, towards which he had at first leaned. He explains his conversion in his "Theological System," No. xlix.

II.

OF LIVING BODIES.

The bodies which are in nature are either animate or inanimate. Living bodies themselves are divided into two categories: 1st. Those which live only of a vegetative life. 2d. Those which are endowed, moreover, with sensibility and live of the sensitive life. Nature, therefore, comprehends three great classes of beings, or, as we generally call them, three great kingdoms—the mineral kingdom, the vegetable kingdom, and the animal kingdom.

After having treated of the essential constitution of the bodies, there remains to consider their life, under its double aspect of vegetative and animal life.

Life has been defined in many ways. We believe, with St. Thomas, that an animal lives when it commences to move of itself. As long as this movement exists in him, we affirm that life continues. Hence, rightly, life has been defined: "an immanent action." Let us pass immediately to the vegetative life.

a. Vegetative Life.

Vegetables or plants are at the lowest degree of the ladder of living bodies, but they are animated and greatly transcend inanimate beings, such as simple minerals, for vegetables are organized bodies—they differ from minerals in their origin and their way of perpetuating themselves. They are generated according to a regular mode, which constant laws determine. Minerals owe their existence only to an incidental action of accidental causes.

They differ, thirdly, in the way they develop and preserve themselves. These radical differences indicate corresponding differences in the substance. There is, therefore, in the vegetable an immanent action, a principle of life. Physics and chemistry cannot explain the phenomena of vegetation.

This vital principle of plants is *one* in itself—there is an active element which presides over all and unifies all; it is at the very bottom of the substance, it is the principle of life.

If it were enough for forming a plant to have recourse to heat, light, or electricity, we do not see why chemists could not have succeeded before now to realize such a progress.

They have been able, lately, to compose some substances similar to those which are found in organic bodies—such as dextrine and glucose—but they have never been able to reproduce vegetable combinations. It is, then, necessary to acknowledge that there is in plants an essential activity, through which they utilize and direct the action of physical and chemical causes for their development, conservation, and reproduction.

There are three faculties in the vegetative life: The *faculty of nutrition*, that is, the faculty of assimilating to oneself, by change of substance, the food appropriated; the *faculty of growing*, by which the living being can develop itself; the *faculty of generation*, or that of producing out of its own substance another living being of the same nature as itself. Generation is not a creation, since it does not produce a being out of nothingness.

b. *Animal Life.*

Superior to plants amongst living beings are animals. These, like plants, have the vegetative life, but in addition, the sensitive life; sensibility is even their specific character.

The theory of the *animal machine*, or automaton, maintained in the sixteenth century by a Spanish physician, Gomez Pereira, and, after him, by Descartes and Malebranche, is repugnant to common sense; hence, the animal has a soul.

The soul of animals is a sensitive soul, endowed with the faculty of perceiving sensible objects, and of perceiving these as good or bad. It is endowed with the faculty of inclining to what is good and of fleeing from what is bad.

Is the sensitive soul in animals one and the same principle as the vegetative soul? Experience shows that the sensitive life, absolutely impossible without organs, demands from the vegetative life this necessary instrument, and, in return, the vegetative life is so connected with the sensitive, that the vegetative not only has need of the sensitive for the choice of aliments, but that the nervous state is of the greatest influence on our digestive functions.

The sensitive and vegetative life in animals is consequently one and the same principle, and this principle is the substantial form.

Animal activity does not surpass the limits of the sensitive life; the most perfect among them, if you except man, possesses nothing of the intellectual life.

This point of the question is more closely examined in the fourth chapter of Psychology.

SECOND DISSERTATION.

. ON THEODICY.

This subject is naturally divided into two parts, in the first of which we treat of the existence of God, and in the second of his attributes.

PART I.—THE EXISTENCE OF GOD.

Some men do not admit the existence of God, and these are called *Atheists*, a name derived from the Greek (α θεος, no God). We may consequently call those who believe in the existence of God *theists*. This first part is, therefore, naturally subdivided into two chapters.

CHAPTER FIRST.

OF ATHEISM.

Atheists are either *speculative* or *practical* disbelievers in the existence of God: the former do not acknowledge his existence; the latter know that he

exists, but live as if they did not know it. Speculative
Atheists are called *negative* when they simply deny the
existence of God, and *positive* when they attempt to
prove that he does not exist: the positive Atheists are
also called *systematic* Atheists.

Note.—There is a difference between Theism and
Deism, although the two words have substantially the
same etymology. *Theism* is the doctrine of those who
believe in God and in his operations, while *Deism* is the
doctrine of those who also believe in God, but entirely
reject divine revelation.

The causes of atheism proceed from the intellect or
from the will; being in the first case (*a*) an imperfect
knowledge, or (*b*) an abuse of certain sciences; and in
the second (*a*) corruption, or (*b*) pride.

§ 1. Is it prudent to remain indifferent concerning the
existence of God?

Such indifference is certainly very unwise; for it is a
question upon which depends our greatest happiness or
our greatest misery.

The Atheists reason in this manner: "I do not know
who placed me in this world; nor do I know what the
world is, or even what I am myself. I do not know
what my body is, or my senses, or my soul, or this part
of me which thinks of what I am now saying. I see
those frightful spaces of the universe which surround
me, and I find myself fixed on a speck of this immensity,
not knowing why I have been placed here rather than
elsewhere, nor why the small space of time which I have
to live has been assigned to me at this moment rather
than at any other moment of eternity. I see immensities
everywhere; they engulf me as an atom, or as a shadow
that lasts but for an instant. All that I know is that I
shall soon die; and yet that which I try most to forget

is this very death which I cannot avoid. As I do not know where I came from, so I do not know where I am going to; I know only that, leaving this world, I fall forever into nothingness, or else into the hands of an angry God: and not knowing which of these alternatives will be my lot, I conclude that it is better for me to pass my life without thinking of what shall happen to me; and believe that I have but to follow my inclinations, without reflection or anxiety concerning what ought or ought not to be done, in order not to fall into eternal damnation, in case that what is said of this be true. Perhaps I might find some light to dissipate my doubts, but I do not wish to take any trouble about the matter, nor do I care to make one step to find this light; and so, looking with contempt on those who trouble themselves with such cares, I prefer to go on and wait without fear for that great event, allowing myself to be carried on quietly to death in the uncertainty of my future condition." Such are the horrible sentiments of the Atheist.

The chief argument of the Atheists is an evident absurdity. They say: If God exists he is infinitely good, consequently there is nothing to be feared. They forget that God is also infinitely just.

§ 2. Are there any evils resulting from the adoption of the theory of the Atheists?

This system is the source of many evils to men, whether considered individually or collectively, that is, as members of society.

1st Atheism is hurtful to men considered as individuals, for it takes away from them all security, all comfort in misfortune, and every hope of happiness. It takes away all security; for in all the labors of life, what gives us courage is the consideration that God will bless our efforts for our own welfare and for that of those dependent upon us. It takes away all consolation and hope, and consequently stifles the voice of nature, to which the pagans themselves gave ear. We find no real happiness in this world, because here every good is mingled with sorrow, and of short duration, because many suffer constantly, and because the thought of death disturbs our joys. Hence Atheism, which takes away the hope of a better world, is hurtful to man, considered individually.

2d. Atheism is also hurtful to men, considered as members of society, for (a) it leaves authority without restraint. (Authority cannot be judged, condemned, and punished by its own subjects.) And (b) it leaves the citizen without morals. (Whence would come restraint against vice if Atheism prevailed? Without God there would be no other life, nor would conscience exist, nor would the laws have any sanction.)

Atheism breaks every bond of union among men. Those bonds are the virtues: gratitude, deference, obedience, sincerity, justice, etc.; and without God there would be no virtue.

§ 3. Is Theism better than Atheism? The observations made above are sufficient to give an affirmative answer to this question.

§ 4. Is Theism safer than Atheism?

A doctrine in which there is nothing to be dreaded, if false, and everything to be hoped, if true, is safer than one in which there is nothing to be hoped for, if true, and much to be dreaded, if false. But such is the case in regard to this question; hence Theism is safer than Atheism.

§ 5. Is Atheism worse than Polytheism?

That doctrine is the worse which restrains our passions the less. Atheism restrains our passions less than

Polytheism, for Polytheism admits the belief in another life. Consequently Atheism is worse than Polytheism.

It is objected to this, that without God, 1st, there would be the natural law; 2d, that religion has been the cause of many wars; 3d, that many Atheists have been good men, while many Theists have been bad men; 4th, that the Atheist is inclined to do evil by his nature only, while the Polytheist is inclined to evil both by his nature and by the example of his gods; and 5th, that it is better to deny God than to attribute to him vices which debase him.

We answer to the 1st, that without God there would be no sanction to the natural law, and without a sanction no law can have force; to the 2d, that religion has been the pretext, but not the cause of war (we may here observe that we speak of religion as being the aggressive power, for religion has often been obliged to defend herself. The cause of these wars was ambition, or a spirit of revenge on the part of princes who were censured by the popes, or some other cause of similar nature); to the 3d, that neither Theists nor Atheists were logical in their conduct, and that therefore no conclusion can be drawn from their conduct; to deduce a general conclusion from exceptional facts is a fallacy *per accidens;* to the 4th, that the Polytheists have some motives for restraining their passions; for example, the belief in another life; and to the 5th, that the ignorance of the Polytheists is not the result of a bad will, that consequently their intentions are good, and that since the intention constitutes the merit or the demerit of our actions, the conduct of the Atheists is worse than that of the Polytheists.

12 *

CHAPTER SECOND.

Of the Proofs of the Existence of God.

Is it possible to give a demonstration of the existence
of God? Every demonstrated truth is one which, not
being immediately certain, becomes such by means of
another. The ordinary process, as we have already said
in Logic, is to pass from the cause to the effect. But it
can happen that the effect is more manifestly known
to us; and, on account of its close connection with the
cause, it might be possible to ascend to the cause, instead
of taking it as our starting-point.

The demonstration of God is a truth of the latter
kind. What we know, first of all, are the divine effects.
God manifests himself in his works. He appears to us,
firstly, as first cause and the creator of the world; and
let it not be said that, because there are no proportions,
we cannot pass from finite effects to an infinite cause,
from the world to God.

The question is not to know the absolute perfection
of God by means of an imperfect world. Our aim is
simply to pass from the world, taken by right of effect,
to God, preëxisting by right of cause.

To demonstrate the existence of God, we may consider the world such as it appears to our eyes. We
may regard the things which compose the world under
general characters, common to all finite beings. One of
the physical proofs of the existence of God is that which
is taken from the spectacle of nature and its admirable
order. Metaphysical proofs are those which have for
their starting-point the essence itself of created beings.

To these two orders of proof is added the moral proof
which results from the universal consent of men. We

will develop, one after another, these different proofs, commencing with metaphysical arguments; and, after having solidly established by it the great truth of the existence of God, we will discuss the others which the seventeenth century held in great honor, and which are generally called "the Cartesian proofs of the existence of God."

ARTICLE FIRST.—METAPHYSICAL ARGUMENTS.

These arguments are so called because they are grounded upon the essence of things, and are drawn from considerations purely intellectual.

Some preliminary notions, more fully explained in Ontology, must be summarily repeated in this connection :

No being exists without a reason for its existence. This reason may come from the nature of the being, or from a cause which is extrinsic to it. A being which has in its own nature the reason of its existence, or which exists by itself out of its own nature, is called a *necessary being*, or a being *a se*. The opposite of a necessary being is called a *contingent being*, that is, a being which has received its existence from an extrinsic cause.

An *infinite being* is one which admits of no limit; it is also called *ens simpliciter*, because it excludes negation in every way. The notion of infinite necessarily excludes that of number or series : the idea of an infinite number or series is contradictory in itself.

First argument, taken from the notion of a necessary being.

Proposition.—*From the existence of a necessary being we conclude that God exists.*

Argument: God exists if there is a necessary being; but such is the case ; therefore God exists.

Proof: There is a necessary being. For among beings now existing, either there is a necessary being or all beings are contingent. But this latter supposition cannot be true; for, if all existing beings are contingent, they must have received their existence from another being: but it cannot be that all existing beings have received their existence, for, if they had, they must have received it from a being taken either outside or inside the collection of existing beings: but neither of these suppositions can be true; for, since none but contingent beings exist, the being upon which they depend cannot be taken outside of them; and it cannot be taken from inside their collection, for then it would be both contingent and non-contingent; it would be cause and effect, prior and posterior to itself, which is a contradiction: there must, therefore, be a being which is not contingent, that is, a necessary being.

Conclusion.—The necessary being is infinite. It is infinite if it has all the perfections, existing or possible, of all existing or possible beings; but such is the case: for all contingent beings come from the necessary being; but perfections existing in contingent beings have absolute perfection for their exemplary cause; hence all perfections existing in contingent beings come from the necessary being. This necessary being must have all possible perfections also, for otherwise these perfections would be possible and not possible at the same time. Therefore the necessary being is the infinite, and the infinite is God.

Second argument, taken from the existence of a first motor.

God exists as first motor, as first principle of all movements. By movements we understand here every transformation caused by the different beings. It is the passage of the power to the act, of the possible to the actual. Undoubtedly there are movements in nature, even in inanimate beings; and that which is possible becomes actually real only when there exists an action of a Being itself actualized in that point of view. Movement, consequently, necessarily supposes a motor *foreign* to the being which is subject to it. But this motor may have movement from itself, or may have received it. It may be a first or second motor. Second motors would never have been actualized if at last analysis they had not found a first motor—a pure act to act on them. The name of God being given to this first motor, the existence of God is demonstrated. This proof, called the proof from *movement*, is the great proof of Aristotle. It is for this reason that St. Thomas, who mentions it the first, calls it at the same time the most manifest.

The degrees of perfection which exist in physical beings manifest to us the real existence of the absolute Perfection. It is evident that there are in nature beings that have but a limited perfection,—beings which we call imperfect, in opposition to a type of perfection.

This type may be, by itself, but an imperfect type, if we compare it to a superior type. But, beyond and above all subordinate types, there must, of necessity, be a supreme type, to which absolutely belongs the notion of perfection.

At all degrees, the type exists before the copy, and necessarily exercises an influence upon its existence as a pattern cause. The efficient cause may not be, sometimes, by itself, the pattern cause, if it be but an instrumental cause; but it is impossible that the principal efficient cause find not in itself the pattern which it realizes. We may say, then, that the very author of an effect involves in himself, and in a very real manner, the perfection which it communicates.

A real perfection, then, supposes a real type; and a subordinate real type, being but a dependent perfection, supposes, in its turn, an ulterior real type, even up to the supreme type, that cannot but be an absolute reality. Consequently, if there is some real degree of perfection, there must also be, *a fortiori*, the real Perfection; and if God is the name by which we designate perfection, God exists.

ARTICLE SECOND.—PHYSICAL ARGUMENT.

The physical argument is taken from the aspect of the universe, and the beautiful order found therein. The Atheists pretend that the world was made by chance, and Epicurus embodied this system in the following manner: From all eternity an immense vacuum existed, and in this vacuum matter was found to have existed from all eternity. This matter was not found collected in one mass, but divided into its primitive atoms. To these atoms Epicurus gives the following properties: They had various forms; they were eternal and necessary; they were indivisible on account of their extreme hardness; they moved in the vacuum in straight lines. It happened that some of these atoms deviated from the straight lines and adhered to other atoms, thus forming various bodies, until gradually the world resulted from this disorder.

We may observe that these principles are quite arbitrary; and that, our definitions of the words necessary and infinite being accepted, these same principles are also absurd and contradictory. Besides, the consequences are false; for, from our definition of the necessary being, it follows, that the world has been created, and created by God; while, from the system of Epicurus, it follows, that the order of harmony, the conversation and reproduction of material beings, are merely the result of the deviations of atoms wandering in a vacuum, in which an infinite matter is found. Who does not smile at such incoherencies! It is needless to say more of this system. Let us come to our argument, and establish the following

Proposition.—*The order of the physical world indirectly proves the existence of God.*

Argument: This proposition is true provided there is order in the physical world, and that this order comes from a being of supreme intelligence; but such is the case, and consequently the order of the physical world proves the existence of God.

Proof.—A. Order is found in the physical world. The parts which constitute the physical world are the planetary and stellar systems, and the twofold kingdom of nature, the inorganic and the organic. In the inorganic it will be sufficient to point out the atmosphere; while in the organic we have the vegetable and the animal creation. In all these we find a beautiful order; that is, the most suitable disposition of means for the end in view.

B. This order comes from a being of supreme intelligence. This assertion is true, provided (a) the author of this order is a being distinct from matter and endowed with intelligence; and provided (b) the cause of this order infinitely surpasses the human mind in intelligence. As both of these are true, it follows that this order comes from a being of supreme intelligence.

(a) That the cause is intelligent and distinct from matter appears from this: Order is a disposition of the means necessary to reach an end; consequently, the

author of this order must be able to know both the end
and the means necessary to reach it; it must then be
an immaterial and intelligent cause, since matter is
inert, blind, and void of intelligence.

(b) This cause infinitely surpasses the human mind
in intelligence. All admit that the order found in the
works of nature is far superior to anything produced by
the human mind. This order is so perfect that the
human mind has never been able to discover all its
perfections; new wonders are found every day, while
many more escape the most ingenious researches.
Hence it appears that this intelligent cause immeasurably surpasses the human mind, and therefore it
must be God.

This argument destroys the system of Epicurus, since
it proves that the order of the universe does not spring
from chance, that is, from a blind cause; it also over-
turns the system of the Pantheists, who pretend that
God is not distinct from matter: but it does not absolutely prove the existence of God, that is, it does not
prove that the intelligence that formed the universe is
infinite, but only that it immeasurably surpasses mere
human intelligence.

NOTE.—From what has been said, we may conclude
that matter is contingent and consequently that it has
been created; hence, its existence proves that of a creator. Matter, we have further seen, is inert; and we
may conceive it as existing without motion: hence,
motion is not a necessary quality of matter, and as
motion exists, we conclude that there has been a prime
mover. These observations will supply the means of
answering the objection raised against the creation from
the axiom *ex nihilo nihil fit.* If "nihilo" here means
a *cause,* the axiom is true; but if the axiom means that

what was merely possible may not become actual, it is false.

A *moral proof* is one drawn from some fact that belongs to the moral nature of man; that is, a fact based on the propensities or opinions which are common to all men. Such proof produces in the mind a certitude not less than that resulting from metaphysical or physical proofs. Hence, the certitude resulting from a moral argument ought not to be confounded with what is called moral certitude, a term which often signifies nothing more than probability.

First argument, taken from the common consent of mankind.

Proposition.—*From the unanimous consent of mankind, it follows that God exists.*

Argument: If at all times and among all nations men have believed in the existence of God, we may conclude that God does exist. But there has always and among all nations been such a belief. Hence, the unanimous consent of mankind proves the existence of God.

Proof: The fact may be established as follows: We may know that all peoples have at all times believed in the existence of God, if we find everywhere and in all ages prayers, temples, altars, sacrifices, and religious rites. But this fact is abundantly proved for ancient times by all the writers, sacred or profane, who deserve our confidence. The fact is as clearly evident for our own times, from the testimony of numberless travellers and writers. No nation, civilized and enlightened, or barbarous and savage, has been found where some form of worship could not be discovered.

This consent is universal, uniform, and constant, and no one denies that the fact to which it testifies is of the greatest importance; consequently this testimony has all the conditions required in the treatise on certitude to constitute an infallible motive of certitude. Therefore God exists.

This proof is complete, and allows us to conclude the existence of an infinite being; because such is the notion, although sometimes obscure, which is found in the minds of all people concerning God.

Second argument, taken from the existence of the natural law.

Proposition.—*The existence of the natural law proves the existence of God.*

Argument: God exists if there is a natural law; but there is a natural law, hence He exists.

Proof: The natural law is that rule, commanding what is right and forbidding what is wrong, which is found in the conscience of every man. Since it is found in all men, it is the voice of truth, that is, the voice of God. But there is no law without a legislator; and since the natural law is implanted in the hearts of all men the legislator must be prior to man and superior to him, that is God.

ARTICLE FOURTH.—CARTESIAN PROOFS OF THE EXISTENCE OF GOD.

They give this name to the proofs which were held in great honor in the seventeenth century by Descartes, especially the proof which is deduced from the idea of the necessary Being.

Descartes, who in this last argument followed St. Anselm, was, in his turn, followed by the philosophers of his time, and above all by Fenelon and Leibnitz.

We will examine these proofs, more specious than solid; leaving aside the argument taken from the imperfection of the human being, this, indeed, is but one side of one of the metaphysical arguments developed in the first article.

1. *Proof deduced from the idea which we have of the Infinite.*

We have, says Fenelon, the idea of the Infinite, and this idea is distinct and well characterized. It is neither the nothingness nor the Indefinite, but the Being without any limitation, the absolute Being.

But, he adds, this notion, which has no proportion with the physical beings and ourselves, cannot be the production of our thought. Moreover, it is repugnant that we could form in a finite mind a resembling image of the Infinite. Hence we ought to conclude that the Infinite Being presents himself to our mind when we conceive him; hence it exists.

Descartes, in his *"Discourse on Method,"* does not go so far in the sense of the vision in God, but says: "The idea of the perfect being given, it is manifestly impossible to admit that we have received it from nothingness. Something cannot proceed from nothing, nor the more perfect come from the less perfect; hence this idea was put in me by a nature which has in itself every perfection."

This argument would be a good one if it were proved that the idea of the Perfect or of the Infinite corresponds to a truth entirely foreign to anything which we know outside of it. But this is not proved; and the perfection conceived by our mind is, after all, the perfection observed in the world. We cannot say that we have an adequate idea of the Infinite, and, moreover, this knowledge is far above the proportion of our weak nature. This first Cartesian proof rests then on a false supposition; it is consequently inacceptable.

2. *Proof deduced from the analysis itself of the idea of the Perfect Being.*

This argument comes from St. Anselm. By the very fact, says this great doctor, that we have the idea of the most perfect being, it exists; it could not be the most perfect being, if it were only possible.

Descartes says substantially the same thing, and gives it the vigorous exactness of a mathematical demonstration (see "*Discours sur la Méthode,*" *IVth Part*). Note III. Fenelon in his turn affirms that the idea which we have of the necessary being implies clearly its actual existence ("*Traité de l'Existence de Dieu,*" *Second Part, Second Chapter*). These arguments are simply the kind of Sophism which is called "*Transitus de genere ad genus*"—to pass from one genus to another.

A definite essence is undoubtedly a source of deductions; the ensemble of the deductions constitutes the essence considered in all its aspects. But the propositions deduced ought to be such as the essence was considered.

If we consider the essence in the ideal order, the conclusions which we deduce therefrom belong to the ideal order.

Here we have the Divine Essence considered as a mere concept. Then its actual existence ought to be the existence considered in the ideal order.

We should, in order to act logically, after having stated that we have the idea of the perfect, not to conclude its reality before we have demonstrated that the perfect is not merely ideal, and this is done by a demonstration *a posteriori.*

The demonstrations of St. Anselm and of Descartes cannot prove the real existence of God, if this existence really actual be not already proved in another way.

Leibnitz gives the same argument under another form. If God be possible, he is. For the first cause cannot be caused, and the perfect cannot be dependent. Then from its sole notion, God exists.

We can reduce this argument to the following words: "God exists, because we conceive him as the necessary being." Under this form the argument does not differ from that which we have just examined in Descartes and Fenelon.

In conclusion, God exists if he has in himself the reason of his existence. In himself and before himself he has in his essence the reason of his existence. For us, the dependent reality, which we observe, affords the only reason on which we can base the existence of the first being. He is *cause*, because *effects* depend on him, and the *reality* of these effects is the unique proof of the *reality* of the cause.

PART II.—NATURE AND ATTRIBUTES OF GOD.

I. NATURE of GOD.

The nature of a being is that which characterizes and distinguishes it from other beings. In order to determine the nature of God, we must find in his being that which comprises him entirely.

"*I am he who am*," "*Ego sum qui sum*," said God to Moses. In this word alone is expressed the nature of God. It is the Being.

Being, with the others, comes from a foreign source, and exists in the subject only by right of *received being*.

In God, Being exists of itself, and has need only of itself to exist.

Aseity (ens a se) is the consequence of the proofs which we have given of the existence of God. God is

13 *

supremely independent in the possession of his being; he is the *pure act* and first cause.

Aseity excludes every idea of substance composed of matter and form. God is immaterial in his substance. He is a pure form. It is in this that spirits approach nearest to his essence.

Aseity supposes more than immateriality; it supposes also absolute perfection. Aseity, confounded with absolute perfection, sums up well the Divine Being, and supposes all his attributes. Consequently it assigns to God a rank apart from all beings; alone he is the Being, while others only participate in it.

Alone he is the Being in its plenitude, while others have being only in a measure and with more or less perfection.

The Infinity of God is but a corollary of his Aseity. Being absolutely the Being, for the same reason he is the infinite Being.

If, in fact, we form a correct idea of limit, it is but a negation of the Being.

Properly speaking, the word "infinite" adds nothing to the word "being," and we say as much of God in saying that *He is*, as if we would call him the *Infinite Being*. In all, God, by nature, is of a supreme independence, and his name answers to the idea of the necessary, the perfect, the Infinite.

II. ATTRIBUTES OF GOD.

An *attribute* is a quality declared to belong to a being; and as perfection is an attribute which it is better to have than not to have, it follows that all the attributes of God are perfect; hence, to speak of the attributes of God is the same as to speak of his perfections.

Perfections are *absolute* when they exclude any limitation, and *relative* when they admit some limitation. The first are found in God alone, and the others in the creation; but God necessarily possesses all absolute perfections formally, that is, as they are, and all relative perfections *modo eminenti*, in an eminent manner.

Concerning the question as to which is the primary attribute of God, we find four opinions. The first is that of the nominalists, who pretend that it consists in the ensemble "cumulo" of all the perfections; others pretend that the primary attribute is the *infinity*, which they call *radical*, and that this attribute is the *exigence* of all perfections. A third opinion, held by some of the Thomists, places this primary attribute in the *actual intelligence* of God. Then comes the fourth opinion, which is the one of the other Thomists, and which is commonly accepted in the school; it consists in asserting that the primary attribute of God is his *aseity* (esse a se), which is the same as the necessity of existing, and in fact the ratio of the aseity is so inmost in God that nothing else can be conceived anterior to it. Suarez develops and defends this opinion of St. Thomas in his Metaphysica.

In God, in fact, the attributes are connected only with the essence, and spring but from it; they participate in his supreme perfection. But we have seen that *Aseity* constitutes the nature of God. If, then, in God, essence takes from itself its own subsistence, it is in itself alone all the substance; and the perfections of this substance is no other than the plenitude of the Being. *Aseity*, or the supreme Being, is then the nature and the foundations of the attributes of God.

The attributes of God are divided into two classes, relative and absolute. The relative attributes are those which are proper to each of the three persons of the Holy Trinity: the discussion of these belongs to theology. The absolute attributes are those which belong to the divine essence.

As we have said, God is a simple substance; the assertion of the contrary would involve a contradiction. The difficulty then is to explain these attributes of God. Is the distinction given above real, or logical, that is, virtual only? Is it real; that is, does there exist in God the same distinction of attributes as there exists in the human soul between the will and the intellect? or, is this distinction virtual only, that is, the result of the action or manifestation of God's attributes, appearing to us as if there was a real distinction in them?

The Scotists teach that there is a formal distinction among God's attributes, and the Thomists affirm the contrary. The doctrine of the Thomists certainly offers less difficulty in reasoning on this mysterious question. St. Augustine, before St. Thomas, gave the second opinion as his own. "No," says he, "there is no formal distinction among the attributes of God; but it is the essence of God which is, at the same time, most simple and most manifold, being a simple multiplicity and a multiple simplicity." In God, the essence draws from itself its own substance. It is, then, to itself all the substance, and the perfection of this substance is none other than the plenitude of the Being.

In God, consequently, the attributes are affixed only to the essence, and holds of it alone. Incapable of any limit, they are distinguished from one another by no real opposition.

However, the terms by which we designate them are not words void of sense. The conceptions which they express have not, it is true, corresponding determinations in the divine Being; but these determinations, though not *formal*, are, nevertheless, *virtually* comprised in the infinite Being.

We shall divide this question concerning the attributes of God into thirteen chapters; treating successively of his unity, his eternity, his immutability, his liberty, his independence and omnipotence, his simplicity, his immensity, his intelligence and knowledge, his wisdom, his sanctity and truth, his goodness and happiness, his justice, and his creation and providence.

CHAPTER FIRST.

Of the Unity of God.

This attribute of God has been denied by the Polytheists and by the Manicheans. The Polytheists admitted a plurality or multiplicity of gods, while the Manicheans affirmed that there are two principals of all things—one bad, who is the originator of all evil, and the other good, who is of course the cause of all good. In order to proceed methodically, let us divide the present chapter into three articles.

Article First.—The Unity of God Proved against the Polytheists.

The forms of Polytheism have been manifold; being denominated Demonolatry, or worship of demons, Anthropolatry, or worship of men, Herolatry, or worship of heroes, Zoolatry, or worship of animals, Idolatry, or worship of idols or statues, and Fetichism, or worship of objects having no determined form.

It is impossible to find out exactly when Polytheism made its first appearance in the world; but it is certain that it has never been general, that, besides the philosophers, the generality of the people had some idea, though a confused one, of the unity of God. It is certain, moreover, that Monotheism was prior to it, contrary to the teaching of some writers who pretend that

Christianity is but a phase of Polytheism. It is clear also that Polytheism did not grow more perfect in the course of time, but it degenerated and engendered general corruption, placing the world on the verge of an abyss, so that, according to the opinion of Bossuet, the world would have relapsed into chaos again if Jesus Christ had not come to save it. It has been asked whether Polytheism sprang from the will or from the intellect. We may accept as the true opinion that Polytheism originated mainly from the corruption of the will.

Against the Polytheists we proceed to establish the following

Proposition.—*God is one.*

1st. We have shown that God is a necessary being, or a being simply, that is, one who has in himself the whole fulness of being, or existence. He cannot therefore be multiple; for if there were any being, or a plenitude of being extrinsic to him, it could not be said that he possesses the whole fulness of being.

2d. The necessary being is infinite; that is, the necessary being excludes any limitation : hence he is one, otherwise there would be limitation.

3d. The unity of harmony which is found in the creation shows that its author and preserver is one.

4th. We may add to the above reasons the consent of nations; for it may be clearly demonstrated that the Pagans themselves admitted the unity of God.

Article Second.—The Unity of God Proved against the Dualists.

We find among the Semitic races, especially in Egypt and Persia, a belief in the existence of two first principles, one the principle of matter, and the other the prin-

ciple of spirit. This Dualism is not that which we
propose to examine in this article, but rather that which
was put forth by Manes in the second and third centuries
of the Christian era, and revived by Bayle in the seventeenth century. These men taught that all evil comes
from the bad principle and all good from the good principle; but their doctrine cannot be accepted, for,

1st. God is one—there cannot be two necessary
beings. The necessary being is infinite; the infinite
being contains the fulness of being or existence: he
cannot therefore be multiple; and hence he is one.

2d. Of these two beings one would be infinitely perfect and the other infinitely imperfect; but imperfection
is a negation, that is nothing; hence the principle of
evil would be infinitely nothing, which is an absurdity.

3d. Laying aside the former considerations, neither
of these beings would be omnipotent, and neither would
be happy, unless they made an agreement with each
other concerning all things which should be done, and
then we should have fatalism, that is, human liberty
would be annihilated.

4th. In conclusion, we will say that this system is
not necessary in order to explain any difficulties in the
mechanism of the world.

ARTICLE THIRD.—THE ORIGIN OF EVIL UNDER A BEING
INFINITELY GOOD.

It is true that it appears difficult to explain the origin
of evil under a being infinitely good; still we cannot
reject the unity of God on account of this, for that truth
has been established.

Let us then make a few considerations concerning this
question of the origin of evil. The evil in the world
is threefold.

1st. The evil which is called metaphysical consists in this, that God has granted more or less perfections to his creatures. It is plain that there is no disorder in this; it is even necessary as the source of order, for this very variety, while harmoniously disposed, constitutes the foundation of that beauty and order in the moral world which excites our admiration. It is the principle of society, the source of heroism, and the origin of all the virtues.

2d. Physical evil consists of the pains which afflict the human body in many ways. These are the consequences of the actual condition of man; and it derogates nothing from the perfections of God, that, though infinitely good, he has established this condition. For it may be demonstrated that the good is greater than the evil, even from this physical point of view, as is evident from the fact that there is no one who does not prefer to live rather than to die. Besides, these evils are the source of moral good to many, and thus become the occasion of eternal happiness: the greatest virtues have their origin in the existence of these evils or pains. Moreover, we know that physical pains are often the result of moral evil.

In a Christian sense the evil does not exist, but as punishment; original sin explains everything; but in this work we consider the question philosophically.

3d. Moral evil is sin. God was not obliged to prevent sin for these reasons:

(a) Not *on account of his sanctity or holiness:* God is holy if he be not sullied with sin and if he hate it; but such is the case.

(b) Not *on account of his justice:* God is just if he have established man in a condition good in itself, and if he do not punish him unjustly; but such is the case.

(c) Not *on account of his goodness*: God is good if he have granted to man liberty, which is good both in itself and in the intention of God; but such is the case.

(d) Not *on account of his wisdom*: God is wise if he have done nothing but for a good end, and have chosen the best means to reach that end; but such is the case. He proposed to reward the virtues of men, and gave them the most efficacious means that they might not abuse their liberty.

The objections to our arguments are taken from the fact of God's foreseeing the abuse which men would make of the liberty he gave them. The principles for refuting these objections are as follows: The intention of God was good, the gift was good, the foresight of God had no influence on human liberty, God helps human weakness, and, finally, all agree that existence, as it is, is better than non-existence.

CHAPTER SECOND.

OF THE ETERNITY OF GOD.

Proposition.—*God is eternal.*

Argument: God is eternal if he be necessary, but God is necessary: then he is eternal.

Proof: We have already proved that God is necessary. A necessary being is one whose essence it is *to be;* and, since we cannot conceive a being without its essence, the necessary being must always have been: hence he is eternal.

If the necessary being were not eternal he would have been produced by another being, for he could not have produced himself, that is, he would be contingent; but we have proved that God is the necessary being, he is then eternal.

14

Several authors have considered the question whether there is succession in the eternity of God. We have seen that the necessary being is infinite, but infinity and succession in the same being involve a contradiction. Succession is composed of moments added to one another, each of course being limited; but the infinite excludes limitation, while succession includes series, a series being a collection of finite beings: hence, the infinite and series, or succession, are terms involving a contradiction. The eternity of God is therefore not successive, but simple, like his own being. God is. For him, there is neither past nor future, but all is present: his essence is *to be*.

CHAPTER THIRD.

Of the Immutability of God.

Proposition.—*God is immutable.*

Argument: God is immutable if immutability can be ascribed only to contingent beings; but such is the case, and hence God is immutable.

Proof: Mutation is the transition from one condition to another, consequently the transition from the possible to the real: hence mutation can be applied only to contingent beings, and the infinite and the mutable are terms involving a contradiction.

In God everything is infinite; hence nothing can be changed, either in his perfections or his decrees; there can be in him nothing which is contingent. God is then immutable.

In order to solve the objections which are advanced against this attribute of God, let it be remembered that in God there is neither past nor future. These words cannot be applied to God, to whom everything is present.

CHAPTER FOURTH.

OF THE LIBERTY OF GOD.

Liberty is the power of choosing. The object of liberty is either an act which brings to its author some perfection or imperfection, or else an act which brings to him neither perfection nor imperfection: hence we see that the object of liberty is within the limits of what is good.

Liberty may be considered as freedom either from external force, otherwise called freedom from coaction; or as freedom from necessity, otherwise called freedom of election.

The acts may also be either exterior or interior. For God, the interior acts are those whose object is himself.

Evidently God is free from coaction; but, in his interior acts, he is not free from necessity.

The liberty of God has been attacked by the Pantheists, who, admitting only one substance, make every phenomenon a necessary modification of God; and also by the Optimists, but these deny God's liberty only indirectly.

We shall divide this chapter into three articles: in the first we shall demonstrate the fact of the liberty of God; in the second we shall explain and refute the doctrine of the Pantheists; and in the third that of the Optimists.

ARTICLE FIRST.—THE EXISTENCE OF THE LIBERTY OF GOD.

Proposition—*God is free in his exterior acts.*
Argument: God is free if liberty is a perfection, and

if no cause could have compelled him to create from necessity; but such is the case, and therefore he is free in his exterior acts.

Proof: Liberty is a perfection; for a being who is free is independent in his acts and the supreme arbiter of what he does; and independence is better than dependence, and consequently an absolute perfection; but God being infinite possesses infinitely all absolute perfections; hence he is free.

God possesses infinitely all the perfections which are found in his creatures; but we are free, and therefore he must be free.

No cause could have obliged God to create from necessity: neither *his happiness* nor *his glory*, for in these he suffices for himself; nor *his internal perfections,* for if this were so we should conclude that God, considered in his essence, is not infinitely perfect, but certainly this would be untrue.

It appears difficult to reconcile the immutability of God with his liberty. Three systems have been formed for this purpose. Each of these solutions is satisfactory, at least in this sense, that each of them sets at naught the objections of our opponents. Now, which one of the three solutions is the best? That of the Thomists is accepted by philosophers whose authority has very great weight, and might perhaps be held as the most probable; nevertheless, besides being obscure, it presents some disadvantages. It is enough for us that both attributes have been proved to exist in God: the difficulties spoken of only serve to show the weakness of human reason.

ARTICLE SECOND.—PANTHEISM.

Pantheism is the system of those who admit the existence of but one substance, which substance, according to them, is infinite. Hence, the Pantheists agree with the Atheists in making matter exist from necessity, and consequently in making it eternal and infinite.

The doctrines of Pantheism may be reduced to these three heads: First, what exists, exists from necessity; second, what exists forms one substance; and, third, this one substance is infinite.

The above principles are evidently false: For, in the first place, it has been proved that there is but one necessary being; and that we are contingent, since we have received our existence. Secondly, there is a multiplicity of substances in the world, if, for instance, there exists an essential difference between my soul and the bodies around me. Again, if there were but one substance, this substance would be either material or spiritual, or at the same time both spiritual and material; but certainly all the substances in the world are not spiritual only, or material only, nor are they at the same time both spiritual and material, for this would be a contradiction. Thirdly, as the infinite is simple, that is, not composed of parts, it is clear that matter cannot be infinite.

The doctrine of Pantheism is pernicious in its consequences, for these reasons: 1st. It takes away all obligation and sanction from the moral laws, since according to this system there is no superior being. We speak thus absolutely, although the Pantheist will say that conventions may be held and their decisions accepted for the sake of peace: we all know that no convention not approved of God can ever find the human

14 *　　　　　　L

conscience. 2d. Pantheism destroys man's liberty, and consequently takes from him all responsibility for his actions; for if matter be necessary, so also are its volitions or modifications—the actions of men, according to the Pantheists, being but modifications of the one necessary substance. 3d. Pantheism would oblige us to admit logically certain consequences which are evidently absurd; as, for instance, that God is a stone, a plant, or a beast.

Pantheism, which in our days has taken a development so fearful in its consequences, is an old error.

In the philosophy of the Vedanta, among the Indoos (fourth century before Christ), Brahma, that is to say God, appears as the only being, undetermined, impersonal, unconscious. All the determinations to which we give a reality are but chimerical appearances.

With the Greeks we find Pantheism in the metaphysical school of Eléa Xenophanes, its founder, abusing the axiom, "Ex nihilo nihil fit," made use of it to affirm the absolute unity of substance.

Pantheism reappeared in the Neoplatonician school of Alexandria. Plotinus, Proclus, and the rest represented God as the only being, whence sprung, by way of emanation, all the things which we consider as distinct from him, but which after all are found in his substance.

This gross error vanished before the full light of Christianity.

In the middle ages, we would in vain cite some obscure names of despised Pantheists.

We have to come to the beginning of the seventeenth century to again meet Pantheism, which Spinosa tried to revive.

Spinosa, of Jewish origin, by birth a Hollander, an

unbeliever as regards religion, maintained that God is the only substance of every thing that exists.

Spinosa had but few followers, and encountered very strong oppositions. It is his system which we have in view in our refutation of Pantheism. It was reserved to our age to behold the expansion of this absurd doctrine.

Germany has been the fertile soil of this new Pantheism.

Kant pretends that exterior objects offer but undetermined matter to knowledge. The distinct forms which render notions different belong only to reason ; objects borrow them from it. Objects characterized by these forms are the object of knowledge: *what is thought* ; but they are the act of the mind which knows: *what thinks* ; Kant preserved the two terms, but this appeared as an inconsequence to his successors.

Fichte pretends that there was but the second term— that *which thinks*, or the *pure me*—which, by an act of reflexion which is essential to it, determines itself as subject and object. Schelling stops at what *is thought*, and of it he makes an *absolute*, in which all distinctions, whatsoever it may be, even the distinction of subject and object, disappears. This undetermined *absolute* is the only *existing*. Hegel puts in the Idea where they meet, the *thinking subject* of Fichte, and the *absolute thought* of Schelling.

The infinite becomes the abstract idea of every determination, the *Idea Being*. Such are the different forms of Pantheism which philosophical pride had endeavored to propagate in place of the pure notion of the true God.

We lay aside the particular absurdities of the idealistic systems of the Germans.

All the Pantheists insist upon the unity of substance ;

there is, according to them, no distinction, except a logical one, between the *ego* and the *non-ego* ("me" and "not me"), that is, there is but a logical, and not a real, distinction between the subjective and the objective. This doctrine of Spinosa and the German philosophers is based upon the following definition of substance, which is ambiguous: "Substance is that which is in se (in itself), and which is conceived to exist by itself; that is, it is that of which we may conceive, without conceiving of some other being by which it might have been formed." Evidently there is here an allusion to the modification, which does not exist independently of the substance, and which presupposes substance in order that it should exist itself.

Pantheism is the doctrine of the French Communists, called Saint Simonists, Phalansteriens, Fourierists, etc.; and it is notorious what calamities have lately resulted from their doctrine in Europe, and especially in France.

Article Third.—Optimism.

Optimism is the system originated by Malebranche and Leibnitz, in order to vindicate the providence of God and to refute the objections of Bayle and others against the goodness of God on account of the evil which exists in the world. Both Leibnitz and Malebranche admit the existence of evil; but according to them the evil is necessary for the perfection of the universe, and does not detract from this perfection. According to Malebranche, God was free to create, and could consequently have refrained from creating. He was also free to choose among several worlds equally perfect that which he wished to form; but, owing to the perfections of his attributes, he was not free to choose a less perfect world, rejecting others more perfect.

According to Leibnitz, God, on account of his wisdom and goodness, was not free not to create, nor was he free to create any but the most perfect world. God could not even choose among several worlds unequally perfect, taking one in preference to another. Still, even when God acts according to what is absolutely required by his attributes, he remains free.

Both systems must be rejected, first, because they destroy, at least indirectly, the liberty of God, notwithstanding the contrary assertion of both philosophers. They must also be rejected because they assume that the ultimate reason for the exterior acts of God is the goodness of the object of these acts; while, in fact, this ultimate reason for God's exterior acts is his own will, for which reason he may choose a less perfect object in preference to a more perfect one, if he wills it, provided this choice be not in derogation of any of his attributes.

Thirdly, their system must be rejected because its assertion that God was obliged to create the most perfect world involves an impossibility : for the most perfect world would be one of such perfection that none more perfect could be imagined ; but the perfection of the world could never be such that a more perfect one might not be imagined ; for however perfect it might become, it would still be finite, that is limited; and what is limited is capable of increase, that is, it is imperfect : hence, the most perfect world must be infinite in perfection, which is an impossibility. The systems of Malebranche and Leibnitz must therefore be rejected.

CHAPTER FIFTH.

Of the Omnipotence and Independence of God.

1st. *Omnipotence* is the power of producing, or of bringing into existence, that which is merely possible. By what is possible, we mean that which does not exist, but the idea of which involves no contradiction.

Proposition.—*God is omnipotent.*

Argument : God is omnipotent if he can do whatever is possible ; but such is the case, and hence he is omnipotent.

Proof : God can do whatever is possible : for either he has this infinite power, or else he can do nothing or only something ; but the latter supposition cannot be correct, since, if it were so, God's power would not be so great as we may conceive it to be, and consequently not infinite. But he is infinite, and hence he can do everything which is possible ; he is therefore omnipotent.

Note.—It is evident that God cannot do what is impossible ; for instance, he could not make a square circle, because that involves a contradiction : the essence of a circle is roundness, and no being can have an essence other than its own ; for, if it could, the being would both be and not be at the same time.

It is also plain that God cannot make what is infinite ; for, if so, the infinite would have a beginning, that is a limitation, but the infinite has no limitation, no beginning, hence it cannot be produced by God.

2d. Proposition.—*God is infinitely independent.*

Argument : God is infinitely independent if he depends on no one for his existence, or for the mode of that existence; but such is the case, and therefore he is infinitely independent.

Proof: Independence consists in this, that the being who is independent depends on no one for his existence, or for the mode of that existence. Such is the case in regard to God. We have demonstrated that he exists in himself (*a se*); hence he depends on no one for his existence. The second part is but a corollary of the first; for if God depends on no one for his existence he is equally independent as to the mode of that existence, since the mode, or modification, necessarily follows the substance.

CHAPTER SIXTH.

Of the Simplicity of God.

This attribute of God has been denied by the Polytheists, the Pantheists, the Materialists, and the Anthropomorphites. These last were heretics of the fourth century, who, taking the words of Scripture in a literal sense, maintained that God has eyes, mouth, hands, etc.

Proposition.—*God is Simple.*

Argument: God is simple if he is infinite; but he is infinite, hence he is simple.

Proof: If God is not simple he is composed of parts; and these parts cannot be infinite, but must be finite. But God himself is infinite, and we cannot admit that a compound of finite parts, the essence of which is to be limited, can constitute a being which is infinite, or the essence of which is to be unlimited. Hence, God is simple; and hence, also, he is not corporeal. This latter conclusion is against the Anthropomorphites.

CHAPTER SEVENTH.

Of the Immensity of God.

We call that immense which cannot be measured. *The immensity of God* is that attribute by virtue of which his presence cannot be limited, or by virtue of which he is present to everything that exists: hence, in this sense, immensity means the same as omnipresence; this immensity has nothing in common with what is called Space; Real space is not distinct from the bodies which exist in nature. Since God is an intelligence, he is omnipresent not only by his knowledge and operations, but also in his Substance.

Proposition.—*God is Immense.*

Argument: God is immense if he is infinite; but he is infinite, hence he is immense.

Proof: We have shown that God is infinite, that is, that he is without any limitation: hence, according to the definition, he is immense. He is therefore substantially present everywhere.

Note.—This substantial immensity of God is not of course a corporeal presence, but a spiritual one, since God is infinitely simple; for the same reason, although God is whole in each part of space, still his substance is not multiple. Finally, we may say correctly that God is everywhere and also that he is nowhere: in saying that he is nowhere, we mean that he does not occupy a limited point of space, or a space of certain distance or dimensions, as creatures do. Here again we meet with a difficulty in explaining how God can be simple and immense at the same time; but we have shown that he possesses both these attributes, and that they do not involve any contradiction.

CHAPTER EIGHTH.

OF THE KNOWLEDGE OF GOD.

Men before knowing must conceive, judge, and reason; but such is not the case in regard to the knowledge of God. He knows, or rather sees, everything. All philosophers admit, first, that God alone knows *himself* perfectly; second, that everything past is present to him, for otherwise his immutability would be destroyed; third, that everything present, even the most secret things, are known to him; fourth, that he knows everything which is possible and that he realizes those same things; and, fifth, that he knows all future things which are necessary, that is, which flow necessarily from the laws established by him.

In regard to those future things which are called contingent, that is, those things which may happen, but which are dependent on the free choice of men, Cicero and many other pagan writers, and afterwards the Socinians, as well as certain modern theorists, have maintained that God has only a contingent knowledge.

But it is certain that God knows all future things, even those which are conditional and contingent; and this may be proved in the following manner:

1st. God is immutable; hence he knows everything, for otherwise he might acquire knowledge, and consequently change.

2d. God is infinite. But if God did not know everything, we might conceive a being more perfect than God, and this would destroy his infinity.

3d. God is eternal. Eternity is the permanence of existence, or being. Eternity is one and simple, and we have proved that it cannot be successive; conse-

15

quently, such words as "prevision," "prescience," and "conjecture" are inaccurate when applied to the eternal being, that is, to God. God is, and, consequently, knows; and neither in his being nor in his knowing can there be any limitation, any priority or posteriority.

4th. All mankind have ever been convinced of this truth.

The scholastics have asked in what way it is that God sees all things, and what is the character of his knowledge. All admit that it is more perfect to know a thing directly than indirectly, or to see a thing in itself, that is, in its essence, rather than in a being distinct from the thing. Hence it follows that God sees himself, and all possible things, as well as all future necessary things, in their own essence.

St. Thomas says that God also sees future free and contingent things in their essence, that is, that he sees them in his eternal and immutable decrees; for nothing, even a free action, happens except by a decree of God, in such a way that in our free actions God is an efficient cause. But Molina and his disciples contend that with such a system it is impossible to defend human liberty; and they say that God sees the future as contingent on the free determinations of his creatures. We can accept either system.

In order to answer objections to the foreknowledge of God, we have but to remember the words of St. Jerome: "The actions of men foreseen by God do not happen because God foresees them, but God foresees them because they are going to happen."

CHAPTER NINTH.

Of the Wisdom of God.

Wisdom is that attribute according to which a being proposes to himself a good end and takes the most proper means to reach that end; but God has this attribute, for, first, he is infinitely perfect; second, the order existing in the world proclaims his wisdom; and, third, we have shown that God possesses in an eminent degree all the perfections found in his creatures.

CHAPTER TENTH.

Of the Sanctity and Veracity of God.

Sanctity consists in the love of what is good and the hatred of what is evil; it is evident that such an attribute must be found in a being who is infinitely perfect.

Veracity, inasmuch as it comprehends infallibility, consists in this, that a being can neither deceive nor be deceived: God being holy cannot deceive, and having a knowledge which is infinite, he cannot be deceived.

CHAPTER ELEVENTH.

Of the Goodness and Happiness of God.

Goodness, or benignity, is that attribute by which a being is inclined to do good to others gratuitously. Evidently such an attribute is a perfection, and consequently it is an attribute of God. This all men in all ages have believed: God has always been called *Deus optimus maximus*—" God very good and very great." To the goodness of God we must refer his mercy, which is rather an attribute in a theological sense, but which is also infinite.

Happiness consists in the enjoyment of the good and the absence of the evil: but God being independent cannot be subject to evil, and being infinitely perfect he must possess and of course enjoy all good. Hence God is infinitely good and infinitely happy.

CHAPTER TWELFTH.

OF THE JUSTICE OF GOD.

Justice is the attribute according to which we give to others what is due to them. God of course possesses this attribute, for he renders to all beings what is due to them—rewards to the good and chastisements to the wicked; if he did not act thus, he would not be equitable, and consequently not infinitely perfect. We might here, if necessary, cite the testimony of men; but all agree on this point.

CHAPTER THIRTEENTH.

CREATION AND PROVIDENCE.

ARTICLE FIRST.—CREATION AND CONSERVATION OF THE WORLD.

We have seen in the refutation of the doctrine of Pantheism the distinction which exists between God and the world. Let us see now how far the world depends on God for its existence.

God is Cause in a higher degree than these causes of which the action is manifested to us by transformations. He is Creator, that is to say, the author of the whole being of all that exists outside of him. The world is a production out of nothingness.

The world, in fact, does not exist by itself, since it

has not the absolute perfection of the necessary Being. It is then the work of the First Cause, of God.

The faculty of creating does not exceed the power of God. Since the first Being is capable to make himself exist, *a fortiori*, he is capable to draw out of nothingness the finite beings.

Creation is a fact, and this fact was accepted by all men, as it is evident from the testimony of the sacred writers as well as from that of the profane historians. Some philosophers, however, have imagined to explain differently the origin of the world. We will give the three principal systems. 1st. The Atomistic Atheism. 2d. The Dualism of Plato; and 3d. The System of the Emanations.

1st. ATOMISTIC ATHEISM.—This system puts aside God and the spiritual world, and reduces everything to the conditions of the material being. It supposes, besides, that matter is eternal, at least in its primitive elements, which cannot be decomposed, and for this reason are called atoms (α, τεμνω). These atoms are infinite in number, and may be combined in every possible way.

This system was professed by Democrites, Leucippus, Epicurus, and Lucretius. Cardinal de Polignac gave an elegant refutation of it in his poem entitled, the *Anti Lucrece*. We have another refutation in the " *Traite de l'Existence de Dieu,*" by Fenelon. Cicero before them had opposed Epicurus in his work, *De Natura Deorum.*

Here are, in a few words, the main contradictions found in this system :

(a) The atoms are eternal, hence they ought to have all the perfections of the Necessary Being.

(b) They could not be multiple, because a number really infinite is a contradictory notion.

15 *

(c) Atoms eternal ought to be immutable.

(d) Their movement should be a necessary one; how, then, could they meet by deviation?

2d. DUALISM OF PLATO.—Plato admits the existence of God, but denies him the power of creating. According to him the world is eternal, but in the state of matter without form. The action of God is confined in the information of this matter according to the ideas which are in him the exemplar of everything.

This system was invented on account of the supposed impossibility of creation.

Here again we have a necessary being without the infinite perfection, and this Being, or God, is the world, eternal according to the teaching of Plato. We have besides another God, whose action on the world is very limited.

3d. SYSTEM OF THE EMANATIONS.—We find this system in the Eastern countries. It was taught by the Gnostics and the Neoplatonicians. The world is but an emanation of the divine substance. This substance either remains divine or degenerates and ceases being divine.

In the first case the world remains God, and it is Pantheism with all its consequences.

In the second case, we should admit the corruption of the divine substance, which is absurd.

Finite being then cannot but emanate from the creatrix power of the Almighty God; consequently there is creation. God is at the same time the efficient cause, the exemplary cause, and the final cause of the world.

God who created everything acts also in order to preserve everything. The creature of which the being is the effect of a cause, could not subsist if this cause would disappear. God preserves *positively*.

ARTICLE SECOND.—THE EXISTENCE OF PROVIDENCE.

Providence is the care which God extends over his creatures; or, it is the action by which he directs his creatures, either the reasonable or the unreasonable, to the end which is proper, to each individually, and to all in general.

The Epicureans, the Stoics, who held the doctrine of fatalism, and some modern philosophers contending, that God's providence would destroy man's liberty, and that God is too great and too high to take such care of us, deny the existence of providence. Against them we establish this

Proposition.—*God's providence exists and extends to all things.*

Argument: The existence of providence must be accepted if it be required by those attributes of God which are believed by all, and which are necessary in order to explain the order of the world; but such is the case, and hence providence does exist, and must extend to all things.

Proof: 1st. All admit that it is good, that it is a perfection, to take care of what we have produced; hence, God, who is infinitely perfect, must have this perfection.

Providence is required by the wisdom and goodness of God. God's wisdom requires that he should do what is necessary in order that his creatures may reach the end he has designed for them; and we are so ignorant, so weak, and so wickedly disposed, that without providence we could not reach this end.

The goodness of God requires that he should do what is necessary in order that we may obtain happiness; but we have just seen that without God's providence we could not reach our end, hence we could not be happy, and God would not be good: but since God is good providence must exist.

2d. All people, in all ages, and in all countries, have believed in the existence of providence, as might easily be shown by the testimony of Christian and pagan writers; and this testimony, so universal, so uniform, so constant, and concerning such an important question, is a criterion of certitude: we may therefore again conclude that providence exists.

3d. The constancy and uniformity of the effects, or rather of the order perpetuated in the world, is, after all, the most striking proof of the care which God takes of his creatures: and if this argument is so clear, and so generally confessed by every one, in regard to the physical world, *a fortiori*, it is likewise conclusive in regard to the moral world.

To these proofs we may add the following consideration: Existence is something contingent to us, since it does not belong to our essence; consequently, existence must be renewed at every instant of our life. Then, in order that we may live, it is necessary that God perpetuate, that is, renew at every instant, the act of his will by which he created us. Conservation is a continued creation; and, so far as God's will is concerned, it is a necessity. But with God, to will and to act are the same; hence the action of God upon us during our life is constant. It is this which the philosophers call the *immediate concourse* which God lends to the actions of creatures.

This *immediate concourse* is the necessary consequence of the *positive conservation*. If a being cannot be at any moment, without the divine influx, it is absolutely necessary that the divine action should intervene in the action of the second cause which produces the being by right of effect.

This *positive conservation,* this *immediate concourse,* is simultaneous: it is God himself watching over his creatures; it is Providence.

In its proper acceptation, Providence shows the plan of the world such as God conceived it from all eternity, and the ensemble of the means by which he works it out.

If we call government the action of a power which endeavors to bring about, in a society, the realization of the order, as traced out by the laws, we might also define Providence to be: the government of the world by its divine Author, according to the law, and in view of the aim he himself has determined.

In order to answer the objections to this proposition, we have but to observe that the preservation of his creatures does not injure the majesty of God any more than their creation; and that such care cannot cause trouble or grief to God, who is infinitely happy and immutable.

ARTICLE THIRD.—CONSEQUENCES OF THE EXISTENCE OF PROVIDENCE IN REGARD TO THE FREE ACTIONS OF MEN.

From the definition given above, it follows that God directs everything in the world towards its own end; and, consequently, that this action must have some influence over the free actions of men. This influence may be natural or supernatural. It is natural when the actions are considered without reference to future life, and supernatural when these actions are considered with reference to future life. This supernatural influence is God's *grace,* a subject belonging to theology.

M

We have here to examine only the natural influence of God over the free actions of man. We shall first consider whether this influence exists, and if so what is its nature.

I. Does this influence of God exist?

The existence of this influence has been denied by several modern philosophers. But that the influence does exist is certain, for (a) God is the primary cause, and this attribute requires that everything which is a perfection in the creature should proceed from God; but evidently the good use of liberty is a perfection, nay, even the greatest perfection in man, hence this good use proceeds from God. Good use here signifies the free and right determination of men, but under the influence of God, since this way of acting, which is a perfection, must proceed from him.

(b) We may here again bring forward the consent of mankind. We all pray to God, that he may guide us, correct us, help us, inspire us, etc.

Evidently, this influence takes place only for the good use of liberty. In regard to its wrong use, God cannot have any influence on man's actions, in the sense that he has granted liberty, of which a bad use is made against his suggestions: his sanctity forbids that he should act in that case, although God concurs *immediately* to all our actions, whether good or bad, inasmuch as they are physical actions.

II. What is the nature of this influence?

The Molinists pretend that this influence is positive and direct, but not on our will, which it neither moves nor determines, but simply helps, and with which it acts in concurrence for the performance of actions, so long as our will remains within the limits of what is good. As this assistance consists in affording a concourse of circumstances the most suitable for the determination, the followers of this system have been called Congruists.

The Thomists maintain that the above system too much restrains the actions of God, who is the primary cause of everything which is a perfection in his creatures; and they contend that the influence of providence is direct even upon the will, but, however, that God, whose knowledge is infinite, keeps human liberty always safe.

It seems difficult to conceive how man's liberty is preserved, according to the system of the Thomists; and equally difficult to understand how the supreme dominion of God is respected, according to the system of the Molinists.

This question, like many others, occasioned by the difficulty of explaining the attributes of God, became the subject matter of many books, which now, as Bouvier says, sleep in the dust, and the question is not solved, and remains insoluble.

There are other opinions, and especially that of St. Augustine, but they are rather theological than philosophical, and consequently we shall omit them, and here finish this treatise on Theodicy, which is the first part of Pneumatology, or spiritual metaphysics.

THIRD DISSERTATION.

ON PSYCHOLOGY.

PRELIMINARY NOTIONS.

The word Psychology is derived from the Greek ψυχή λόγος, and signifies a discourse upon the soul. We may define this branch of pneumatology to be the science which has for its object the general knowledge of the human soul.

The soul, notwithstanding its union with the body, is a true spirit. It possesses an activity independent of the organs; consequently, it can be made the subject of a distinct science.

There are on the soul traditional notions; and such a science is not at all to be despised: but we can know it by another way—we can verify by our own observations the exactness of the sum of belief that we already possessed.

Reason for determining the nature of the soul does not start from a definition *a priori*. The proper method to follow is that of analysis or observation.

It is conscience, or the intimate sense, which is the means of psychological observation. This conscience is not the moral conscience, or the practical rule of our actions; psychological conscience is but the witness of what takes place in us: it is our inner eye.

Psychological conscience is sometimes *spontaneous* and sometimes *reflected*. It is spontaneous when it perceives its object without arresting the mind by an effort of reflection. It is reflected when, by an act of voluntary attention, it dwells on its object in order to study and know it better.

Conscience has not the disadvantages which the senses have, since the latter are bound to material organs.

On the other hand, psychological observation is more difficult than sensible observation, and that for several reasons:

1st. It is a fact of experience that our mind stays more easily on sensible things. Spiritual things require to be represented, for fixing our ideas, in some way to our imagination. Now, this labor of imagination is not always easy and prompt: it begets distraction and fatigue.

2d. The field of conscience is more confined; for, whilst in the sensible order objects present themselves in great number to our senses, but one soul, our soul, offers itself to the conscience of each one of us.

3d. The labor of reflection is possible only later on in life; and then, to distinguish amongst the phenomena which present themselves in crowd to our mind, must we use the process of analysis; and that is not an easy thing to do.

4th. As this science is connected with the practical part of life, we are interested sometimes in not understanding, or in ill-defining anything. The remedy to these difficulties is the habit of attention and of recollection, no less than the uprightness of the mind.

Psychology is divided into two parts: the first treating of the human soul more according to experience than reason; and the second treating of it more according to reason than experience. The first is called experimental psychology, and the second rational psychology. We shall treat of these two parts in succession.

PART I.—EXPERIMENTAL PSYCHOLOGY.

Experimental Psychology may be defined to be the science which treats of the faculties of the human soul by the method of experience. According to this definition we shall naturally divide the subject of experimental psychology into as many parts as there are faculties of the human soul.

We find in the soul three faculties, or general attributes; namely, activity, which is the fundamental
16

attribute, and the sensibility and the intellect, which are the faculties that excite the soul to action.

Since activity is not put in motion in the soul until it is first excited by the sensibility and the intellect, we shall treat first of the sensibility, next of the intellect, and afterwards of activity.

CHAPTER FIRST.

Of Sensibility.

The sensibility of the soul may be considered either in general or particular.

Sensibility, in general, is the faculty by which the human soul experiences emotions which are ordinarily pleasant or unpleasant. A pleasant emotion is called *pleasure*, and an unpleasant one *pain*.

The elements of sensibility are two. As soon as the soul perceives a sensation it instinctively turns to the object causing the sensation; we have therefore two elements, the sensation perceived and the reactive motion of the soul: in the first case the soul is passive, and in the second it is active, but this activity is instinctive and necessary.

This sensible emotion is merely passive and subjective, and is thus distinguished from the intellectual perception, which is a modification of the soul merely passive, but also objective; because the intellectual perception represents an object as distinct from the modification itself.

The reactive motion of the soul is called by the moralists *motus primo primus*, and its ordinary appellation is *appetite*. This reaction is *attractive* when the emotion is agreeable, and repulsive when it is disagreeable.

The source from which these attractive and repulsive emotions, or all the appetites of our soul, proceed, is the love of ourselves.*

Sensibility, in particular, is exterior and physical when the emotion is produced by the action of the organs of sense, and interior when this emotion is produced without such action.

(A) *Physical sensibility* is the power of experiencing sensation. By *sensation* we understand the emotion which the soul experiences on account of some action of the organs of sense. Three elements, then, are found in physical sensibility: the organic impression which precedes and causes the sensation; the sensation itself; and the appetite, or the reaction after the sensation.

---

* This faculty has been introduced among the moderns. A faithful analysis of the facts of sensibility shows that there is not here a faculty distinct from the two other faculties. What is taken as a faculty is but the echo, in the sensitive life, of the two others.

Sensibility, in its proper acceptation, is the faculty which the animal has of perceiving, by means of organs, corporeal beings; these acting on us produce an impression which is transmitted to the brain, the centre of all the sensitive organism; and the result is a *sensation* or sensible perception.

These facts of sensibility have the name of *sensations*, if they relate to an organ or to a determinate place. They are called *sentiments*, if they affect the body in general without being anywhere localized. We have the sentiment of the peril which our imagination presents to us. Those impressions do not come from the external world; but they are communicated from our inner self through the sensitive imagination. Our organism, moreover, undergoes the rebound of all that effects, in good or evil, our intellectual soul.

That is precisely what we wish to express when we say of a man that his sensibility is moved. A man wounded in his dignity *feels* the injury made to him.

Sensibility, then, gives us the knowledge of the good or of the noxious beings, and calls forth in us a movement of attraction or of repulsion.

(a) The organic impression is the impression made on one of the organs of sense by an external body, and transmitted to the brain by the nerves.

The senses are five in number: taste, touch, smell, hearing, and sight. No sensation is experienced before the impression made on the organ of sense has reached the brain. The brain is an organ consisting of a soft, whitish, nerve-like substance, situated in the skull. That part in the upper front part of the head is the direct and immediate organ, not only of physical sensibility, but also of interior sensibility, of the intellect, and even of the will; so that if that part of the brain is removed or paralyzed the man loses his power of feeling, of understanding, and even of controlling the acts of his will.

The brain is divided into two parts, or lobes, one on the right side and the other on the left, and each part is subdivided into many smaller ones. Upon these divisions the system of the phrenologists is built.

The nerves are either sensitive or motive. The sensitive nerves are those that transmit the impressions made on the organs of sense to the brain; and the motive nerves, or motors, are those that serve, as we might say, as the tools of the will. How these impressions are conveyed to the brain, and how the desires of the will are carried back again, are questions to which no answer has been given.

(b) *Sensations.*—From what has been said it is easy to see the difference between sensation and the organic impression, which causes sensation. Sensations are either pleasant or unpleasant; and our power of knowing by means of the nerves the place of the impression enables us to determine what part of the body feels pleasure or pain.

There are some sensations which we may call indifferent. Although in morals no human act is indifferent in regard to salvation, yet we may accept the opinion of a large number of authors who consider many of our sensations as indifferent, that is, as affording neither pain nor pleasure, or, at most, very little of either pleasure or pain.

(c) *Appetite.*—Appetite is the reactive motion of the soul after it has experienced a sensation, whether agreeable or disagreeable. It is now customary to call the appetite resulting from an unpleasant or repulsive sensation a *repugnance.* We can now readily understand the difference between sensation and appetite.

It is not by sensation only that appetite is excited in the soul: the remembrance of a sensation is sufficient to produce appetite.

Appetites are *periodic*, as that of hunger, etc.; and *accidental*, as that for a certain kind of food, etc.

It is obvious that the end to be obtained by appetite is the preservation of the body.

(B) *Interior sensibility* is the power of experiencing sentiments. A *sentiment* is the emotion produced in the soul by an intellectual notion. A sentiment differs from a sensation in two respects: first, a sentiment is produced by an intellectual notion, while a sensation is produced by an impression on the organ of one of the senses; and, second, the nature of the resulting emotions of pleasure or pain are different.

The reactive emotion arising from a sentiment is called *passion.*

Passion is an emotion of the sensitive soul. It tends to produce itself every time that a sensible good, even when only apparent, has impressed us. Between the sensation of pleasure or pain and passion there is a link

16 *

which the will cannot break asunder. Nevertheless, the will, by the action which it exercises on the brain and on our external movements, allows us to govern our passions. To be sure, passion itself exercises on the will an influence which the latter does not always resist. The attraction of the sensible good is sometimes very powerful. The duty of man is to labor with all his might, in order to maintain in the mind the supremacy of the will. Let us never enter into a compromise with an unsubdued flesh, and let us beware to gratify it. Let us take delight in entertaining our mind with elevating things. To triumph in this contest is to secure a moral greatness. All effort in that direction is an act of virtue. Consequently virtue alone constitutes true greatness.

Passion is also the name frequently given to *sensible* or *sensitive appetite* (and we call here *appetite* the faculty which we have of tending towards good. This appetite is called *sensitive* in the life of the senses, and *reasonable* in the intellectual life).

Bossuet gives the following definition of the Passions: "They are motions of the soul, which, under the sensation of pleasure or pain coming from some object, either real or ideal, tends towards it or shrinks from it." Hence the "stimulus" of the passions is the sensible good, and this good speaks only to our senses, to our imagination; and reason having nothing to do with it, the impression produced by it upon us holds sway, and we suffer the motion which is its consequence; it is a motion of passion (pati—to suffer).

It follows that all the passions may be resumed in these two words: attraction and repulsion, or love and hatred. *Sensitive appetite* is divided into *concupiscible appetite* and *irascible appetite*.

Concupiscible appetite is that in which the object is simply considered as present or absent. According to Bossuet, six passions belong to this appetite: love, hatred, desire, aversion, joy, and sadness.

Irascible appetite is that in which the desired object offers more or less difficulty. According to Bossuet, five passions belong to this appetite: courage, fear, hope, despair, and anger.

Passions are natural to us; they are not essentially bad; governed by reason, they become a powerful help to us.

Sensitive appetite has for its object only the sensible good; the object of the *reasonable appetite* is not only the sensible good, but also the spiritual and the absolute good.

Reasonable appetite inspires itself with reason, and guides itself by reflection.

In order to distinguish the movements of the reasonable appetite from the passions, properly so called occasionally, we give to them the term of *affections.*

When this appetite is produced after a deliberation, it is *the will* (voluntas), which supposes three elements: 1st, *self-possession;* 2d, *deliberation;* 3d, *resolution.*

Interior sensibility considered in relation to its object is threefold in character: 1st, in relation to the personal affections, 2d, in relation to social desires, and 3d, in relation to those sentiments which involve a certain conception of pure reason.

(a) Personal affections. These are the dispositions, good or bad, with which we regard our fellow men; and which determine us to wish them good or evil; they are accordingly either benevolent or malevolent.

The benevolent affections are either particular or general, and the others universal. The particular benevolent affections are those of the family, friendship, gratitude, commiseration, etc. The general benevolent affections are charity, love of country, etc. Among the malevolent affections we may mention rivalry, envy, etc.

The principal distinctions between the benevolent and the malevolent affections are: first, a benevolent affection is always accompanied with an agreeable emotion; second, a benevolent disposition is natural to man; and third, in regard to the object, benevolence is more extensive than malevolence.

(b) Social desires. These are emotions of the soul by which we are inclined to seek for certain advantages that are found only in society, as reputation, power, etc. These desires may be reduced to five: 1st, the desire for social companionship, which is natural to all men; 2d, the desire of knowing; 3d, the desire of acquiring esteem and consideration; 4th, the desire of superiority; and 5th, the desire of property. These words need no explanation.

(c) Sentiments involving some conception of pure reason. There exist within us certain sentiments which originate in the soul by the influence of the conceptions of pure reason; as, for example, by the conceptions of the ideas of *truth*, of *beauty*, of the *infinite*, etc.

The chief sentiments of this kind are: the sentiment of truth; the sentiment of beauty, or the æsthetic sentiment; the sentiment of goodness, or the moral sentiment; the religious sentiment; and the sentiment of the infinite. There is such an affinity between the objects of these sentiments and our intelligence that the soul cannot perceive them without experiencing some agreeable emotion, and this emotion is called the love of truth, of beauty, of goodness, etc.

CHAPTER SECOND.

OF THE INTELLECT.

We have already, in Logic and in the Introduction, examined most of the notions concerning the intellect, and we shall now only briefly recapitulate them.

The intellect is the thinking power. The faculties of the intellect may be divided into two classes, the perceptive faculties, by which the mind perceives, and the reflexive faculties, by which the mind makes use of these perceptions. This chapter is, therefore, divided into two articles, to which we shall add a third on the nature and origin of ideas.

ARTICLE FIRST.—THE PERCEPTIVE FACULTIES.

There are two kinds of perception, the perception of contingent things, otherwise called experimental perception or experience; and the perception of necessary things, otherwise called rational perception or pure reason, or simply reason.

(A) The experimental perceptive faculties are: Consciousness;* memory,† to which may be added what is called the association of ideas; and the perception of the senses.

The association of ideas is the concatenation of several ideas owing to some relation existing between them.

These relations may be natural or arbitrary, according as they exist in the very nature of things, or depend on our will.

The principal natural relations are:

1st. *Resemblance*, when two objects, or their ideas,

---

* See Logic, Second Motive, page 85.
† See Logic, Sixth Motive, page 96.

resemble each other by some essential marks, or some accidental qualities; the mind naturally goes from the one term to the other.

2d. *Opposition*, when we bring objects or ideas nearer so as to construct them.

3d. *Simultaneity*, which relation takes place when objects present themselves to us as existing simultaneously in the same time or at the same place.

There are, moreover, in ideas other natural relations which it is sufficient to enumerate: The relations of the *cause* to the *effect*, and of the *effect* to the *cause*; of the *substance* to the *attribute*, and *vice versa*.

Arbitrary relations are far more numerous and more varied. We establish them according to our fancy, and they can only be useful to us by a special agreement made with others.

It is well to observe here that there is an essential difference between sensation and the perception of the senses. As we have said, sensation is a phenomenon purely subjective. For instance, the sensation of smell is altogether an affection of the soul, and represents nothing distinct from this sensation; for if there were a representation of something accompanying the sensation it would not belong to the sensation itself, but to the perception or the imagination. The perception of the senses, on the contrary, is a phenomenon both subjective and objective, which represents something which is outside the soul. The confusion of these two notions was the origin of sensism.

The errors generally attributed to the perception of the senses come from three sources: 1st, dreams and delirium; 2d, affirmation of more than the senses perceive; and 3d, weakness or unsound condition of some of the organs of sense. To avoid mistakes from these sources, we should affirm nothing more than we really perceive, and if possible use more than one sense to observe the same phenomenon. Besides, we should renew our observations under different circumstances.

(B) The rational perceptions are, first, ideas, or rational conceptions, the principal of which are those of being (*idea entis*), of unity, of infinity, of substance, of cause, of truth, of beauty, and of goodness, concerning all of which we have already spoken sufficiently; and, second, the necessary truths, or the principles of pure reason, which we have explained in the Dissertation on the motives of certitude.

ARTICLE SECOND.—THE REFLEXIVE FACULTIES.

The reflexive faculties are those by which the soul exercises its activity upon the perceptions. They are, as we have explained in Part First: Attention, abstraction, judgment, reasoning, imagination, and the expression and transmission of thought by language.

We will say a few words only in respect to *attention* and *imagination:*

Attention is the application of the mind to an object in order to know it. Attention directs the intellect and belongs to moral activity; it implies at least love of truth, which is the good of our intellect.

There is a certain attention preceding knowledge; it is the *attention of investigation,* or attention properly called.

There is another one following knowledge; it is the *attention of complacency;* it is the enjoyment of the soul in the discovered truth.

Attention is necessary, and on it depends the perfection of the intellect. Attentive intellect is the only intellect worthy of man, and the one only which is fruitful. Its acts assume various denominations. The intellect *observes* when applied to real facts of the experimental order. It *reflects*, when reverted on itself so as to better establish its ideas. It *meditates*, when the reflection is prolonged and extended to a regular series of ideas. It *contemplates*, when, having attained truth, it calmly delights therein.

Attention is *spontaneous* or *voluntary*, inasmuch as it is produced by a spontaneous act or a formal resolution. Voluntary attention is: *Application*, or work of the mind. Application necessitates rest, which becomes *idleness* when not preceded by application. Idleness is innate in us, and it must be checked from infancy; the means to effect this vary according to circumstances.

Distraction is the absence of attention. It is twofold: *Dissipation*, which causes the mind to wander towards every subject without applying itself to any, and *abstraction* or *preoccupation*, which is attention restrained exclusively to a certain kind of ideas or a special aspect in an object.

The imagination is that faculty by which the soul represents to itself an object under a sensible form, without the present or actual exercise of the perception of the senses. The imagination may be creative, as well as reproductive; for we may by imagination represent to ourselves certain intellectual notions under sensible forms.

The imagination is affected by the vicissitudes of the body and the influence of physical agents more than any other intellectual faculty: it is modified by the influence of age, temperament, sickness, manner of living, and diversity of climate.

When the imagination is well directed it affords much aid towards the happiness and moral improvement of mankind; but when badly directed, especially when sustained by the reading of novels and bad books, its influence is most pernicious.

This faculty does not suppose a spiritual soul: the vital principle of animals suffices.

Imagination takes also the name of fantasy (φαντάζω), whence is derived the term fantastic, which we use in designating a man who never consults but the whimsical dreams or the fancies of his imagination. The brain is its proper organ. It is a sensitive faculty distinct from the understanding, although both be closely connected together.

Dreams are the effects of the imagination; it happens that during sleep the external organs are alone inactive, whilst the internal organ is active, and allows imagination to exercise itself.

Various causes disturb sleep, and dreams ordinarily relate to what has impressed us whilst awake.

The expression and transmission of our ideas by language is a subject which must be treated more fully.

(a) *General Notions.*

Language, in general, is any sensible sign by which men may communicate to one another their thoughts, feelings, and affections: it is either natural or acquired.

Natural language is that which men use and understand without any previous instruction; such as gestures, looks, shouts, etc. This kind of language, which is also called gesticulation, is very expressive in certain circumstances, but generally is too vague, uncertain, and incomplete.

Acquired language is that which can neither be expressed nor understood without previous instruction

17.   N

and knowledge of the native tongue. This kind of language is either spoken or written. Spoken language, being uttered by the tongue and other organs of speech, is language properly so called, or the *tongue*, as we say the English tongue, the French tongue, etc.

Language is natural to men, in the sense that they have suitable organs for its use; but it is also conventional, in the sense that the meaning given to the sounds issuing from the organs of speech is fixed almost altogether by the agreement of men.

It is clear that spoken language is far more useful than that which we have called natural language, or gesture.

Written language is a collection of fixed and permanent figures, by the use of which men give expression to their ideas. It is of three kinds: ideographic, or picture writing (as the figures in arithmetic, algebra, geometry, and chemistry); alphabetic; and hieroglyphic, which is a mixture of the other two.

(b) *Language Considered in Relation to Thought.*

Language is not the producing cause of our ideas, but it is necessary in order that the human intellect should attain the degree of perfection of which it is capable. In regard to abstract and purely intellectual ideas, language is necessary to develop and preserve them; for it is impossible without language to meditate upon things which do not belong to the sensible order, as, for instance, God and his attributes, etc.

In order that the language be well composed, it is necessary that it be full, clear, and harmonious. The rules to be followed in its use are given in the text-books on grammar.

(c) *The Origin of Language.*

The inquiry on this subject is twofold: we have first to consider the question of fact, and secondly that of possibility.

First.—The Question of Fact.

I It is certain from Genesis that God gave to our first parents a supernatural knowledge of articulate or spoken language.

II. The most ancient traditions of all nations agree in admitting the existence of what they call the golden age, during which God conversed with men and instructed them.

III. All history is silent concerning an invention of language.

IV. The study of philosophy has shown conclusively that all languages have had a common origin, or that there was a primitive language which furnished the roots of all other tongues; and it is surely more simple and reasonable to explain this fact by the supernatural gift of language to man in the beginning, than by the invention of a first language, which must have been imperfect and incomplete, and which consequently could not have been the original of all languages.

Second.—The Question of Possibility.

Is it possible that our first parents could of themselves have invented language?

I. All the materialists and sensists affirm that our first parents could have done this. Some Christian philosophers hold the same opinion, and say: First, that men can naturally express what they feel by some external signs, and consequently that, if they can think before speaking, they can manifest their thoughts by spoken language; but, they further assert, men can think before speaking, and hence could have invented language. Secondly, they say, that by attention men can have ideas of individual things, and afterwards express these ideas in words; then pass from this point to abstraction, generalization, etc., and so gradually form language.

II. De Bonald is the principal defender of the opinion that it is impossible that men should have invented language; and most of the Catholic philosophers side with him. They say, first, that without language it is impossible to acquire reflexive ideas of immaterial things; and this is proved by daily experience, and by the mental state of the deaf and dumb who have not been taught an artificial language, as well as by the state of mind of certain unfortunate persons who have lived in the wilderness without human society from their infancy. Secondly, as is shown in the case of children, abstract and general ideas, even of material things, cannot be acquired, except gradually and with the knowledge of the language: these ideas require reflexion, and reflexion requires words. Thirdly, in order to invent language it would first be necessary to know its law and structure; but these cannot be known without reflexion, and the same difficulty occurs as before. Fourthly, language could not be invented by one man, since he could not be understood by the rest of men, nor could he obtain their consent to use the language formed by him; nor could it be invented by a number of men, for this would suppose an agreement, and no agreement is possible without language. Fifthly, they conclude language cannot have been invented gradually, since it forms a whole of which all the parts exist at the same time.

Neither of these opinions is sufficiently conclusive.

Either, however, may be accepted without opposing the Catholic doctrine.

ARTICLE THIRD.—THE NATURE AND ORIGIN OF OUR IDEAS.

1st. *The Nature of our Ideas.*

We have already spoken of this subject in *Logic;* but there we considered ideas especially in regard to the objects which they represent. We have now to examine the question subjectively, and inquire whether our ideas of things, corporeal or incorporeal, are only modifications of the mind representing objects to itself; or whether they are images distinct from these modifications and also from the objects represented. According to the first hypothesis, there are but two things to be considered in connection with the idea, namely, the subject and the object, while, according to the second hypothesis, there is, besides the subject and the object, an image, which is a medium between the two. Philosophers are divided in opinion on this question. Arnauld, Thomas Reed, and Scotists advocate the first hypothesis; while Aristotle, Democritus, Malebranche, Locke, and the Materialists defend the second. Some of these latter consider the medium to be a material image, which is absurd.

It seems probable that the first hypothesis is the correct one; for the other is entirely gratuitous, and besides does not solve the difficulty, which is: How does the soul, a spiritual substance, see corporeal things? This difficulty reappears on the introduction of the medium.

2d. *The Origin of our Ideas.*

Ideas are pure, or rational, when their objects are necessary things, and empiric when they represent con-

17 *

tingent things. But as empiric ideas come from experience, we need not here inquire of the origin of this
sort of ideas, but only of those which are pure, or
rational; besides, ideas ought not to be considered as
abstract, but as concrete, for undoubtedly abstract ideas
come from abstraction.

The question then is: What is the origin, or the
source of concrete rational ideas, such as the idea of
existence, of unity, of truth, of substance, etc. There
have been three opinions entertained by philosophers
concerning the origin of ideas: That of the Sensists,
that of the Idealists, and the one of the Traditionalists.
We will then unfold the scholastic system, which to us
appears the true one. We will take no notice of the
system of the Materialists, ancient as well as modern;
for they have been effectually refuted by what has been
said concerning the immortality and the spirituality of
the soul. Consequently we will disregard Epicurus,
Lucretius, Helvetius, and De Holbach, and will immediately turn our attention to the school of the Sensists.

(a) *The System of the Sensists.*

Sensism is due to Locke, but above all to Condillac.
It is the system of those who derive all our ideas, even
rational ideas, from the senses. Their axiom is: There is
nothing in the intellect which was not first in the senses.
All the Sensists agree that at the time of its creation
the soul is like a sheet of blank paper, void of all ideas.

There is a difference between the Materialists and
the Sensists; the former contend that the soul is a
material substance, the latter do not.

This system ought to be rejected, if it is true that
rational ideas cannot come from the senses; but it is
true that these ideas cannot come from this source,

either directly by the perception of the senses or indirectly by reflexion: for the senses perceive only bodies and their phenomena; and reflexion, acting upon ideas of contingent things, can derive nothing from them but what they contain, that is, what is contingent and mutable. Consequently, reflexion cannot derive from ideas of contingent things the ideas of truth, infinity, justice, etc., the objects of which are necessary and immutable things. This conclusion is strictly logical, and established upon the principle of contradiction.

Sensism is one of those theories which flourish during times of abasement and degradation. When man lowers himself to the level of the brute, he feels the necessity of making his position regular. He then embraces with pleasure despicable systems to legitimate this practical disorder.

According to the doctrine of the Sensists, man, in fact, does not substantially differ from the animal, as Condillac makes no difficulty to avow. Why, then, if it be so, should he have a superior destiny, a nobler end, than sensible enjoyment? The system of the Sensists, to be consequent with itself, ought to resolve itself into pure materialism. Since we have, according to this system, but mere sensitive faculties, we can know only what falls under our senses. Then it follows that what is outside of the sensible order either does not exist at all, or does not fall under our knowledge. Consequently there can be no spiritual objects, or, at least, we have no means of ascertaining their existence. On what plea, then, could the Sensists attribute to man a spiritual soul? Well could Leibnitz, taking hold of the formula which Sensists so much abuse, *Nihil est in intellectu quod non prius fuerit in sensu*, add, *nisi ipse intellectus*.

(b) *Idealistic Systems.*

Idealism makes too little of the conditions of our animality and tends to elevate us to the dignity of pure spirits. To idealism belongs the theory of Innate Ideas and Ontology.

1st. *Theory of Innate Ideas.*—The first upholder of the theory of Innate Ideas was Plato. According to him, the souls preëxisting to the bodies possess all their ideas by the intuition of type-ideas, which he supposes to be eternal. Besides, have these type-ideas a self and independent existence? Are they a part of the divine substance? It is difficult to determine, with any degree of exactness, the opinion of Plato on this point, and it is not here the place to discuss it. Be that as it may, the souls, according to that ancient philosopher, were in possession of their ideas when they were united to their bodies. This union, which was a chastisement, had for result the obscuration of their knowledge; and they are now reduced to the necessity of laboriously recalling their former reminiscences. Thus it is that, according to Plato, rational knowledge is but a reminiscence.

Descartes, without admitting with Plato the preëxistence of the soul, supposes, nevertheless, that from the first instant of their existence they possess, already awakened, by the will of the Creator, if not all their ideas, at least the principal ones. Leibnitz modified the opinion of Descartes in this, that he admitted but a single idea innate in us, the idea of the being. Now, thereby, he understands not the mere notion of the being in the abstract, that is, the most extended, as well as the least perfect notion; but the notion of the being adorned with all the perfections of which it is capable. This notion would imply all the sciences, and it would require but to deduce them therefrom.

The opinions of Plato and Descartes, in what they have in common, may be formulated as follows: Ideas are in us without us: they precede all intellectual acts which are proper to us.

This theory, in the first place, is a gratuitous supposition, which is not at all necessary for the solution of the question in debate. Moreover, this theory is in contradiction with the nature of our being, in which, by the reason of the union of the body with the soul, the simple power necessarily precedes actualization. This theory becomes absurd if, with Plato, we want to apply it, without any reservation, to all ideas, and as to the system of Leibnitz, it necessarily leads to pure idealism.

2d. *Theory of the Vision in God—Ontologism.—* This theory has for author Malebranche, who expounded it in his work entitled "Recherche de la Connaissance."

Malebranche found during his life but few adherents. A few expressions of Bossuet, in the fourth part of his work, "Knowledge of God and of Oneself," seem to lean towards that opinion, as do certain passages of St. Augustine himself, whom Ontologists fain to designate as their chief. However, it is not difficult to give the true sense of those passages. We could less easily justify Fenelon in certain passages of his treatise "On the Existence of God;" but it is only just to remark that he treats nowhere this question *ex professo*, and that he, probably, would have given a more precise turn of expression to his thought, had he been called upon to make a choice of opinion.

The theory of the vision in God has been taken up again with ardor in our time: it has been the subject of a very lively controversy in Catholic schools.

This theory may be formulated in the following propositions: 1st. The object of our rational knowledge is not the idea considered as a form or modification of our soul. The soul is not the limit of intellectual knowledge. Ontologists affect to suppose that this is the scholastic theory, and hence the name of Psychologism, which they give to it. 2d. Knowledge has for object the being properly so called (*ens simpliciter dictum*). Hence the name of Ontologism. The being so known has, besides, all the characters relating to rational knowledge. The being is universal, absolute, necessary, eternal, infinite. 3d. There is no being having these characters outside of the Divine Being, consequently it is God in his real existence whom reason apprehends when it knows. 4th. In the immediate knowledge of God our intellect can know nothing. God being known, on the contrary, we know more or less explicitly all truth; for his essence contains all the absolute types of the finite beings; and that is precisely where we perceive them. 5th. Ontologists distinguish a twofold knowledge: the direct or habitual knowledge and the reflex knowledge. The direct knowledge has God for object. It is necessary to us; it is in our essence; but we are not conscious of it. The reflex knowledge relates to creatures formed from the divine ideas which serve as types. Creatures, as rationally understood, exist only in these types and by these types. Reflex knowledge, of which we are conscious, supposes them the former, and cannot exist unless it is preceded by it.

In conclusion, we say that in this theory reason does not know, in a created light, which participate in the divine light; but that it knows directly the divine light itself.

Such is the system of the Ontologists: it cannot withstand a serious criticism.

In the first place, the idea is not, according to the scholastics, an intellectual knowledge: the idea is a sign, and consequently the medium by which the mind is placed *en rapport* with its object.

The scholastics do not absolutely exclude God from the origin of our knowledge; for our understanding is but a secondary cause; it cannot act, except by the impulsion of a first cause—God. The object of the understanding itself could not be completely isolated from God. God does not intervene directly as an illuminating principle; but He is everywhere concealed behind secondary causes.

This vision of the Divine essence, if it existed, would exist without our knowledge, and so we would be the plaything of a strange illusion.

This vision in God is without proportion with our nature. It would be already above the reach of a pure spirit; and, *a fortiori*, would it transcend the reach of a spirit united to a body.

This theory does not distinguish the natural order from the supernatural; it prepares the way to Pantheism, and finally Ontologism has been condemned by the Holy See on the 18th of September, 1861, when a decree emanated from the Sacred Congregation of the Inquisition declared that no one could safely teach seven propositions, many, if not all, of which relate to this system.

(c) *System of Traditionalists.*

This system was devised to oppose Rationalism.

De Bonald, and later de La Mennais, were its principal exponents. Traditionalism exaggerates the part which teaching or tradition obtains in the development of the intelligence. They contend that without this exterior help our understanding would be deprived even of the first elements of our knowledge, that ideas come to us only through contact with society and through language.

De Bonald did not, however, go so far as to attribute to language a creating influence on our ideas; but he evidently mitigated this absurd assertion in speaking of intellectual germs latent in our mind. We will content ourselves with making a few remarks on this system.

What are those germs of which de Bonald speaks? In what do they differ from innate ideas? Upon what basis does he place himself to demonstrate their existence? These are questions upon which the illustrious writer should have explained himself with great precision.

De Bonald attributes to language effects which it is not capable of producing; language, so long as it is not in the mind attached to a conceived idea, is nothing but a mere sound, without any signification whatsoever.

We can think without the aid of language: experience and the study of our nature lead us to this conclusion. It could not be proved that it would be impossible for man to invent language.

As regards the influence of teaching on the development of our mind, we must seek it in the judgments rather than in the formation of our ideas.

Without calling in question the great utility, the moral necessity of tradition, we should not go beyond that nor make our whole intellectual life depend from it.

(d) System of the Scholastics.

The sensualistic theory and the theories of the Idealists, which we have just considered, are false: the former, because it allows too much to the senses; the latter, because they exaggerate and misconceive the forces of reason. Between these extreme errors may be set, as the true solution, the theory of the Scholastics, otherwise called the theory of Aristotle and of the peripatetician school. The Scholastics, in the first place, lay the point of departure of our intellectual knowledge in sensible knowledge. They do not, however, pretend, as the sensists do, to assimilate and confound one with the other; but they contend that we have never known anything rationally, if the operation of the understanding has not been preceded by the perception of the senses, which serve, so to say, as instruments for its exercise.

Experience is in accord with their sentiment. Every time, in fact, that we wish to conceive intellectually it is a fact that we recall a sensible object to give form to our idea.

We come to the same conclusion when we consult the nature of man. The essence of our being is animality rendered rational by a form which is intelligent, whilst at the same time it serves to animate the body. Consequently, if it be true that "the operations follow the being," we begin by knowing sensible things in order to rise afterwards by our reason to abstract and general notions. Thus it is that we pass from sensible beings up to metaphysical notions and to the knowledge of the essence of spiritual beings.

Such is the point of departure, according to the Scholastics, of rational knowledge. Thus it is that they understand, with Aristotle, the famous axiom which has been so misconstrued by the sensualists: "*Nihil est in intellectu quod non prius fuerit in sensu.*"

18

To show, now, how we enter into full possession of our ideas, that is to say, to explain intellectual knowledge, the Scholastics distinguish a twofold faculty, or at least a double point of view in the same faculty: the possible intellect and the agent intellect.

The possible intellect is the understanding in power of ideas, in the condition, then, of *tabula rasa*, until it be informed by determinate conceptions. This possible intellect exists: it is the primitive state of our reason; but in order that this possible intellect be not perpetually inactive, we must have recourse to a force capable of rendering sensible representations actually intelligible, and that is the function of the agent intellect, so called because its operation is such that it acts by itself in presence of the objects of knowledge; it is a force of abstraction essential to our intelligence. The function of the intellect is to constitute, by abstraction, the intelligible which the possible intellect actualizes and informs.

The agent intellect is the eye of our inner self; it perceives images, ideas, and renders them intelligible.

The difference between that eye and the material one consists in this, that the latter does not derive light from itself, whilst the understanding becomes the luminous focus for the possible intellect. This theory is the one most conformable to experience. It could not be rejected except through blindness and obstinacy.

CHAPTER THIRD.

Of Activity.

Activity is the power or faculty of acting: it is both interior and exterior. Interior activity is the soul's activity, considered independently of its action on the body; while exterior activity, on the contrary, is the soul's activity, considered with reference to the movements of the body: exterior activity has therefore been called the motrix faculty.

Interior activity is twofold, free and spontaneous; the latter must not be confounded with the soul's passivity.

Spontaneous activity is exercised in two ways, from instinct and from habit. Instinct differs from habit in this, that instinct proceeds from nature, while habit is the result of a frequent repetition of the same acts. Instinct is found in animals as well as in men, and in children as well as in adults. Animals act nearly always through instinct. Men, on the contrary, are directed by reason in almost all their actions. However, in the adults, there are certain actions which proceed from instinct.

Instinct which is not modified by reason remains stationary. And that is what takes place in animals.

Infancy is the period in the life of man when instinct principally acts; but it decreases in proportion as he advances in years, without, however, disappearing entirely.

There remain always in man certain instincts; some of which are physical: they are the instincts of the body and those of the soul.

The former manifest themselves in those circumstances when reason alone could not supply the wants of man, as the action of the eyelids, the maintenance of the equilibrium of the body.

As to the instincts of the soul, it will suffice to make mention of the *desire* for *happiness*—that instinctive natural propensity which precedes all reflection and all deliberation; the *inclination to believe* on the testimony of others; and also *the belief in the constancy and generality of the laws of nature.*

Habit has been defined as the disposition to act acquired from a frequent repetition of the same acts. The soul and the body have each their own habits. It is evident that actions proceeding from mere habit are not free in themselves, though they may be so indirectly, that is, in their cause.

Each power of the soul is naturally inclined to accomplish those acts which properly belong to it; but by itself alone it does not incline towards any of them in particular: all are equally indifferent to it so long as it does not complete itself by a certain modification, whose effect is to create a new circuit in the general movement which characterizes it.

That manner of being of a power is what we call its habit. Habit produces uniformity in operations; it renders acts more prompt and rapid. Habit finds in the accomplishment of its acts the satisfaction of a want, and is, therefore, a real enjoyment.

There are *innate habits:* they are those which we bring with us in this world; and there are also *acquired habits*, or those which we ourselves contract.

Habit is a quality of the activity; it exists only in the powers of the rational soul. It creates a particular direction in the activity which must direct itself in different ways, and that is found only in the understanding and the will.

The sensitive powers are not susceptible of states which modify them; considered in themselves, they are invincibly attracted by the allurement of the present good. But it is another thing, if we consider the sensitive powers and the body as the instruments of reason and will. In this case, they follow the rational faculties in the direction of their habits.

There are, in relation to the subject, intellectual

habits and moral habits, according as the latter are relative to science or to the will.

Moral habits are either good or bad, according as our will makes a good or bad use of its liberty.

The habit which conforms itself to duty is called *virtue;* and the contrary habit, *vice.*

Education consists in fostering the innate good habits in creating new ones, and in preventing and correcting bad ones.

Free activity, or the liberty of the soul, will now be treated at large, forming the chief part of this chapter. The other subjects belong directly to theology.

The Freedom of the Human Soul.

We first give a definition of the will: The *will* is that faculty by which the soul chooses the good proposed to it by the intellect and avoids evil. Hence we conclude that nothing is willed unless it first be known.

The will is either necessary or free. In the first case, the one who wills cannot refrain from willing, and this is will properly so called; in the second case, one may refrain from willing that which is proposed by the intellect and choose something else, and this is called freedom. Freedom, therefore, is the power either to will or to refrain from willing; or, more simply, it is the power of choosing.

The will of man tends to good. If this good would manifest itself to us in its entirety, we would not be free, but it manifests itself only indirectly by means of those things which we call good.

These relative goods have not the reason of end, but that of means. As they are imperfect, they are susceptible of being multiplied.

The will, instead of being determined *ad unum*, re-

18 *   O

mains free in its choice of the multitude of diverse forms which the understanding conceives and which the judgment appreciates. It is precisely in this that liberty consists. Liberty, consequently, is the exemption from all necessity in the choice of the will.

On account of this choice there is an abyss between animal and rational life.

Liberty is not the exemption from all constraint; constraint limits our exterior activity, impedes the exercise of liberty, but does not destroy it in its substance. The exemption from constraint is an extension of interior liberty.

Liberty is not an absolute independence.

This is modern liberalism; the teaching of Satan and of the revolution.

Obedience and liberty are not incompatible. The command is simply proposed to our reason. Now, to consult our reason, and for this to take the aid of another's wisdom, even of a law, does not take away our liberty.

The obligation which results from a law exercises a certain pressure upon us, but it leaves us free.

Sanction also is nothing but a stimulant; it is not a necessitating motive.

Among the philosophers who have denied the freedom of the will, we find, first, the Stoics, who were strict fatalists; second, the Pantheists, who cannot admit freedom without being in contradiction with themselves; third, the Manicheans, who pretended that we do good or evil according as the good or the evil principle inspires us; fourth, the Mahometans, who are fatalists; fifth, several modern religious systems which teach that we are predestined to do good by grace, and to do evil by concupiscence, thus confounding the notions of the

voluntary and the free, and of course destroying freedom; sixth, the followers of Cousin and Gall, who indirectly teach fatalism; and, seventh, the Materialists,
whose system, like that of the Pantheists, destroys
human liberty.

NOTE.—Euler and some other philosophers have contended that freedom is essential to spiritual substances.
We feel constrained to deny this, and to say that God
might have created us without liberty, at least without
the liberty of doing wrong.

We have now to discuss the question as to whether
we have the liberty of choosing, and will proceed to
prove the

Proposition.— *The human mind is truly free.*

Argument: That ought to be admitted as true which
is proved to be true by the testimony of consciousness,
by the consent of mankind, by the absurd consequences
of fatalism, and by reason; but such is the case with the
above proposition, and hence the human soul is free.

Proof: First. Consciousness. We have seen that
consciousness is an infallible motive of judging of the
present state of the soul. Now, we feel sure that in
many of our actions we are free: we perceive that there
is an essential difference between the actions which are
performed with deliberation and those which are done
without deliberation. The remorse that follows our bad
actions helps us to make this distinction more evident.
We may therefore conclude that the freedom of the will
is proved by our own consciousness.

Second. The consent of mankind is a clear and powerful proof in this case. We find everywhere, and in
all ages, laws, treaties, rewards, punishments, etc.
Among themselves men naturally use entreaties, threats,
exhortations, etc. Even the fatalists do not deny these

facts, although they pretend to believe that this general persuasion proceeds from necessity. But we cannot admit that God, in his wisdom and love of truth, would permit all men to remain in such a state of delusion; and we therefore hold this consent of mankind as conclusive in favor of the freedom of the human soul.

Third. If the doctrine of fatalism were admitted, we should be but machines, deprived of reason. It would be absurd to speak of reasoning, deliberation, prudence, wisdom, etc., or of a distinction between virtue and vice or good and evil. There would be no merit in being a poet, an orator, or a philosopher, since necessity would compel certain persons to fill these positions. No one is willing to admit the existence of these consequences, which, however, are logically true if we are not free.

Fourth. Reason. We might here use an *argumentum ad hominem*. Would those philosophers who deny the existence of human liberty refrain from asking for punishment for any one who should strike or rob them? And yet, if they were logical, they would not consider those persons guilty who do these things. The illogical conduct of the fatalists themselves then shows that we are free.

We conclude:

1st. That the existence of our freedom is as clear as that of our thought.

2d. That the denial of our freedom leads to the denial of certitude itself.

3d. That the existence of human freedom must be considered a primary truth.

It is in the doctrine of the moderate fatalists that we find objections raised against the existence of human freedom. By moderate fatalists we mean those philosophers who, considering the strength of our physical nature, blinded more or less as it is by ignorance, habit, or prejudice, exaggerate its influence over the determination of the will.

That this influence exists, and is in some cases very strong and very pressing, is of course true; but it can never have such power over our determination as to make us act from necessity. We may always ascertain that we have been free, even in those actions in which our temper, our habits, etc., have had most influence over us.

Divine order is, after all, the supreme direction of our moral activity. In our individual being, consciousness sufficiently enlightened is the guiding principle. In society, the mission of authority consists in the establishment of the general order and the realization of the common good. Consequently the direction of the individual or of society ought always to be inspired with the absolute order, if not, it ends with an apparent order and a real disorder. Individual caprice, royal caprice, people's caprice can never be erected into laws. This absolute order shows itself with its unchangeable principles, which are the basis of authority.

These principles should be kept inviolable, and it is for this reason that there is a need of some absolute and indisputable infallibility somewhere.

This infallibility cannot be found in Reason as it is now in the state of fallen nature. And where should we look out for it but in Revelation, this divine remedy to the infirmity of our mind.

But living Revelation is the Church, the Church and the Pope are but the same thing: " *Ubi Petrus, ubi Ecclesia.*" The infallibility of the church is consequently the crown of social order, whatever it may be.

PART II.—RATIONAL PSYCHOLOGY.

CHAPTER FIRST.

OF THE NATURE OF THE HUMAN SOUL, OR OF ITS SIM-
PLICITY AND SPIRITUALITY.—REFUTATION OF MATE-
RIALISM.

The soul is a substance. Life, in the diverse modifications it assumes in animated beings, may be but an
accident. But here, as ever, the accident has a relation
to a substantial principle. Underlying the vital acts
which we observe, there is the vital activity which remains, by essence, identical to itself.

Is this activity the corporal substance? Has the
body the power to produce vital motions? If it were
so, where would be the distinction between animate
and inanimate bodies?

It is evident that there are living bodies; but the
principle of life in them is not the material principle
which begets space.

As vital principle of our body, the soul would at
most be an element of the substance. For a stronger
reason is it a substance, if life, whose principle it is, is,
by the very nature of its operations, independent of the
body and of its organs. Now, that is the character of
the spiritual activity of our rational life.

Our soul, in virtue of its spiritual nature, has in itself
a proper reason of subsistence ; and that renders its separate existence possible. From that point of view, it is
made assimilable to the pure spirits.

The soul, reduced to a singular existence in the subjects really existing, supposes, joined to the pure substance, a principle of individualization; and as it is, by
its nature, rational, this principle will be a person.

This personality is a real entity; and, in this respect, Kant is mistaken in making the personality of the soul to consist in the consciousness which the soul has of itself.

Consciousness is a mode of the human nature; it requires a subject which, by its subsistence, permits it to excite and act.

Consciousness perceives our personality, but does not create it. Descartes is wrong also when he says: "We are, because we think;" this signifies that the *me* (ego) in man is the thinking being.

The person supposes the body and the soul—a compound nature. The *me* is the body and the soul, but united hypostatically in the person.

The person is what makes us to be "*juris proprii;*" it is the principle to which all the acts of the body and the soul relate.

Personality, therefore, begets *responsibility*. The soul is immaterial, because it is simple and spiritual. As simple, it is not subject to space and divisibility. As spiritual, it is even not subjected, by essence, to be but the informing principle of matter.

Those philosophers who admit the spirituality of the human soul are called Spiritualists, and those who deny it are called Materialists. Besides the school of Epicurus, we may rank among the Materialists, Locke, La Mettrie, Voltaire, Cabanis, Helvetius, d'Holbach, and Diderot.

Among the ancients many admitted the spirituality of the soul, as Cicero and Aristotle.

Proposition.—*The soul is a simple substance, and absolutely distinct from matter.*

Argument: Two substances cannot be identical when they have opposite properties; but such is the case in regard to the soul and matter.

Proof: In order to prove the above proposition we will establish the fact that the soul is endowed with three properties which matter cannot have: the power of thinking, that of judging, and a free will, or activity.

I. *The soul has the power of thinking*, a power which cannot be found in any material substance, that is, in a substance which has extension and is capable of division; for if a material substance could have the power of thought, (1) the whole thought must be located in the whole substance, or (2) in each part of the substance, or (3) in one part only.

The first hypothesis cannot be accepted; for if it were true we should have to admit that thought may be divided into as many parts as there are in the substance, and consequently there would be no part which would be conscious of the whole thought or perceive its entire object.

The second hypothesis is equally absurd; for if it were true, the thought would be multiple, instead of divisible, but we feel that our thought is one.

The third hypothesis is also inadmissible, because the same difficulties come back. This part of the matter would itself be matter, and consequently divisible, and of course the thought must again be either divisible or multiple, and this is against the general conviction and feeling of our consciousness that the power of thinking is simple.

II. *The soul has the power of judging.* In order to compare there must be a comparer who examines the two notions to be compared; this comparer, therefore must have the attribute of unity; but unity cannot be found where there is divisibility, that is, in matter. Hence this power belongs to a simple substance.

III. *The human soul is active.* We have proved that

we are free; to be free is, first, to be active; but matter has no activity, being inert by nature: hence the soul must be an immaterial substance.

We might add other observations to the above: First, that taken from the identity of the thinking principle within us. We are conscious of this identity. We feel that we are now the same beings that we have ever been; and yet our bodies have been changed many times, being constantly renewed.

Second, that taken from the consciousness which we have at the same time of several sensations of a different character: I see, hear, smell, taste, and touch at the same time, and am conscious that it is the same principle that perceives these various sensations. If, according to Epicurus, this principle were nothing else than the organs of the different senses, I could be conscious of but one sensation at the same time.

Third, that drawn from the consent of mankind may be added to the above, and we conclude that the immateriality of the soul is proved.

In order to answer the objections made against this proposition, let us observe that from the mutual influence of the soul and body over each other we cannot conclude that the two substances are identical, for these reasons:

(a) There is no contradiction in the action of a spiritual substance on a material one. (b) As God, who is a spiritual substance, acts upon material creatures, so may the soul act upon the body. (c) Many examples show these substances to be different; as very often a powerful mind is found in a weak and feeble body. (d) The body is to the soul what a musical instrument is to a musician: the musician tunes his instrument by degrees, and so the soul acts on the body during all the periods of our existence.

19

From what has been said we may conclude, first, that the soul is a substance endowed with activity, sensibility, intellect, and freedom ; and, second, that it is a substance which is a unit in every man, simple and always identical with itself.

We have seen in the first chapter what constitutes the immateriality of the soul, viz., its simplicity and spirituality.

It would be well to observe that there is a difference between simplicity and spirituality. Simplicity excludes extension and divisibility. A substance is spiritual not only when it is not material, but also when it is independent of matter and not united to any corporeal organ.

Simplicity, with reference to the soul, excludes plurality of number, for the soul is not a collection of several distinct forces, but it is in us a force unique.

The soul excludes every idea of extension and divisibility. Our own conscience is perfectly aware of the unity and identity of the soul. There are also in the body identity and unity. These, however, are but imperfect. In order that they be perfect, they must be placed in another principle simple, active ; which perseveres so as to maintain unity in all changes and periods.

The nature of thought also shows the simplicity of the soul. That which we have said concerning the nature of the soul more than refutes the doctrine of *Materialists*. This system, which admits but extended substances, would not find adepts if it did not otherwise recommend itself. It is the absence of responsibility which it engenders that causes many to adhere to *Materialism*.

It would be tiresome to enumerate all the fastidious objections opposed to the immateriality of the soul.

1st. The soul, they say, does not differ from the body,

because we cannot imagine a substance without extension.

There is nothing wonderful in our incapability of imagining such substance. Still there are things which reason conceives, such as pure spirit, the human soul, etc.

2d. The soul diffused throughout the whole body also has extension. Our own conscience reveals the contrary, in which we find nothing that implies a contradiction.

3d. The soul is associated with the body in all its changes, and therefore is confounded with it.

It is unnecessary to admit the confusion of substances in order to explain these facts. To admit that they are closely united, and at the same time distinct, is sufficient.

4th. Dynamical materialism attributes to matter a necessary activity, consequently there is no spiritual activity.

We here find a conclusion more extended than the premises permit. We have said that matter can be a formal cause, and is therefore capable of a true activity; but there is a vast difference between the activity of material beings and the vital activity of the soul.

Phrenology bears some relation to materialism. This system, developed by Gall, ascribes to the brain a determining influence on the rational life itself. Everything in man depends on the constitution of his brain.

There is assuredly a close relation between the brain and the soul; but it is absurd to subject forcibly to fixed laws phenomena which depend only on spiritual activity.

CHAPTER SECOND.

OF THE ORIGIN OF THE SOUL.

There have been two errors concerning the origin of the soul. Pythagoras, most of the Stoics, and Epictetus considered the soul as a part of the divine substance coming from it through emanation. The Manichæans, according to St. Augustine, and the Priscillianists, according to St. Jerome, held the same teaching.

Others taught that the soul was propagated through generation by the parents, as the body is propagated; these were called the Traducians. Tertullian and Apollinaris held this opinion, and for some time St. Augustine himself defended it, using it, for the purpose of explaining more easily the transmission of original sin, against the Pelagians. The hypothesis concerning the preëxistence of the souls was held by some philosophers in two different ways: 1st. Some, especially among the ancients, thought that our souls had existed in another anterior life, and that they were united in this present life to such or such body, according to the way they had behaved in the former life. This doctrine was prevalent in Chaldæa, in Egypt, and generally in all the Eastern countries. This dogma, under the name of *metempsychosis*, or *transfiguration of the souls*, was taught by Pythagoras and his disciples, and is found in our days among the Indians, the Japanese, and the Siamese.

Socrates also taught the doctrine of the existence of a former life, giving as an argument in its favor that when men learn the first principles of the sciences they seem to remember what they have known before. Plato adopted this teaching.

Origenes taught that all the souls were created by God at the beginning, and placed in some spiritual world; but on account of some crimes they were sent into a corporeal world and imprisoned into human bodies. This doctrine was condemned in the fifth ecumenical council.

The hypothesis concerning the preëxistence of the souls was accepted and taught by Leibnitz and some of his disciples. According to this learned author, all the souls created by God at the beginning were deposited under the form of germs in Adam. Leibnitz gave this theory as the only way, according to him, of explaining the transmission of original sin.

Contrary to this, we say that every soul is created immediately by God.

First, the souls are neither uncreated beings nor parts of the divine substance, because in the first case they should be necessary beings, and have all the perfections of the necessary being; and, secondly, the divine substance is simple.

It is false to say that the souls of children are generated out of the souls of parents. This could not be done by the generating soul through communication of a part of its own substance, because the soul is a simple and immaterial substance, and to assert that this is not done through communication of some part of the substance of the generating soul is equally false, for in this case it should not be a generation, but a creation.

The preëxistence of the human souls cannot be admitted. This doctrine cannot stand the test of reason. It is gratuitous. It cannot agree with our notions about God's wisdom. It is in opposition with the common teaching of theologians.

We say, then, that the soul is created immediately by God, and united to the body at the very moment of its conception.

CHAPTER THIRD.

VARIOUS SYSTEMS ON THE UNION OF THE SOUL AND OF THE BODY.

1st System. SYSTEM OF THE PHYSICAL INFLUX.— This system, attributed to Euler and strenuously defended by the disciples of Locke, makes the union of

19 *

the soul and of the body to consist in the reciprocal action of the two beings, one upon the other.

This action gives to the body a complete actualization independently of the soul, since before it can act it must be.

The soul itself does not act upon the body in the manner that a form penetrates a primary matter, in order to cause it to pass from the power to the act; but in the manner of a motor.

The soul would cease to be one of the two substantial elements of the human compound, and behold dualism in us.

2d. SYSTEM OF THE PLASTIC MEDIATOR.—The second system, that of a plastic or operating mediator, is taught by those who believe that there is between the soul and the body a middle substance, by the aid of which the soul and the body mutually act upon each other. According to the philosophers who teach this doctrine, this mediator is an active and incorporeal substance, but is deprived of sensibility and intelligence.*

3d. SYSTEM OF THE OCCASIONAL CAUSES.—The third system, that of occasional causes, is the one taught by Malebranche. According to this system there is no real action of the soul upon the body, or of the body upon the soul : but the operations of the mind are only occasions, and these being present God himself acts upon the body ; in like manner, the *modifications* of the body are occasions, which being also present, God modifies the mind, that is, excites sensations in it.

---

* This system rests on no serious foundation. It was invented by an English philosopher of the seventeenth century, Cudworth by name. This mediator is neither purely body nor purely spirit ; evidently it is as difficult to assign a reason for this intermediary as to account for the union of the two elements in our substance.

4th. SYSTEM OF THE PREËSTABLISHED HARMONY.—
The fourth system, that of a preëstablished harmony,
is the system of Leibnitz. This philosopher teaches
that there is no direct action of the soul upon the body,
or of the body upon the soul ; nor does God act directly
upon the body on account of the operations of the mind,
nor upon the mind on account of the modifications of
the body ; but He so disposes, or prepares, both body
and soul at the time of their creation that the whole series
of volitions of the mind answers, in the most perfect
harmony, to the whole series of the motions of the
body.

The fourth system does not differ from the third in
regard to the present difficulty, which is to determine
whether there is a mutual influence of the soul and the
body on each other. Both systems deny that there is
any such influence, and in this respect they do not differ,
although in other respects they differ greatly. In each,
however, especially in that of Leibnitz, we do not see
how human freedom would be safe.

The hypothesis of Malebranche has, in the first place,
the mischief, as Leibnitz used to say, " of causing the
intervention of the ' Deus ex machinâ' in a natural and
common thing."

It destroys the substantial unity of our being in completely separating the two constitutive elements. It
even renders their union impossible in supposing them
associated only in the common action which God exercises on each of them.

Moreover, how could we, according to this system,
affirm the coexistence in the same place of the soul and
of the body ?

If, according to this system, all the natural causes
are only occasional causes, we must deny all created

activity. God would be the only cause. Would not such a system open the way to Pantheism?

The system of Leibnitz breaks asunder, also, the unity of our being: he does away with all link between the soul and the body, and substitutes thereto the ideal links of a divine conception. He does in no way account for the coexistence of the body and the soul in the same place. The soul might be in Rome and the body in Paris; yet the accord among all the movements would be no less perfect. Now, what right thinking man would admit that that is enough to establish the human unity?

It is impossible, we repeat, to reconcile this system with liberty; for before this divine preordination what will be our part of initiative and independence?

This system, besides, cannot be suspected of idealism. Wolf, a disciple of Leibnitz, acknowledged it. "Even," said he, "if the visible world should not exist, our soul would represent it to itself in the manner as it does now." And, in fact, the soul a stranger to its own body would be so, *a fortiori*, to the external world, with which it corresponds neither directly nor by intermediary means. Leibnitz seems to have recognized the inanity of his hypothesis: in his correspondence he alludes to it as a plaything of his mind, and a vain exercise of scientific imagination.

CHAPTER FOURTH.

NATURE OF THE UNION OF THE SOUL WITH THE BODY.

We have said that bodies are compound substances. They contain in themselves an element which needs a foreign act in order to be realized, and another element which, *in actu*, by itself actualizes by influence that to which it is joined. The former, a material principle, furnishes a matter to the action of the latter, which is the formal intrinsic principle. The concourse of these two principles begets *the first being*, or substance-principle of subsequent operations. In the unity of the human compound, the soul, without ceasing to have its own proper and spiritual life, is, at the same time, the form of the body. This truth is not a mere philosophic truth, it is a truth of faith as defined by the general council of Vienna.* This dogmatic definition has been reaffirmed by Leo X., in the fourth council of Latron; and Pius IX., in his encyclical letter to the Archbishop of Cologne in 1857, in condemning the error of Gunther, confirmed the same doctrine.

Union is not, then, a mere relation or coördination of two complete substances. It is made in the innermost of the being. Its link is a substantial link. The union of the mind and of the body has its principle not only in personal reality, but also in substantial reality. The body needs the soul in order to exist, to live. The human nature, after the adjunction of the soul to the body, is then but a sole nature.

Consequently there is in man unity of the vital principle. The three modes in which life manifests itself

---

* All doctrine or proposition which would rashly deny or put in question that the substance of the rational or intellective soul is *truly* and *by itself* the form of the human body, we do condemn it, with the approbation of the Holy Council, as *erroneous, and opposed to the truth of the Catholic faith*, defining,—in order to show to all the truth of the faith in its purity, to shut all the issues of all errors and to prevent them from being introduced,—that whosoever would henceforth have the presumption to affirm and uphold with obstinacy that the rational or intellective soul is not *by itself and essentially* the form of the human body, must be looked upon as a heretic.

P

in created beings are met in us, and we must reduce them to one vital principle only.

This being said, we proceed to lay down the following proposition :

Proposition.— *The soul has a direct influence upon the body, and the body upon the soul.*

Argument: If the existence of this mutual influence is not shown to be impossible, and if it is even proved by many facts that the influence does exist, then the proposition must be accepted as true; but such is the case, and hence the soul has a direct influence, etc.

Proof: 1st. It has never been shown that the existence of this influence is impossible. When we say that the soul can act directly upon the body, we do not mean that it acts materially, for it is a spiritual substance; but we mean that the soul has a natural power of moving the body. That the existence of this power of spirit over matter is not impossible is evident from the fact that God, who is a pure spirit, does move material substances.

That the influence of the body upon the soul is a passive one is evident from the fact that the body, being matter, is inert of itself. The body is like an instrument in the hands of a workman; it acts, or has influence, upon his will in proportion to its degree of fitness and perfection. Besides, it has not been shown that the forces of attraction and repulsion, existing among the molecules of matter according to the arrangement made by God, do not exercise some action or influence upon the soul.

2d. Many facts and circumstances prove the mutual influence of the body and the soul. These facts are :

(a) *The testimony of consciousness.* Whenever I move my body I am conscious, not only of my will to move my body, but even of a certain effort of the soul to move it, and I clearly perceive that the movement of my body responds to the effort of my soul.

(b) *The universal persuasion of mankind.* All men are convinced that the human will is the moving cause of bodily action, and also that the body reacts upon the soul. This testimony, as we have proved, is a sufficient argument to establish certitude.

(c) *The unity of human personality.* Personality, in man, is a union between the soul and the body, so complete that they form one individual, who attributes to himself all the actions of the soul and the body—who can say with equal correctness *I* think and *I* walk. It is clear that we could not thus express ourselves if we did not know and feel that our actions are indeed our own, and not the result of the actions of God in consequence of the volitions of our mind or the movements of our body.

(d) *The power which the mind has of directly perceiving corporeal objects.* This has been established in *Logic*, in treating of the evidence of the senses. The existence of this power shows that the senses have a direct influence upon the soul. The first system may therefore be now considered as fully proved to be the true one.

NOTE.—In regard to the consequences of the union of the body with the soul, there are two kinds of phenomena; the first ones are the result of the influence of the body upon the mind, as has been noticed in *Experimental Psychology*, in treating of sensation, memory, etc., when both soul and body are in a normal condition, and in treating of delirium, etc., when they are in an abnormal condition; and the others are the result of the influence of the mind upon the body, as it has been said in treating of the changes of the voice, countenance, etc., when we wish to show the feelings of the soul, in other words, when the influence of the soul is exercised upon the body.

CHAPTER FIFTH.

OF THE IMMORTALITY AND THE DESTINY OF THE SOUL.

It has been shown that the soul and the body are two substances, entirely distinct and different. The dissolution of the body does not involve that of the soul, since the soul is not divisible, that is, is not composed of parts. The dissolution of the body does not necessitate the annihilation of the soul; for if such were the case it would be because the soul could not exercise her faculties without the body; but this is not so, for there are in the soul many faculties which by their nature have no connection with the body : such are the faculties of thinking, judging, reasoning, etc. Hence we may conclude that the soul may outlive the body. This property of the soul is its immortality.

Immortality is a consequence of immateriality, and especially of the spirituality of the soul. Consequently, is it denied by the Materialists, who feel the necessity of warding off the thought of the future life as too importunate to a guilty conscience.

The immortality of the soul is also suppressed by the Pantheists, who give to man but an illusive personality, awaiting the day when he will go to lose himself in an eternal oblivion in the bosom of that universal being who subsists unconscious and undeterminate.

But is not the soul, at least, victim indirectly of the corporal disorganization, as is the soul of animals that necessarily disappear at the moment when the organism is dissolved?

There are two kinds of forms. Separated forms, which are the pure spirits; and inferior forms, which by their union with primal matter beget living bodies. The former subsist by themselves; the latter, to subsist, need materialized beings. The human soul holds from the ones and the others.

As an animal form, it would tend like the souls of animals to disappear by way of indirect corruption; but this reason of perishing cannot prevail on the reason of subsisting, which belongs to it by the superiority of its nature.

We are, besides, conscious that such are not the conditions of our soul. The animal has for aim in life only the present hour. We consider the being and life on a vaster aspect. We feel the want of being, and the innate desire of perpetuating our species. The soul continuing to subsist continues to remain active and to act in conformity with its spiritual nature.

Deprived of organs, it becomes incapable of sensitive operations, but not of intellectual operations. Sensitive life is in no way indispensable to intellectual life, as considered in itself. Often even sensitive life has for effect to constrain and paralyze intellectual life.

The soul, then, has nothing in itself which is opposed to its immortality. There is in its being no defect which sooner or later would condemn it to die. But might it not have exterior causes of destruction to fear?

No created cause is capable of destroying the soul. The soul being free from all composition, created causes cannot destroy it by corruption. On the other hand, being powerless to create they are likewise powerless to

20

annihilate. They could not any better destroy the soul by annihilation.

The power to destroy, like the power to create, is a divine power.

Since the soul may outlive the body, there must be another life; at least, the above remarks will justify us in concluding that the existence of another life is possible. Does this life then exist? This question properly belongs to *Ethics*, and we shall only consider it briefly in this place.

The existence of another life is rendered necessary, 1st, by two attributes of God, his justice and his wisdom. Note IV. 2d. It is shown by the desire born with us to enjoy a felicity not to be found here, and which must be found somewhere. 3d. It is proved by the natural inclination of men to seek for reputation, glory, and immortality. 4th. It is proved by the common consent of mankind, who have always in their treatment of the dead shown their conviction of the existence of another life. It cannot be objected to this that the testimony of a good conscience, or the hope of a reward, are a sufficient sanction to the natural law; for experience shows that a time comes for some men when these impressions are of no avail. 5th. It is proved by the consequences which would be the result of the contrary belief.

Note.—The eternal duration of the other life is not in contradiction to reason.

CHAPTER SIXTH.

Of the Souls of Animals.

Besides God, the angels, and the human soul, there is the inferior soul of animals. By this soul we mean the principle by which the animal has its life. Let us examine, first, what are the faculties of this soul, and, second, what is its nature and destination.

ARTICLE FIRST.—THE FACULTIES OF THE SOULS OF ANIMALS.

The soul of animals is endowed with the faculty to perceive sensible objects—to perceive them as being good or bad. It is endowed with the faculty to direct itself towards what is good, and to fly from what is bad. These two faculties sum up the sensitive life, which is but a rough draught of the intellectual life.

In order to accord to animals a sensitive life, it is then necessary to recognize in them perception, or to employ the received term, sensation; and with the sensations the appetite, that is, the activity.

(a) *Perception* or *Sensation.* Animals have a physical sensibility which is superior in acuteness to that of man, as that of sight in the eagle. They have physical appetites as men have. In some of them we find desires and passions, as the inclination to live in society, emulation, ostentation, envy, and avariciousness. We find in some animals affections, that is, sentiments either good or bad.

By the organs of sense they perceive certain qualities of many bodies placed before them ; and this perception produces a conviction which excludes any doubt, as in the case of oats placed before a horse. Hence they have consciousness of their own sensations and operations. They are capable of being attentive, as a hunting dog scenting game. They have memory. A horse will after years recognize a road through which he has once passed. Some animals have imagination ; and this is the only way of explaining their dreams. Many animals have the power of expressing themselves exte-

riorly, or of communicating their sentiments.   It would
not be unreasonable to admit in them something more
than attention, in fact a sort of calculation on their part,
in order to explain some extraordinary phenomena.

(b) *Activity*.   Some of the actions of animals are
spontaneous and others voluntary ; some proceed from
instinct, some from choice, and others again from acquired habits.

Instinct in animals takes the place of reason; certain
actions of theirs, as we have said, proceed from choice,
as, for instance, a dog will abstain from food for fear of
a stick with which he is threatened.

The difference between men and the inferior animals
is (1) that men are endowed with reason, which belongs
to the nature of the human soul ; consequently, by their
nature men are superior.   It is by reason that men distinguish what is good, true, beautiful, etc., and it is certain that the lower animals cannot make these distinctions.   (2) The lower animals are incapable of morality : having no moral liberty, their actions are not characterized by moral good or malice.

ARTICLE SECOND.—THE NATURE AND DESTINY OF THE
SOULS OF ANIMALS.

It is evident that there is in all animals some immaterial
substance.   We must believe this (1) since they are endowed with the faculties which belong to a sensitive soul.

Such substance ought to be immaterial, because the
above faculties are essentially different from the properties found in matter.

We may therefore reject the doctrine of Descartes,
who says that beasts are mere machines, and also the
doctrine of some modern dreamers, called philosophers,
who pretend that men are not superior to beasts.

The soul of beasts exists only in view of the body which it animates, and it would not be able to survive, the organism being no more. But what becomes of it?

The soul of beasts does not end by annihilation. Annihilation takes place only when the being is wholly destroyed, and the soul of beasts is not, properly speaking, a being, but an element of the animal being, which continues to subsist in a different manner after a substantial transformation. It does not end by a true corruption which would be proper to it only, for corruption takes place only in the transformation of matter; and the principle of animal life, not being compound, does not transform likewise, in its being considered apart, consequently it remains that it disappears indirectly by the effect of the corruption of the whole animal being.

20 *

PART III.

ETHICS; OR, MORAL PHILOSOPHY.

PRELIMINARY DISSERTATION.

The Ultimate end of Man.—Definitions.

MORAL philosophy is that science which directs the free actions of man towards his ultimate end.

The *end* in general is the object which is intended by an action.

This end may be either *proximate* or *ultimate.* The *proximate end* is that which is immediately aimed at by the agent; the *ultimate*, that unto which the will holds, any relation to another end being removed.

The acts performed by tho agent in order to attain this end are called the effects of the end; they are: *volition, intention, deliberation, consent, election, prosecution.*

What, then, is the ultimate end of man?

The will cannot bend towards evil, considered as such. Evil is not a being, and the object of any appetite is some being: a being, inasmuch as it is a being, is good.

Man acting deliberately always intends some end. The end is always first in the intention and last in the execution.

The last end of man is happiness—it is that which he aims at in all his actions. This happiness, which is the object of man's will, is a perfect one, and hence ought to be his ultimate end; for it is this that satisfies his whole nature; were it not so, man would tend towards some absent good, to say which would be an absurdity. Besides, the very fact that man in all his deliberate actions tends towards some end, there ought to be an ultimate one, that is to say, one which, as it were, is entirely independent of any other, which is loved for itself. Because, as says St. Thomas, in the series of ends, they do not proceed from infinity "to infinity." Man cannot have two ultimate ends at the same time. The ultimate end is that which satisfies the whole will, so that nothing else can be desired beyond it. There cannot be two ends of this kind. No created object can be the ultimate end of man, because nothing can give full satisfaction to his faculties, neither wealth, nor honors, nor pleasure, nor science, not even virtue, because virtue, being the habitual direct tendency towards the end proper to human nature, of course is not its own end.

Hence, God only is the ultimate end of man; since no created object can be this end, God alone, the infinite being, can be its object.

The intellect and the will cannot be satiated but by the knowledge of the sovereign truth and the love of the sovereign good. God is "Summum verum" and "Summum bonum." Daily experience shows that man cannot attain his ultimate end in this life. Perfect happiness is impossible in this world, but we can find and enjoy some imperfect happiness which consists in inward peace and tranquillity. These can be obtained only by habitually directing our tendencies towards the ultimate end. Hence, wicked men, although abundantly possessing the goods of this world, cannot be happy, because they are in need of the very foundation of happiness.

Virtuous men, even when suffering, are happy, and, although they feel their pain, still they are consoled and comforted by the testimony of a good conscience, and by the firm hope of an eternal reward. This happiness then cannot be taken away from us against our will.

In order, therefore, to be happy in our present condition, we must practice virtue and subdue our inordinate passions.

The words *Ethics* and *Morals* have the same meaning: the first comes from the Greek *ἦθος*, and the second from the Latin *mores*.

Ethics is the practical science which directs human actions toward honesty.

Human actions are those which we perform as human beings, that is, with the knowledge of the intellect and the consent of the will. Actions performed without this knowledge or consent are called the *actions of man* (*actus hominis*).

We have already said, in *Ontology*, that there exists in the world a twofold order, the physical and the moral.

Beings deprived of their liberty necessarily follow the order assigned them by their Creator; so that if there is disorder, the disorder cannot be attributed to them as the cause thereof: consequently they deserve neither praise nor blame.

Beings endowed with liberty are responsible for their actions; according to their own wish, they follow or refuse to follow the order assigned them: and this is the first principle of human actions. Human actions may be considered both in general and in particular; hence the division of this Part into two dissertations.

FIRST DISSERTATION.

ON HUMAN ACTIONS IN GENERAL.

Human actions are considered in general when they are examined abstractly, that is, the special state of man being laid aside.

We have first to examine whether there are actions which are good and others which are bad, also what is the source of each and how we may make a distinction between them. Hence the division of this dissertation into three chapters; in the first of which we shall treat of the difference between good and bad actions, in the second of the principles of these actions, and in the third of the rules making distinctions between them.

CHAPTER FIRST.

OF THE DIFFERENCE BETWEEN GOOD AND BAD ACTIONS.

It would be useless to give rules of conduct if there were no difference between good and evil. We must consequently first determine whether there is such a difference, and if so, whether there is any natural obligation of doing good and avoiding evil. In order to proceed methodically we shall divide this chapter into five articles. In the first, we shall examine whether there is any difference between good and evil; and in the second, whether there is an obligation to do good and avoid evil, that is, whether there is a natural law; in the third, we shall establish the fact of the promulgation of that law; in the fourth, we shall prove that the law is immutable; and in the fifth we shall show what is its sanction.

ARTICLE FIRST.—THE DIFFERENCE BETWEEN MORAL GOOD AND MORAL EVIL.

This difference has been denied by Epicurus and his disciples, by Hobbes and Spinosa, and by the modern deists, as Helvetius, La Mettrie, and d'Holbach. Their principles are, first, that man has received no useless faculties from nature, and consequently that what is possible to him is also lawful for him; and, second, that, in order to obtain security for themselves, men made an agreement to abstain from actions which might be injurious to the general welfare, from which, they say, resulted the distinction between good and evil.

But we affirm that there is an essential difference between good and evil, as there is an essential difference between truth and falsehood; and, to prove this, we will establish the following

Proposition.—*Moral good and moral evil are essentially different.*

I. We prove this proposition first by its own evidence. What the mind clearly perceives as existing does really exist. But we clearly perceive the difference spoken of in the proposition; it therefore does exist. For instance, the mind clearly perceives that it is right to honor our parents and wrong to insult them. The knowledge of this difference being a primary truth, its existence cannot be directly demonstrated.

II. In the second place, we prove this truth by the unanimous consent of mankind. That this consent exists we may know by daily experience, by the annals of all nations, and by the language of every people. We may, moreover, prove it by the manner of acting of those whose advantage it would be to deny the existence of this difference. There is not a wicked person who would not like to call his bad actions good, if he could do so; and the very fact that he tries to do it shows that he admits that there is a difference between good and evil. The remorse which he feels is the best evidence of the truth of the proposition. It may further be proved by the manner of acting of those who deny theoretically the existence of the difference; for these same deists, like all men, praise virtue and condemn vice. Since then this general consent exists, since it concerns a matter of great importance, and since it is in opposition to our passions, it must be an infallible motive of certitude. As we have said in *Logic*, such a consent could not come from education, prejudice, or agreement; it must therefore come from nature, and is consequently the expression of truth.

III. Thirdly, we prove this proposition by noting the absurd consequences of the opposite doctrine. If this difference did not exist, then good and evil would be the same; but this is in contradiction to the common sense of men and their practices in daily life. If this difference is not essential, but the result of an agreement, it would follow that to-morrow men might agree that it is right to insult our parents and wrong to honor them, which is evidently absurd. Hence we conclude that there is an essential difference between good and evil, that this difference is based upon the essence of things and upon the first principles of morals, and that neither God nor man could alter them.

The principles of morals are of course the same for all men. However, in regard to the application of these principles we find a great diversity of opinion; and, in regard to their remoter consequences, even the most learned men do not agree. All peoples, for instance, know that it is right, and even obligatory on us, to honor our parents; yet nations are found where men think it an act of kindness to kill their parents when they become very old. The love of parents for their children has also been strangely abused by those who, through fear of future want or misery, think it allowable to kill their own offspring. Objections to our proposition may be answered by the aid of these remarks.

ARTICLE SECOND.—THE OBLIGATION OF DOING GOOD AND AVOIDING EVIL, OR THE EXISTENCE OF THE NATURAL LAW.

The word law is probably derived from *ligare*, to bind. A *law* is a precept which is common to all, just, stable, given by a superior, sufficiently promulgated and sanctioned.

Law is a precept, and not an advice; common to all and consequently different from a mandate, which is made for certain persons; just, for no one can command that which is unjust; stable, because it is not a transitory act, permanence being essential to it; sufficiently promulgated, for it must be made known, and this can be done only by promulgation; given by a superior, a legitimate superior only having the power to command and to exact obedience; sufficiently sanctioned, for otherwise the superior could not realize his end.

There is no superior unless there are subjects.

The power to command supposes the obligation of obedience.

The obligation of obedience to law is not deduced

from human reason, considered in itself, but from the supreme dominion of God. The obligation of obedience to a law cannot be deduced from the human reason considered absolutely; because, in order to impose an obligation, two wills are necessary, the one of a superior, having a right to command, and the other of an inferior, who is bound to obey: but the human will, considered abstractly from God, is not that of a superior, all men being naturally equal; hence the human will cannot create an obligation. The obligation must therefore come from the authority of God; and when a man commands he does so as holding the place of God: *omnis auctoritas a Deo*, all authority proceeds from God.

Consequently, according to the Atheists there could be no obligation of obedience.

From all eternity, God sees the supreme order of the essence and relations of things. This order constitutes the law which is called moral, when considered in reference to free and intelligent beings; and the disturbance of this same order constitutes moral evil.

The supreme reason existing in God, determining in a fixed manner what may be done and what may not be done, is called the eternal law. The eternal law is therefore the will of God commanding the maintenance and forbidding the disturbance of the natural order of things.

The natural law is a participation of the eternal law by rational creatures. We may define it to be a precept by which God commands us to fulfil the duties which arise from the nature of things; the necessity of which our reason may know, either by itself or by the aid of another being.

Proposition.— *There exists a natural law.*

I. We might first give as an evidence of this truth

21   Q

several passages of the Holy Scripture, quoted or found even in the writings of pagans, as that of Psalm xxxiii. 15, *Diverte a malo et fac bonum*, avoid evil and do good.

II. We have seen that there exists in the world a supreme order, but it is impossible to admit that God does not take care to have that order respected and observed by his free creatures: to admit that God looks with indifference on all our actions would be to deny his wisdom, his sanctity, etc.

III. If we except the Epicureans, we find that the legislators and the peoples of all ages have believed that God regards the actions of men, in order to reward the good and punish the wicked; and we know that such a consent is an infallible motive of certitude.

ARTICLE THIRD.—THE PROMULGATION OF THE NATURAL LAW.

I. There is no one having the use of reason who does not perceive within himself the presence of a light by the aid of which he can discern good from evil, and judge surely that some of his actions are right and others wrong. This light, found in the minds of all men, must come from God, the author of nature, and must therefore be the means of showing us what is his will. Thus the natural law is made manifest to us, and this manifestation is its promulgation, and creates for us an obligation of obedience. No form is required for such promulgation: it is sufficient for us that the will of God has been made known to us.

In the same manner the first precepts of morals are made evident to our souls. However, this light, which is merely rational, is exceedingly feeble in some men, and in others it is almost obscured, especially concerning several consequences deduced from first principles. In order to help our natural weakness God has further enlightened our minds by revelation, by the authority of the Church, and by tradition.

To conclude, we may say that conscience, even when aided by education, could not discover many things which by deduction belong to the natural law: it is therefore no wonder that many philosophers, not enlightened by revelation, have given forth so many absurd and even monstrous systems.

II. It has been a question whether, in the present state of things, there can be an invincible ignorance of the natural law. By invincible ignorance is understood such an ignorance as cannot be removed by the ordinary help of nature and grace. The contrary is called vincible ignorance. Some rigid doctors have contended that there can be no invincible ignorance, even of the most remote consequences of the violation of the natural law; because, they contend, these consequences are essentially bad, and no one can be invincibly ignorant of what is essentially wrong.

This opinion is generally rejected. We know that this invincible ignorance exists, since we see the most learned doctors, as St. Thomas and St. Bonaventure, giving contradictory solutions to questions resting on the natural law. But concerning the primary precepts of the natural law and the proximate conclusions deduced from them, there is of course no invincible ignorance in any man with the use of his reason.

III. The judgment of the mind concerning the morality of an action performed, or about to be performed, by it is called the conscience. Hence in Ethics we do not consider the conscience merely as a faculty, but also as an operation.

As this subject belongs to theology, we shall here content ourselves with a few general remarks.

Conscience is either true or false, certain or doubtful.

A true conscience is one which declares lawful or unlawful that which really is so; a false one being, of course, the contrary.

A certain conscience is one which judges prudently, and without any fear of probable error, that some action is good or bad. Hence we may see that a certain conscience may not be a true one; such a conscience, when in error, is said to be invincibly erroneous.

A doubtful conscience is one which abstains from judging, because it perceives on both sides opposing reasons.

1st. It is plain that a true, or at least a certain, conscience must be the rule of all our actions.

2d. It is never allowable for us to act against our conscience, even if it should afterwards appear that our conscience was in error; for to act against our conscience is to be willing to commit sin.

ARTICLE FOURTH.—THE IMMUTABILITY OF THE NATURAL LAW.

The immutability of the natural law consists in this, that what is declared good by the natural law can never become bad, and *vice versa*.

Proposition.— *The natural law is immutable.*

This is proved, first, by the intrinsic goodness of certain actions, and the intrinsic badness of others.

Certain actions, as the honor due to God, are perceived by us to be so intrinsically good, and others are perceived to be so intrinsically bad, that never, in any hypothesis, can they be otherwise. Hence the law which commands us to observe this necessary order is immutable.

In the second place, the moral axioms, or the first principles of the natural law, are necessary truths, just as the mathematical axioms are necessary truths. The principle, "We must give to every one what belongs to him," is as necessarily true and immutable as the axiom, "The whole is equal to the sum of its parts." Hence the natural law is immutable, and can suffer neither dispensation nor derogation.

Some facts of Holy Scripture have been quoted against the truth of this proposition; as the command of God to Abraham to kill his son, and to the Israelites to take the vessels of the Egyptians. In the first there was no violation of the natural law, for this law forbids us to inflict death on our fellow-men by private authority; but God, being the supreme master of our lives, may, in virtue of his divine authority, command any one for a just cause to take away the life of another. In the case of the Egyptians, the Hebrews merely took back what was their own. In neither case, therefore, was there any dispensation or abrogation of the natural law.

ARTICLE FIFTH.—THE SANCTION OF THE NATURAL LAW.

By the *sanction* of the natural law, we understand the reward bestowed on those who observe the law, and the punishment inflicted on those who violate it. In regard to this sanction we proceed to prove the following propositions:

First Proposition.—*God has established a sanction for the natural law.*

God being infinitely wise and powerful, has taken the proper means to secure the observation of the laws which he has established. But, considering the natural disposition of men, it is evident that a sanction is necessary for the enforcement of the natural law; for if left

21 *

to his own inclinations man will not obey unless he
forces himself, and he will not force himself unless he is
compelled to do so: for this compulsion duty is not
always a sufficient motive; rewards and punishments
must be provided. Hence God must have established
a sanction for the natural law.

Second Proposition.— *The natural law has some sanction even in this world, but this sanction is incomplete and
even void if separated from the sanction of another life.*

1st. The natural law has some sanction even in this
world, that is, some reward is bestowed on those who
observe the law, and some punishment is inflicted on
those who violate it; for experience shows that virtue
makes a man happy, so far as it is possible to be happy
in this world, and, on the contrary, that vice makes him
unhappy.

2d. This sanction, in the present life, is incomplete;
because it is not in strict proportion to the merit of
virtue or the demerit of vice; and because, as we all
know, there are many virtuous actions that have no
reward in this world, and many vicious ones that receive no punishment.

3d. Moreover, this sanction, in the present life, is
almost void if separated from the sanction of the future
life. Virtue makes one happy because it brings peace
of conscience, and vice renders one unhappy because it
is followed by remorse of conscience; but if we remove
the certitude of another life this peace and this remorse
would have no real foundation.

All admit, when they speak seriously, that the desire
of enjoying a good name among men, the intrinsic
beauty of virtue, and the deformity of vice, are not
sufficient motives for securing the observance of the
natural law.

We may conclude, from these considerations, that there is another life; and that that life will be eternally happy for the good, for God can never cease to love them; and eternally unhappy for the wicked, this eternity of punishment not being repugnant to the justice, wisdom, or goodness of God. This last conclusion, concerning the eternal duration of rewards and punishments, has always been believed by the generality of mankind.

NOTE.—It is worthy of inquiry whether one who observes the law on account of its sanction, that is, on account of the hope of reward or the fear of punishment, performs a good moral action.

We must distinguish: 1st. He who abstains from evil on account of mere hope or fear, but retains the desire to do evil if the sanction were removed, does not perform a good action, because his will is evil. 2d. He who observes the law on account of the hope of reward or the fear of punishment, but also with the desire of thus doing his duty, performs a good action, for he does good on account of the duty resting upon him. 3d. He who observes the law on account of the hope of reward or the fear of punishment, without considering the question of right or duty, does not indeed perform a bad action; but his action is less perfect than that of the man who acts on account of duty.

CHAPTER SECOND.

OF THE PRINCIPLES OF GOOD AND BAD ACTIONS.

These principles are the sources of goodness and wickedness; they are, the intellect, liberty, and the will.

1st. It is certain that in order that an action be good

or bad, it is necessary the intellect should know it to be such before it is performed. An act done without the knowledge of the intellect is not a human action.

2d. It is also certain that liberty in the actor is necessary for the morality of a human action. If the actor is not free, the act cannot be considered his own. An act done through necessity must be charged, not to the agent, but to the cause which determined him to act.

3d. Again, it is certain that the will only is the cause and the foundation of sin; as it is also the cause and the foundation of virtue. The will, understood in this sense, is consequently human liberty in exercise.

The will considered in the act is either simple or free. Its operation is called volition.* Volition is itself either simple or free. It is simple when there is knowledge of the intellect and consent of the will; it is free when besides these two there is also deliberation. Hence what is free is voluntary, but what is voluntary is not necessarily free. For instance, we seek our happiness voluntarily, but not freely. It is free volition only which is the principle of our actions.

Volition is direct when something is positively and in itself intended by the agent; and indirect when something is willed, not in itself, but in the cause of which it is the effect. For instance, if one burst a shell for mere amusement, and thus accidentally kill a man, he does not will the death of the man directly, but indirectly.

Volition is perfect if it does not suppose any repugnance of the will, otherwise it is imperfect. An example of imperfect volition is that of a merchant at sea who throws his goods overboard for fear of shipwreck.

---

* This word means here what the authors express by *voluntarium*.

The causes which may diminish or destroy the freedom of the will are : force, fear, error, ignorance, and passion.

CHAPTER THIRD.

RULES FOR DISTINGUISHING GOOD FROM BAD ACTIONS.

It is clear that we must avoid everything which is bad, but that we are not obliged to do everything which is good, as this latter would be impossible. Hence, the precept to avoid evil is negative and universal, whereas the command to do good is affirmative and particular. The first obliges always and in all cases ; while the second obliges always, but not in all cases. The questions which belong to this chapter are all theological, and are fully examined in the treatise on "Human Actions."

SECOND DISSERTATION.

ON HUMAN ACTIONS IN PARTICULAR.

Man, as a moral agent, may be considered in three points of view, in his relations with God, with himself, and with his fellow-men. Hence the three varieties of his special duties.

Duty means the same as obligation. It is a moral restriction of the natural powers of a person. This is called a moral restriction, because duty imposes not a physical, but a moral restraint.

This restriction is the result of the power which one being has either of doing something without hindrance from another being, or of exacting something from that other being : this last power is called *right*. Hence right is the cause or origin of duty; they are correlative, and one cannot exist, or be conceived, without the other.

Right is then the lawful authority of one being to do something, or to exact something of another being. From this definition, it is easy to conceive how duty results from right: First, if a being has lawful authority to act in a certain manner, all other beings are bound not to impede his action; and, second, if a being has lawful authority to exact an action from another being, that other being is bound to perform the required action.

The duties of men are of three kinds, according to the division given above: duties towards God, towards themselves, and towards one another. There can be no other kind of duties, as, for instance, towards beings without reason; for such beings can have no right, and hence there can be no obligation in regard to them.

CHAPTER FIRST.

Of the Duties of Men towards God.

The duties of men towards God, taken altogether, are called *worship*. Concerning this we have two questions to examine, 1st, Is man bound to worship God? and, 2d, Did God supernaturally reveal to man the manner in which He must be worshipped?

This second question, which is theological, is fully discussed in the treatise "On Religion," in theology. Here we have to examine only the first question, which we shall do by establishing the necessity of religious worship, and by giving the causes which induce men either to neglect or to corrupt that worship.

ARTICLE FIRST.—THE NECESSITY OF RELIGIOUS WORSHIP.

Worship is both interior and exterior. Interior worship is the sum of all our duties towards God, in so much as they consist in certain interior acts of the mind, as to love, to submit our will to the will of God, etc. Exterior worship is the outward manifestation of our interior worship; and is itself either private or public. Private worship is that paid to God by men in their own name; and public worship is that rendered to God by men as members of society.

Concerning the necessity of religious worship as thus explained, we establish the following propositions:

First Proposition.— *Man is bound to give interior worship to God.*

Man is bound to act towards God in accordance with the attributes of God and man's own condition; and both of these require an interior worship of man towards God.

1st. The attributes of God. God is infinitely perfect, and must therefore be loved by his creatures; he has supreme dominion over all things, and must therefore be adored: but love and adoration are both acts of interior worship.

2d. The condition of man. Man having been created by God, is obliged in return to give to him, as to his last end, all his actions and even his being itself; having been the object of the divine favor, he is obliged to return thanks to God; and being in need of divine assistance, he is obliged to ask the help of God: but the direction of our actions towards God, thanksgiving for favors and petitions for help, are all acts of interior worship. Hence the proposition.

Interior worship consists, first, in loving, for love being the noblest faculty of the soul is also the first; and second, in obeying, for obedience is the proof of our love. Besides these duties, adoration, offering one's self to God, thanksgiving and prayer are so many acts of interior worship.

Second Proposition.—*Man is obliged to render to God an exterior worship.*

This proposition may be proved, first, by the necessity there is for this worship, in order that we may be assured of the reality of our interior worship; for man cannot feel deeply without showing what he feels by some exterior signs. Hence, where there is no exterior worship there may be doubt whether there is any interior.

It may be proved, in the second place, by the necessity of exterior worship for the preservation of the interior. Experience shows that the sense of religion is not long retained in our mind unless it is stirred and warmed, as it were, by exterior signs.

Thirdly, exterior worship is necessary, because it is the tribute paid by our body to God, as interior worship is the tribute of the soul. Both owe worship to God, who is the author of both soul and body.

Third Proposition.—*Man is bound to give public worship to God.*

This proposition is proved by these two considerations: 1st. Public worship is necessary for the preservation of both interior and exterior worship; experience shows the truth of this, especially in the case of ignorant and uncultivated persons. 2d. Public worship is the tribute due to God by the moral body called society; and, besides, society, as a body, having need of assistance, must seek it from God.

Fourth Proposition.—*The necessity of interior, exterior, and public worship is proved by the unanimous consent of mankind.*

This is a fact which no one can deny; and this unanimous consent is an infallible motive of certitude. Cicero says: "Each state has its own religion;" and Plutarch, "No one has ever seen a place without worship."

NOTE.—The principal signs that constitute, as it were, the essence of exterior and public worship are: vocal prayer, singing, certain reverential motions and postures of the body, sacrifice, and burning of incense.

When man frequently fulfils his duties to God he acquires an ease and pleasure in worship which soon becomes a habit. This habit is called piety, or a religious disposition.

Piety is therefore the virtue which inclines men to give to God the veneration and worship, both interior and exterior, which is his due. There is, however, a difference between piety and a disposition to fulfil our religious duties. This religious disposition is the state of mind of one who is unwilling to omit to render to God the worship which is due to him; while piety disposes one not only to render to God the worship which is due to him, but also to do this with fervor and great reverence.

Piety is both interior and exterior: the first is a habitual intercourse existing interiorly between God and the soul; the second consists in exterior practices of devotion. Piety is true and solid only when it is both interior and exterior. Solid piety is the most sure foundation of morality.

22

ARTICLE SECOND.—THE CAUSES WHICH INDUCE MEN EITHER TO NEGLECT OR TO CORRUPT THE WORSHIP OF GOD.

I. The causes that lead men to neglect divine worship are of two kinds: those that lead them to deny even in theory the necessity of divine worship, and those that induce them to omit this worship in practice. Of the first kind are atheism, and a false opinion of providence, as in the case of those who deny that God wants any worship, or that he cares for it. Of the second are indifference in matters of religion, very common as we all know, and the slavery of the passions; this slavery is very much opposed to the worship of God, as it is a true idolatry. Very many of these idolators are found in the world.

II. The causes that alter and corrupt divine worship are: idolatry, superstition, and lack of solid interior piety, that is, lip-worship instead of heart-worship. These causes corrupt not only divine worship, but also public morals. This is especially the case with idolatry: the pagan world furnishes a most shameful example of the fact.

CHAPTER SECOND.

OF THE DUTIES OF MAN TOWARDS HIMSELF.

These duties may be reduced to two: the obligation of preserving the life of the body, and that of cultivating the faculties of the mind.

ARTICLE FIRST.—THE OBLIGATION OF PRESERVING THE LIFE OF THE BODY.

To preserve his life man must avoid suicide, and not otherwise expose himself without sufficient cause to the danger of losing his life or his health.

I. *Suicide.*

Suicide is the act of a man who willingly and knowingly kills himself. We will first proceed to show that suicide is unlawful, and secondly, that the arguments which are brought forward to justify it are futile.

First Proposition.—*Suicide is unlawful.*

That is unlawful which is contrary to the destiny intended for man upon earth, and which is opposed to the glory of God, to the good of society, and to the natural propensities of men; but such is suicide.

1st. Suicide is contrary to the destiny intended for man upon earth. The present life is a time of probation: this follows from the fact of human liberty, and that of the existence of another life. For, since man can do neither good nor evil, and consequently gain merit or demerit, and since he is destined for another life which will be eternally happy or eternally miserable, it is evident that the present life is a time of probation. That it is not lawful for a man, by his own authority, to diminish the time of this probation imposed by God, is also clear; because it must be unlawful for a creature to oppose the end designed by his creator, and because it is essential to the nature of probation that its duration be not left to the choice of him who is in the state of probation, but rather of Him who has established the probation.

But by suicide a man diminishes the time of his probation, since he voluntarily deserts the station in which he has been placed by God. Hence suicide is, in the first place, contrary to the destiny intended by his Creator for man upon earth.

2d. Suicide is opposed to the glory of God, since man by continuing to practice virtue glorifies God, whereas if he commits suicide he voluntarily refuses to serve

God, and thus opposes himself to the promotion of God's glory.

Suicide is also opposed to the good of society; for if suicide were declared lawful there is no doubt that many would persuade themselves that it would be better for them to die, and thus numbers of useful members would be cut off from society.

Suicide, finally, is opposed to the natural propensities of men: it is opposed to common sense, for all men admire and esteem those who are patient and resigned in the sufferings of this life; it is opposed to our instinctive love of life, and this love being acknowledged by all men must be the voice of nature, which it is unlawful for us to disobey.

Observation.—Suicide is a most cruel act to one's self, since it hurls him headlong into the midst of the greatest calamities. He who is guilty of this crime dies in the actual commission of a bad action, and consequently puts it out of his power to make any atonement for the wrong which he does. His fate is the most deplorable that can befall a human being.

Second Proposition.—*The arguments in favor of suicide are futile.*

This proposition is a corollary of the first; if suicide be unlawful, then all arguments in its favor must be vain. We shall, however, completely expose the fallacy of all these arguments. Some declare that suicide is lawful, because, they say, life is a gift which we can renounce; others pretend to believe it an act of courage; others, again, affirm that it is a right of nature; and others, finally, would persuade us that it is an act quite indifferent in its character.

First reason: That life is a gift of God which we may renounce whenever it is useless to us and to others, and, *a fortiori*, whenever it becomes an intolerable burden.

Life is not a mere gift, granted without any condition and to be renounced whenever we please. By the very fact of our existence we are bound to serve God, not as we will, but as He wills; and, consequently, as long as He keeps us in this life, we must serve Him, and we are never allowed to change, by our own will, that way of serving Him, by passing into another life. Hence we cannot lawfully renounce the gift of our own existence.

Nor is life ever useless to man. Whatever be his condition he can always make himself more and more worthy of that future beatitude for which this present life is a preparation.

Nor even when life seems to be an intolerable burden is it allowed to man to take it away. Whatever be the sufferings which make life seem intolerable, they can never constitute a motive for committing suicide; on the contrary, the greater the trials of this life the better are they to enable us to reach the end for which we have been destined, and indeed life, in order to be a probation, must be burdensome.

Besides, it is not true that life is ever entirely intolerable; for the trials of life are never so great that man may not bear them, provided he has firm confidence in God. The examples of many good persons have amply proved this in their sufferings. If, therefore, one who does not believe in the existence of Providence finds himself unable to bear the ills of this life, he cannot bring forward his unbelief as a lawful cause for committing suicide.

Second reason : That suicide is lawful and praiseworthy because it is an act of courage.

22 *   R

Such was the assertion of the Stoics; but it is not true, for the man who kills himself because he cannot bear his trials does not perform a courageous act, but a cowardly one, as even the pagans themselves acknowledged.

Third reason: That suicide is a natural right, as J. J. Rousseau and other deists have pretended.

This is false, since men cannot have received from nature a right which is in opposition to the design which their Creator had in view, namely, as we have seen, that this life should be a time of probation. Suicide is opposed to this design of God, and hence cannot be a natural right.

Fourth reason: That suicide is an act indifferent in its character, as Montesquieu, Voltaire, and the Encyclopedists have affirmed, since, says Montesquieu, suicide does not disturb the order established by divine Providence.

We have shown, in our answer to the third reason and elsewhere, that suicide does disturb the order established by Providence, since it is opposed to the end designed by God; hence it is not an indifferent act.

From the answers given above, we may conclude, first, that it is not lawful to kill one's self in order to avoid a more cruel death; and, secondly, that it is not lawful to commit suicide even in order to avoid the danger of committing sin, for to him that confides in God the occasion of sin is never insurmountable.

II. *Danger of Losing Life or Health.*

1st. It is clear that we are not permitted to expose our life when there is not a good reason for so doing, which reason must be of equal gravity with the danger incurred. Consequently, it is not lawful to expose our life for mere amusement.

2d. It is clear, on the other hand, that it is lawful for us to expose ourselves to a probable or a certain danger of death, provided there is a reasonable cause for so doing, the gravity of the cause being in proportion to that of the danger. We may expose our life in order to obtain a greater good, as for the welfare of the State, or to preserve the life of another.

3d. It is further clear that such exposure of life is not only lawful, but even praiseworthy.

4th. And, finally, it is clear that sometimes it is not only lawful and praiseworthy, but even obligatory for us to expose ourselves to certain danger of death. This is always the case in reference to our duties; for instance, a soldier must keep his post at any risk, and a priest must attend his sick parishioners, even when they are dying of pestilence.

Observation.—Although certain trades and occupations are unhealthy, or otherwise endanger life, yet on account of their general utility it is lawful to follow them, even though this utility be of mere temporary importance.

What we have said concerning the danger of losing life may also be applied to the danger of losing our health.

ARTICLE SECOND.—THE OBLIGATION OF CULTIVATING THE FACULTIES OF THE MIND.

Proposition.—*We are all obliged to cultivate and perfect the natural faculties and aptitudes of our mind.*

God gave us those faculties and aptitudes only that we might use them for promoting his glory and the good of ourselves and our fellow-men. In order to promote the glory of God, we must cultivate the seeds of virtue which have been implanted in our heart; and in order to do good to ourselves and our fellow-men, we must cultivate those aptitudes which we have received for following some occupation useful to mankind.

The faculties which we must cultivate are the intellect, the sensibility, and the will.

(a) *Culture of the Intellect.*

The intellect is cultivated by the acquisition of knowledge; and this knowledge may be necessary, useful, or hurtful.

1st. Necessary knowledge. Every one should acquire that knowledge which is necessary to enable him to attain his end, in other words, that knowledge which concerns the general duties of men. These duties are nowhere so clearly pointed out as in the Christian doctrine. Every one should also apply himself to the study of those things which concern his special duties in life.

2d. Useful knowledge. By useful knowledge is meant, not that which is necessary to enable us to discharge the duties of life, but that which may enable us to discharge these duties in a more perfect manner. But the acquisition of that knowledge which is only useful should never interfere with the acquisition of that which is necessary. A knowledge of the liberal arts and the sciences constitutes what may be called useful knowledge.

3d. Useless or hurtful knowledge. It is not lawful to waste our time in the acquisition of useless knowledge; and the acquisition of hurtful knowledge, such as may be had from the reading of bad books, is positively forbidden: for by such knowledge the intellect is weakened and corrupted, and we are prevented from attaining the end for which we have been placed in this world.

NOTE.—In order to acquire sound knowledge, we should, 1st, be careful not to study too many things at the same time; 2d, with the assistance of some experienced person, we should choose the best books, and read them with the most serious attention; and, 3d, we should take particular notice of everything important which we come across in reading.

It has been made a question whether the study of the arts and sciences is hurtful to morals; and also whether it is profitable for people in general to engage in the study of the sciences and the liberal arts.

First question.—J. J. Rousseau, in a discourse delivered at Dijon, tries to show that the study of the arts and sciences corrupts good morals; and, consequently, of course, that this study does not improve the morals. Against these assertions, we establish the following

Proposition.— *The culture of the arts and sciences does not of itself corrupt the morals ; on the contrary, this study exerts a powerful influence in favor of good morals.*

1st. That these studies do not corrupt the morals is evident from the fact that the arts and sciences are good in respect to their object, which object is the development of a series of truths from certain principles, or the expression of the beautiful in the physical and the moral order, or some other equally good and proper end; and the object being always thus proper and good, the study which has this object in view cannot be corrupting to the morals.

Experience also shows the falsity of Rousseau's assertion; for how many learned men are there whose honesty and purity of morals are as remarkable as their attainments in science.

Even Rousseau's own confession refutes him; for he has said in another discourse that he put forth the above paradox for the sake of vanity.

2d. The culture of the arts and sciences even improves the morals. History shows that the ferocity of men has always been in proportion to their ignorance.

We have shown that of itself this culture does not corrupt morals: it may, however, do so incidentally; and hence we sometimes see learned men whose conduct instead of being virtuous is exceedingly vicious. These men abuse their knowledge, and the more learned they are the greater is the abuse of which they are guilty, according to the maxim: *corruptio optimi pessima* (the worst corruption is that of the wise). But from this abuse of knowledge certainly nothing can be proved against knowledge itself, or against the culture of the arts and sciences.

It is objected against this proposition that the Egyptians, Greeks, and Romans became wicked as they became more learned.

Intellectual culture had nothing to do with this, for the arts and sciences flourished in those countries long before the people became corrupt. Many examples may be given, on the other hand, of nations that became great and illustrious in consequence of the spread of knowledge among them; as the Franks under Charlemagne, the Italians under Leo X., etc.

It is said also that many ancient nations remained invincible so long as they remained ignorant; as the Persians, the Romans, etc. The inference that science caused the weakness of those nations is false; for it has not been proved that the study of science lessens the warlike spirit. And even supposing that such culture had weakened the courage of those peoples, we should still have to examine whether they were less happy after this warlike spirit declined than they had been while their heroism rendered them invincible: for, as the most courageous people are often the slaves of the lowest vices, it is certain that a warlike spirit alone is not sufficient to cause the other virtues to flourish in a nation.

Second question.—Whether it is profitable for people in general to engage in the study of the sciences and the liberal arts.

That it is profitable for all people to know how to read and write, and be acquainted with the common branches of knowledge, is something which we all know by experience. Reading especially is very useful to help them in the acquisitions of the religious knowledge which is indispensable to them. But it may perhaps remain a question whether it is always profitable to children in humble circumstances to be instructed in those arts and sciences which will be of no service to them in the sphere of life in which they have been placed by Providence; for such studies generally serve only to disgust them with their condition, without enabling them to rise above it, unless indeed they are possessed of great natural talent.

(b) *Culture of the Sensibility.*

The various propensities of the sensibility may be reduced to two: love and hatred. The first was called by the ancients the concupiscible appetite, or the appetite of desire; and the second the irascible appetite, or the appetite of anger.

1st. Love should be directed towards the supreme good, and diverted from all bad or dangerous objects.

The supreme good is God, and all created good must be loved for his sake, and in proportion to the degree of its perfection, or its approach to the supreme good.

Love should be diverted from every bad and dangerous object, that is, from everything which could prevent man from attaining his end. Among these dangerous objects are, bad books, most theatrical exhibitions, public balls, masks, etc.

2d. Hatred must be overcome by the repression of the irascible appetite, so that it may not become a habit, which would be so much opposed to our own happiness and to the good of others. In order to correct this natural disposition to anger, which is the source of hatred, we should always think well of our neighbor's intentions and abstain from showing any external marks of ill-humor.

(c) *Culture of the Will.*

The will is the first and constitutive faculty of human morality. Its culture is of even more importance than that of all the other faculties, since they serve only for the perfecting of the will. The culture and good use of the will consists in avoiding evil and doing good; and, consequently, this culture is the final object of the whole science of Ethics.

CHAPTER THIRD.

OF THE DUTIES OF MEN TOWARDS ONE ANOTHER.

The first question that presents itself in this connection is whether man was created for society, or not. When this has been answered we will consider the duties of men in their relations with society.

Society is the union of many persons for the purpose

of attaining certain ends by their united efforts. Since society is threefold, domestic, civil, and universal, we shall consider the different duties of men in reference to this threefold society.

Preliminary Article.—Destiny of man for the state of society, and consequences resulting from this state.

(A) Destiny of man for the state of society.

We here propose to give our chief attention to the refutation of Rousseau, who pretended to believe that man was not destined for the state of society, and that the state of society is actually hurtful to him, since it is the source of all the calamities and all the vices in the world.

Proposition.—*Man was born to live in society with his fellow men.*

Argument: Man was born for that state which is required by his propensities and his necessities; but his propensities and necessities demand that he should live in society with his fellows, and hence he was born for that society.

Proof: 1st. His propensities require the state of society; for all men have a certain inclination to live in society, an inclination which we call the desire of society: now this propensity is natural to man, since it is found in every man and is inherent in the human mind itself. That this propensity is *universal* is evident from the fact that men have always lived in society. In the beginning, as soon as mankind became too numerous for the family form of government, they established among themselves a sort of public polity, by which the supreme authority was placed in the hands of one or more persons. From this fact, which is well established by history and tradition, we conclude that man was created to live in civil and political, as well as in domestic society.

23

This propensity is inherent in the human mind; for experience shows that nothing is more tedious to man than solitude. Consequently, the propensities of man prove that he was born to live in society.

2d. Man's necessities require the state of society. Domestic society is necessary for the development of man's intelligence and morality. A few examples of persons who have lived in the forests like wild beasts prove the truth of this assertion.

Civil society is necessary to man for the complete development of his faculties. To fully develop his aptitude for the cultivation of the arts and sciences, man must have imitation and emulation, which are to be found only in civil society. The wants of man therefore render society necessary to man, and consequently prove that he was born for society.

Principles to be observed in answering objections:

(a) The abuses sometimes found in society, as the tyranny of rulers and the slavery of those subject to them, do not prove that the state of society is injurious to man; because, first, these abuses are not essentially connected with society, since they are not found everywhere; and, secondly, the abuses of tyranny and servitude would be greater and more frequent in the savage state than they are in the state of civilized society.

(b) Sickness and other infirmities, which are sometimes said to be more frequent in a state of society than in a savage state, do not show that the state of society is hurtful to man; because, first, temperate and sober men, no matter where they live, are generally in good health; and, secondly, although the dwellers in the wilderness are often stronger, they are not happier than those in civilized society, for happiness is found only in the development of all the powers of the body and the mind, especially those of the latter, which are but feebly developed in a savage state.

(B) Consequences resulting from the state of society. —Inequality of condition in life, and right of property.

Men cannot live in society with one another unless there be some inequality of condition among them, and unless the right to acquire and own property be recognized.

(a) Inequality of condition.

Here again we have to refute Rousseau, who taught that this inequality is an evil and contrary to natural right. This doctrine has been accepted and taught by St. Simon and his disciples, who have labored to do away with every privilege of origin, condition, sex, and nationality. To refute this system we propose the following

Proposition.—*Inequality of condition among men is not opposed to natural law.*

Argument: That which necessarily results from man's nature, and from his destiny to live in society, cannot be contrary to natural right; but such is the case with inequality of condition among men, hence this inequality is not opposed to natural right.

Proof: First, this inequality results from man's nature, since that nature subjects children to parents, the younger to the older, the weaker to the stronger, the ignorant to the learned, etc., and thus establishes unequal conditions among men; secondly, it results from the destiny of men to live in society; for no civil society can exist unless there be rulers and magistrates, the executors and defenders of the laws, which the citizens are bound to respect, and consequently unless there be among the citizens the inequality resulting from the necessary exercise of authority.

(b) The right of property.

We have already given the definition of *right*. The right of property, or property, is the lawful power of doing something or of requiring something to be done for our own benefit, and of preventing others from using that right. The things that form the object of property are either movable or immovable; that is, capable of being moved from place to place without serious injury, or incapable of such movement.

The right of property has been lately attacked by the Communists, whose system has been reduced to the following words: " La propriété c'est le vol," our property is whatever we wish to take. Against this false doctrine we establish the following

Proposition.— *The right of property is a lawful right.*

Argument : That is lawful which necessarily results from our activity, which has been acknowledged as lawful by all men, and which is necessary for the existence and well-being of society.

Proof : 1st. This right naturally flows from our activity ; for when a man by his own activity and industry has improved some portion of matter which was not before occupied by another, he has, by that very fact, attached to the matter something which is his own, and which cannot be taken from him without depriving him of what is his, and consequently without injuring him. Hence the right necessarily results from our activity.

2d. The lawfulness of the right of property has been acknowledged by all men. History shows this.

3d. Without this right domestic society is not possible. This society would be destroyed if parents could not feed, educate, and provide for the livelihood of their children; but it is plain that they could not perform these duties if they had not the right of property, and consequently could not make donations, wills, etc.

4th. Civil society also is impossible without this right; for the industrious will cease to exert themselves as soon as they find that they have to divide the fruits of their toil with the lazy. Hence the truth of the proposition.

Corollary.—We may conclude that the right of property does not originate in civil authority, although this authority may direct and regulate it: civil authority should protect, but never destroy this right.

It is objected to the proposition that the soil is necessary for the exercise of human labor; and, consequently, that being thus necessary for the generality of mankind it cannot become the property of any particular man; and hence that no one can have any exclusive right to property.

The minor of this argument is false: for as soon as any one by his own labor has improved anything which was not before occupied, he has the right, as we have shown, to retain that thing as his own; otherwise he would be deprived of the fruits of his own labor. Nor can it be said that it is lawful to take property thus improved on account of the right which every one has to make use of some part of the earth: for we cannot admit that there can exist any right in opposition to another prior and well established right. Hence some part of the soil may become the exclusive property of one person.

23 *

CHAPTER FOURTH.

ARTICLE FIRST.—INTERNATIONAL RIGHT "IN GENERE."

Having developed the questions concerning the right of property, we deem it proper to add here a few remarks on the right of nations (jus gentium).

This expression has been variously interpreted. According to some authors, it is that right which holds good among the various nations.

Like civil right, it contains two parts, viz., the general principle of the natural law, applied to nations, and positive laws. This distinction is not accepted by all. Some authors of great authority, such as St. Thomas, Suarez, and others, teach that the right of nations (jus gentium) belongs to the positive right (jus positivum). Note V. According to them, the right of nations is that which, necessity exacting and usefulness requiring it, is set on the same footing by all or almost all. The positive right, says St. Thomas, is divided into the civil and the national. They are both human and derived from natural law.

They consider as belonging to national rights the right of war, of alliance, of reducing to slavery free men taken during the war, of commerce, of burial, and, according to many, of property. The principal reasons in favor of this opinion are the following : natural right is grounded on the necessity of nature, and its object embraces intrinsic goodness and badness. But this is not found in national right, as is evident from slavery. The end of both is different ; the one has in view human nature, the other society. Natural law is innate to us and independent of the human will, but national right finds its force only in the manners of those who use it, and not without the wish, or at least the tacit consent of men. It would be easy to show that this doctrine cannot be absolutely accepted; for some part of the right of nations belongs to natural law.

ARTICLE SECOND.—INTERNATIONAL RIGHTS IN PARTICULAR.

We shall here rapidly enumerate these rights.

All civil societies, considered separately, and outside of particular facts, have the right of self conservation, government, and administration. A civil society is an independent, moral person, who has within its own authority the complete principle of its operation, and is consequently able by itself to attain its proper end.

Civil societies ought to be united together in the bonds of mutual love; and of course each society in the enjoyment of this right should find the basis of peace and prosperity.

Every society has the right of property. A moral person, like every individual, needs to look out for its own sustenance.

The high sea cannot be lawfully occupied by any nation. No society can be forced by another to exchange its own products.

Nations are bound to abide by the alliance and treaties agreed upon between them. Nations are not allowed to lie any more than individuals, for this would be against the natural law.

When the right of nations is violated, war is licit. The war, however, ought to be public, that is to say, declared and carried on by social authority; its cause ought to be a just one. It ought to be carried on, not only with every means which might make it efficacious, but also with moderation during its entire duration.

Intervention of arms and violence borne against the affairs of another people are not allowed, unless it be done by the request of a legitimate authority. When a nation is unjustly attacked by another it has the right of asking for help, and no one can lawfully prevent any people from rendering the desired help.

It is not lawful to make war with a nation for the purpose of preventing it from violating the moral law, whenever this violation does not infringe the rights of other people.

DUTIES OF MEN IN THEIR RELATIONS WITH SOCIETY.

ARTICLE FIRST.—THE DUTIES OF MEN IN RELATION TO DOMESTIC SOCIETY.

Domestic society is the union of husband and wife, together with their children, besides servants and other immediate dependents, all forming one family. Domestic society is therefore threefold, conjugal, parental, and *herile*.

(a) Conjugal society is that established between husband and wife by marriage. The first end of marriage is the birth of children, that the number of those who love and honor God may be thus increased. The second end of marriage is that each one may find in the society of a consort help and support, in order to bear more easily the burdens of life. Two other ends, less perfect but not unlawful, may be added to these: marriage is contracted to enable each one to avoid more easily the sins of impurity ; and also sometimes in order to have heirs to name, properties, and dignities.

The choice of a partner for life should be attended with the greatest care : first, by asking light from God ; secondly, by seeking the advice of parents ; thirdly, by endeavoring to choose a person remarkable for piety and virtue; fourthly, by observing, as far as possible, a similarity of age, condition, fortune, etc.; and, fifthly, by being honest and truthful towards one another before the marriage is contracted.

The duties of married persons are: mutual love, conjugal fidelity, mutual obedience, and mutual help.

(b) Parental society is that existing between parents and children, especially in reference to the education of the latter.

The duties of parents towards their children consist, first, in providing them food, raiment, and shelter; second, in teaching them the elements of the Christian doctrine and giving them habits of piety and morality; third, in giving them an education suitable to their condition and talents; and, fourth, in providing them with the means of making their own livelihood.

The duties of children towards their parents consist in honor, respect, love, obedience, and assistance. Note VI.

(c) *Herile* society is that existing between employer and employed, for their mutual advantage.

The duties of employers consist in treating those in their employ with humanity, kindness, and justice; in keeping the contracts or agreements made with them; in watching over their moral conduct; and in giving them opportunities of attending to their religious duties.

The duties of servants to their masters consist in reverence, obedience, and fidelity. Note VII.

ARTICLE SECOND.—THE DUTIES OF MEN IN RELATION TO CIVIL SOCIETY.

We shall first make some general remarks concerning civil society, and then speak of the duties of men as members of this society.

8

I. *Civil Society Considered in Itself.*

(A) Nature and forms of civil society.

Civil society is an association of men living together under the same supreme power, in order to derive from it certain temporal advantages. By these last words civil is distinguished from spiritual society.

Civil society is threefold in form : monarchy, aristocracy, and democracy ; according as the supreme power resides in one man, in several citizens, or in the whole people.

Monarchy (μὸνος ἀρχή) is the form of civil society in which the supreme power resides in one man, who is called king, emperor, etc. The monarchy is either elective or hereditary.

Aristocracy (ἄριστος κράτος) is the form of civil society in which the supreme power is in the hands of an order of citizens of high rank : when the number of those thus holding the supreme power is but few, we have what is called an oligarchy (ὀλίγος ἀρχή), but this word is generally used in a bad sense.

Democracy (δημος κράτος) is the form of civil society in which the supreme power is placed in the whole body of the citizens ; certain classes, however, are often excepted.

Some forms are called mixed governments, as the limited monarchy, called also a constitutional government.

Every form of civil society has its own advantages, but also, on account of the passions of men, its disadvantages ; and it may be said that no one form is equally suitable for all peoples.

(B) The supreme power in civil society.

By the supreme power in civil society is meant the

power which governs that society without any subordination to another power residing in the same society.

The necessity of such a power is evident; but we must examine several questions in reference to it: (a) What are the characteristics and attributes of the supreme power in civil society, (b) what is the origin or foundation of this power, (c) by what means it is acquired, and (d) what are the causes for which it may be taken away.

(a) Characteristics and attributes of the supreme power.

This power must first be independent of any other authority residing in the same state, for otherwise it would not be supreme; and, second, it must be one, for otherwise there would be a perpetual struggle, and consequently civil war, anarchy, and ruin.

The attributes proceed from the duties and rights which pertain to this society. They are of three kinds, legislative, judicial, and executive: these attributes of framing laws, of pronouncing judgment, and of carrying laws and sentences into effect, are incidental to the supreme power.

(b) Origin or foundation of the supreme power.

Whence originates this power of making laws and punishing those who do not obey them? Some say that it originates in the will of the people, who confer upon the magistrate the authority necessary for the exercise of his office. Others contend that this supreme power in civil society derives its authority from the will of God, who, having destined man for this society, has for this reason established supreme power, and attached to it the right to compel obedience. This latter opinion is the one entertained by the Christian philosophers; and, to prove it to be correct, we establish with them the following:

Proposition.— *The supreme authority in civil soci-ety comes ultimately from God, and not from the people.*

(1) This authority does not come from the people: for, as we have before said, to create an obligation two wills are necessary, one of a superior and the other of an inferior; but the will of the people is not that of a superior, since all men are by nature equal; conse-quently, neither the will of one man nor that of several, considered abstractly from the will of God, can impose any obligation upon another man. Men may choose one man, or several men, to exercise the supreme au-thority; but they cannot confer any authority, since they have none.

(2) The supreme authority comes from God. Since God wills that all men should live in civil society, he must have established a supreme authority, for without this authority civil society cannot exist. God therefore wills that a supreme authority exist among men; hence he creates it, and it comes from him and not from the people.

(c) Means by which the supreme power is acquired.

This question is twofold: How was supreme power acquired in the beginning; and how is it acquired now, when society is formed and consolidated?

1st. Four opinions have been entertained concerning the manner in which supreme power was acquired in the beginning: The first of these is that authority was acquired by election; the second opinion is that the su-preme authority in civil society is but an extension of the paternal authority; according to the third opinion, men wanting protection acknowledged themselves de-pendent on others more powerful than they were; the fourth opinion is that God intervened directly and thus established supreme authority.

The fourth opinion is brought forward gratuitously, and we reject it in like manner. The second and the third opinions, unless they be considered substantially the same as the first, may also be rejected; for acknowledgment of superiority and paternity does not of itself constitute supreme authority, or even the right to exercise this authority, unless an election take place, that is, unless the people choose their rulers; and this is the first opinion, which is the true one.

2d. How may supreme authority be now acquired, that is when society is already formed?

Four means are considered lawful for such an acquisition: election, succession, victory in a just war, and prescription. The first three of these need no explanation. In regard to prescription it is held that a ruler who is at first a usurper may, after a time and under certain circumstances, exercise a lawful authority. The lawfulness of such authority is grounded on reason and the consent of the people.

Reason teaches that one who has for many years exercised supreme power, even though originally a usurper, ought not to be deprived of this power at the imminent risk of greater calamities. In such cases God will confer supreme authority, because the welfare of the people is the supreme law.

The consent of the people also shows the lawfulness of prescription: it is recognized everywhere now, and we find examples of it in almost every country.

(d) Causes for which supreme power may be taken from a ruler. ·

These are: first, abdication; second, expiration of the term of election or appointment; third, expulsion after defeat in an unjust war; fourth, revocation on the part of the appointing power; fifth, removal for causes pro-

24

vided for in the constitution, as was the case in some parts of Germany during the middle ages in regard to princes who forfeited their power on becoming heretics. Concerning these five causes there is no controversy.

But it has been made a question whether insurrection against constituted authority be a lawful cause for taking away supreme power from a ruler. Three opinions have been given in answer to this question. The first is that of J. J. Rousseau, who pretends that a people may revolt against their rulers and expel them for any cause whatever. Rousseau logically deduces this opinion from his system concerning the origin of power, but the consequence is as false as the premises. The second opinion is that of Suarez, Bellarmin, and others, who say that in case of tyranny it is lawful to revolt against a ruler and expel him. A third opinion is held by Bossuet and others, who teach that it is never lawful to revolt against a ruler, however tyrannical his government may be. These two opinions may be defended; still it must be confessed that the opinion of Bellarmin, though more plausible in theory, is rather dangerous in practice, being fraught with fearful consequences. Note VIII.

II. *Duties of Men Considered as Members of Civil Society.*

(A) Duties of all citizens to their country: First, they must obey the laws; second, they should exert their talents for the good of their country, by following some occupation useful to society ; third, they must contribute from their wealth to the support of the government (by taxes, etc.) ; and, fourth, when necessary, they must even sacrifice their life for their country.

(B) Duties of magistrates: First, they are bound in

all their actions to aim at the good of civil society; second, they should strictly follow the dictates of justice, by bestowing offices and honors on the most deserving, by inflicting punishments in proportion to crimes, and not tolerating any conduct opposed to the public welfare, and by refraining from wronging the people by granting injurious monopolies, and from wronging foreign nations by unjust treaties or alliances. To these should be added two other duties: those placed in supreme power should become thoroughly acquainted with the science of government in all its departments, and above all they should always show a good example in all things.

(C) Duties of citizens towards their chief magistrates. These duties are respect and obedience to their authority; for, as we have seen, this authority comes from God.

Article Third.—Duties of Men towards One Another.

These duties may be reduced to two: to do unto others as we would have them to do unto us, and not to do unto others what we would not have them do unto us. The first are positive duties and the others negative.

I. *Positive Duties.*

These may be named in the following order: First, we must love our fellow men, since we are all the children of God; and, second, we must do good to them, for idle charity is unavailing. The good works which we must perform for other persons are both spiritual and temporal.

A certain order should be observed in our charity.

According to St. Bernard, the rule of charity is that those in most need should receive first. In other cases we should prefer those who are near to us in blood, friendship, or religion. "True charity begins at home."

II. *Negative Duties—Duels.*

Negative duties are those that prescribe something to be avoided. We must avoid everything which may injure our neighbor, either in soul or in body.

We injure the souls of our fellow men by scandal; and we injure their bodies, first, by homicide, or by mutilating, wounding, or striking them (but evidently there is no injustice in injuring, or even killing, an unjust assailant); second, by stealing from them or otherwise injuring their property; and, third, by injuring their good name.

Duels.—A duel is a private combat between two persons, according to a previous agreement, the place, time, and arms being also agreed upon. Against this unholy practice we establish the following

Proposition.—*Duelling is opposed to natural right.*

Natural right forbids us to kill another, or to expose our own life, without sufficient reason. But he who fights a duel endangers his own life and that of his adversary without sufficient reason. The reason given must be, for instance, to prove one's innocence, to avenge an injury, to preserve one's honor, or to show that one is courageous; but none of these reasons is a sufficient cause for engaging in a duel: for, first, the innocent one may be killed, and thus it may be made to appear that he is guilty; secondly, no one has a right by his private authority to avenge himself; thirdly, honor cannot be acquired by a duel—it is rather a mark of heroism, and consequently of honor, to bear injuries with patience ; and, fourthly, true courage is shown by practising patience, and by reserving the sacrifice of one's life for the acquisition of something preferable to life itself, as the safety of our family or our country.

Observation.—Duelling, which is forbidden by the natural law when undertaken by private authority, may become lawful when performed under the direction of the magistrate for the good of the state, as when David went forth from the army of Saul to challenge Goliath to mortal combat.

The Church forbids duelling under pain of separation from her communion.

To answer objections, let us observe that there are two kinds of honor, true and fictitious : true honor is that founded on virtue, and fictitious honor is that based upon the opinions of men. We must defend true honor, even at the risk of life ; for virtue is preferable to life itself : but fictitious honor ought not to be preserved at the risk life, for human glory is no virtue. True honor never requires a duel for its preservation ; on the contrary, it requires that duelling should be avoided.

Some persons object that no one is obliged to suffer the loss of his reputation. This is false : if fame among men cannot be preserved without violating natural right and divine law, let it perish.

They add also that sometimes, especially among soldiers, a duel cannot be avoided without serious inconvenience, and consequently that in such a case it is allowed. Again the consequent is false : no inconvenience can render that lawful which is wrong in itself and forbidden by the natural law.

They still add that he who refuses to engage in a duel lowers himself in his own estimation. This objection is not a serious one : such a man should modify his

24 *

opinion of himself, for it is a false one; his error cannot make duelling lawful.

The above exposition of our duties is deemed sufficiently developed for a course of philosophy. Let us close by saying that it is not enough for us to know our duties, we must practise them; otherwise, our knowledge, being without good works, would only make us worse in the sight of God. With the help of God, let us endeavor to bring forth fruit by the practise of good works, so that being more wise we may be more virtuous.

NOTES.

Note L., p. 66.   According to St. Thomas:—In physical sciences, abstraction excludes only the individuality in material beings; our mind generalizes without, however, going out of the notions which are provided to its observations by contingent existences. In mathematical sciences, abstraction considers only the pure notion of extension, passive and inert.   Hence the sciences concerning the continued extension—the multiple extension and the blind force—geometrical sciences, arithmetical and mechanical sciences.   In metaphysical sciences, abstraction rises above every material essence, to the concepts common to every being, and even to the immaterial substances—God and the soul.   Spiritual life is, besides this, a more abstract point of view, which is divided into two other ones, knowledge and appetite.   Hence the logical sciences and the moral sciences.

Mr. Ampère more recently has also proposed an objective division, according to that of St. Thomas.   He commences by dividing all sciences into cosmological sciences and noological sciences.   Each division is subdivided, as may be seen in the following tableau:

COSMOLOGICAL SCIENCES.	MATHEMATICAL	Arithmetic and Algebra, Geometry, Mechanics, Astronomy.
	PHYSICAL	Physics, Science of Industry, Geology, Science of the Mines.
	NATURAL	Botany, Agriculture, Zoology, Science of the Amelioration of Races.
	MEDICAL	Medical Physics, Hygiene, Nosology, Practical Medicine.

NOOLOGICAL SCIENCES.	PHILOSOPHICAL	Psychology, Logic, Theodicy, Ethics.
	DIALEGMATICAL	Grammar, Literature, Esthetics, Science of Education.
	HISTORICAL	Political Geography, Archæology, History, Science of Religions.
	POLITICAL	Legislation and Jurisprudence, Military Science, Political Economy, Science of Administration.

Note II., p. 101. Rules for determining the degrees of probability. When we have to determine the degree of probability for some event, a double hypothesis may be assumed, that is, the number of cases in favor of the event or against it is known or not known. In either case the following rules will suffice.

RULE I.—When the number of cases in favor of the even and those against it are known, the degree of probability may be expressed by an arithmetical fraction, of which the denominator should be the total number of the possible cases, and the numerator that of the cases in favor of the event. Thus, for instance, the degree of probability that number 7 shall be obtained at the first throw of two dice bearing on their sides the numbers 1, 2, 3, 4, 5, and 6, may be expressed by the fraction $\frac{6}{36}$ or $\frac{1}{6}$. The number 7 may be obtained through six various combinations of the dice, that is, by $1+6$, $2+5$, $3+4$, $4+3$, $5+2$, and $6+1$. But the total number of the combination for the two dice is 36, because each of the six sides of one dice may be united with the sides of the other dice in six different ways, which produces 36 combinations.

Corollary.—With this rule we may easily find out whether a game of chance is just or not; it is necessary, in order that it be a just one, that the chances be equal for those who play.

The same thing may be said about lotteries. There ought to be an equal probability of gain or loss for those who play, or a right proportion between the value of the lots and the number of the chances. This, however, should not be required with lotteries established for charitable purposes.

RULE II.—When the number of cases is not known, then the probability of some event is to be sought by experience, that is, by finding out how many times, in a certain number of cases, the event in question took place, in order to conclude which shall be the probability that this event will happen again. Let us suppose, for instance, that some balls, the ones black and the others white, are all contained in the same box, and we want to know which is the probability that the first ball taken out shall be a black one. Since we know neither the total number of the balls, nor that of the black ones, we cannot apply here the first rule; but the probability shall be found by taking out successively several balls, and then counting which was the number of those thus taken out and of the black ones. If, for instance, the number of those taken out be 60, and that of the black ones 20, the probability of taking a black ball may be expressed by the following fraction, $\frac{20}{60}$, or else by $\frac{1}{3}$.

Corollary.—This rule may be useful for fixing up the premium in contracts of insurance against fires, shipwrecks, etc. If, for instance, out of 1000 ships having sailed for the same place, 10 are shipwrecked, the premium shall be worth a hundredth part of the value. These remarks and examples are given more fully in the "Logique" of S' Gravesande, and in the work "Logica" of Ubaghs.

Note III., p. 148. Here is the reasoning of Descartes. A definition of a triangle is given to me, I cannot conclude that it exists, because this existence is not included in it; but I may conclude that the three angles are equivalent to two right angles, because this truth is contained in the definition, in the essence itself of the figure.

If, he adds, I examine again the idea which I have of a perfect being, I find that its existence is included in it, in the same way that it is included in the idea of a triangle that its three angles are equal to two right angles. . . . Consequently it is as certain that God exists, as any demonstration of geometry can be certain.

Note IV., p. 230. The constitution of beings shows the thought of God in their regard. If they are made to understand, it is because

He wishes them to be reasonable; if made to feel, it is because He calls them to animal life. Likewise, if they are subject to dissolution, it is because God destined them one day to destruction. On the contrary, however, if there be in them no cause of destruction, it is because He does not wish them to perish. God, to show his dominion and give an irrefutable sign of his intervention, can consent that the established order undergo some accidental derogations; but beyond this any changement made without a sufficient end would show indecision, caprice, a want of power, but especially of wisdom. Hence it is ridiculous to say that God, after having made the soul to be immortal, would amuse himself in destroying it. The annihilation of the soul would no less be in contradiction with the goodness of God. In fact, it is impossible to explain otherwise than by divine action the innate desire we have of happiness. We tend towards happiness with all the strength of our minds, and there we wish to be aloof from all cares and anxieties. But were our soul to end with the body, temporal things only would be our happiness, and they should in that case suffice to content our ambition. But how is it that these temporal goods seem vain and unworthy of us? How is it that the greatness of the soul consists in despising them? Why would their duration, which is always short, be at the same time always uncertain? "A happy life which we are able to lose," says Cicero, "is not a happy one. Is it possible to trust the strength and stability of that which is essentially fragile and unstable? But to doubt the perpetuity of one's goods is to fear to become misfortunate by losing them. And to be the victim of such a fear, is it not in itself a continual misfortune?" Supposing, then, that God had not made the soul immortal, He would have left us to the greatest deceptions. Would this be worthy of his goodness?

The justice, as well as the goodness and wisdom of God, require that the soul be immortal. Justice consists in giving every one his dues. He who makes good use of his liberty, and glorifies God by faithfully following his law, cannot in justice be treated like unto him who takes pleasure in offending his Creator. Virtue and vice have not the same destiny. The same way that there are different degrees in virtue and vice, so there should also be different degrees in their reward or punishment. Does the present world represent us virtue invariably honored and rewarded, vice despised and punished?

Therefore there is another life after this one of trials, and the one we now enjoy is but a prelude of another where order will be revenged by the eternal happiness of the just and the eternal misery of the wicked.

Note V., p. 270. Here are the words given in the Index III. Rerum at the end of the "Summa Theologica St. Thomæ Aquinatis. —Editio Sexta, Luxemburg." "Jus positivum duplex, scilicet, jus gentium, et jus civile; primum derivatur a jure naturali, ut conclusio; secundum vero, per modum determinationis. 1. 2. quæstæ 95. 4. c, ad 1."

Note VI., p. 273. The conjugal contract excludes the plurality either of wives or of husbands, not only a simultaneous, but even a successive one, as long as both parties to the original contract are alive.

Successive plurality is caused by divorce, and simultaneous plurality is called polygamy. When a woman has several men at one and the same time, this kind of polygamy is called polyandry; and when a man has several wives, we have polygamy properly so called. Polyandry is absolutely contrary to nature, for it is evidently opposed to the end of marriage, which is the generation and education of children. This doctrine is so evident that all nations have always held polyandry in horror.

Polygamy is less conformed to the end of marriage, and therefore is not lawful. Polygamy is in opposition to the properties of matrimony, which is a society that requires mutual love and intimate communication of affections; but this could not be obtained with the plurality of wives, because it would not then be complete and reciprocal. Polygamy is opposed to perfect justice; the wife gives herself wholly to her husband, there ought therefore to be reciprocity.

Polygamy leads to tyranny from the part of the husband, and consequently in such a family there can be no peace, and this is in itself contrary to the proper education of children. Matrimony is a perpetual state, as we may see by the mutual promises made by the two parties interested. The end of matrimony, as well as the peace and security of families, require this perpetuity. Experience shows the truth of these doctrines.

Note VII., p. 273. We may add here a few remarks about slavery. Slavery is the condition of those who owe their services to some person forever, and who have no right of requiring for their labor any other reward but food, shelter, and clothing.

Slavery among the Pagans was so absolute that slaves were considered as mere *things* (res non personæ), and consequently neither justice nor charity was due to them. This kind of slavery, as it existed among the ancient Romans, is an evident violation of the natural law; but slavery, as we have defined it, is not contrary to natural law; for if it were so, it is because in this state the slave would cease to be a *man*, or could no more attain his end; but neither of these suppositions can be admitted; then the state of slavery is not contrary to natural law.

The titles by which a man may acquire the right to all the labors of another man are: 1. Free tradition; 2. Purchase or donation; 3. Captivity by war; 4. Birth. The duties of slaves are those of servants.

Note VIII., p. 278. It does not seem to be out of place here, to give the thesis which we find in the book "Elementa Philosophiæ Moralis," of Rev. Father Jouin, S. J., upon the doctrine concerning the supreme authority of the people.

First Proposition.—The doctrine concerning the essential supremacy of the people is absurd. We do not pretend to say that authority can never reside in the people; the democratical regime is lawful; but we deny that the people always possess this authority, and that they can never lose it, although they conferred the exercise of this authority on a king or an emperor. In one word, we affirm that supreme authority is not essential to the people.

Proof.—This doctrine supposes a social contract, according to the mind of J. J. Rousseau, that is to say, it supposes that democracy is the only lawful form of government, and that the people always confer supreme authority on the rulers of society. It supposes, moreover, that the princes are but the delegates of the people, and that they may, according to their will, be removed from the exercise of that authority; and, finally, it supposes that the people can change, as they please, any form of government. But all this is false and absurd; hence a doctrine established on these principles is false and absurd.

In order to solve the difficulties, it will be enough to notice the confusion in the words given by the defenders of this system: "Social authority resulting from the nature of society, belongs to society." If they mean by these words that social authority is a part of society, and its constitutive and essential element, it is true; but if they mean by them that social authority is the property of those who form society, this general proposition is false.

Second Proposition.—Universal suffrage exercised by the people and considered as a right is an absurdity. The right of universal suffrage essential to the people is grounded upon the hypothesis of the essential supremacy of the people. But this is absurd; hence this right is equally so.

PRINCIPLES FOR THE SOLUTION OF THE DIFFICULTIES.

1st. The right of universal suffrage, taken strictly, is altogether absurd, for in this case it should be practised by every one, even by women. But this right restricted to the citizens, or to those who may be citizens, is lawfully exercised in the democracy; but it does not necessarily concern all the citizens under every form of government, since it is only under the democratical regime that citizens possess supreme authority.

2d. Men are not for society, but society is for men, that is, society ought to procure the common good to its members; but it does not follow that these members are allowed, whenever they choose, to change the form of government, for it belongs to society to defend all the rights of the citizens, and evidently society cannot do it if its members may, whenever it pleases them, trample its rights under foot.

3d. Sometimes it is better to change the form of government. In this case, let the people, by lawful means, propose its wants to the prince, so that this change may be made, not by arms and sedition, but peacefully. If there be necessity for the people to have a change, the prince will surely concede it; should this necessity not exist, it belongs to the prince to see what may be granted in actual circumstances, for it is he and not the people who has to see to the order of society. Besides, experience teaches that such changes, when they do not take place properly, are rather a source of evils than one of advantages.

4th. The end of civil society is to protect the rights of the citizens and to promote common good. This being done by the civil authority, the citizens cannot require any more. They cannot oblige the prince to grant them another form of government, because they think that this could work better.

25   T

5th. It is not always by changes in the constitution that a remedy can be afforded to the evils of society. The fact that there are abuses in the actual form of government, does not give the right to the citizens of asking or introducing with violence some changes in the constitution. Examples could be given to illustrate this.

This right of universal suffrage, so much praised in our time by the so-called reformers of society, shall become the cause of the ruin of many governments. How can we believe that the vote of an ignorant and prejudiced man has as much value as that of a well educated and learned one? Is there not also a difference between the vote of him who owns no property and that of the rich man? With the universal suffrage we have the government of majorities, and when infidelity reigns supreme among these majorities, the government must turn into anarchy and tyranny.

Here again we could illustrate what we say, and the last term of universal suffrage in a society where religion is either banished or persecuted, is Socialism or Communism.

THE END.

www.ingramcontent.com/pod-product-compliance
Lightning Source LLC
Chambersburg PA
CBHW020859020726
47497CB00005B/1485